STOLEN EMBERS

SEVERED FLAMES
BOOK TWO

ANNIE
ANDERSON

STOLEN EMBERS
Severed Flames Book Two
Annie Anderson
Published by Annie Anderson
Copyright © 2024 Annie Anderson
Edited by: Angela Sanders
Cover Art by: Tattered Quill Designs
All rights reserved.
Paperback ISBN: 978-1-960315-67-0
Hardcover ISBN: 978-1-960315-68-7

SANDGRAVE

BONEFELL

EVERHOLD

SEVILAVA

PERDER LUCEM

DIREVEIL

GIROVIA

TARRASCA

FESTIA

THE CONTINENT OF
CREDOUR

For all my girlies who reside firmly in defiance. Here's to standing up, sowing chaos, and being ourselves.

We can never be caged.

It is not in the stars to hold our destiny but in ourselves.

— WILLIAM SHAKESPEARE

CHAPTER 1
VALE

A twig snapped under my foot, gouging the tender skin as I raced through the dense trees, dodging withered branches and deadfall. But I couldn't stop. The rushing of water drew me through the forest, calling me to that unknown place I so desperately needed to be.

Nyrah.

There was no other reason to be here—lost in this bit of nowhere—if not for my little sister. Unbidden, I screamed her name, praying that just this once, I would get an answer. But through the darkness, all I got back was stillness.

And stillness in a place like this was a very bad thing.

I never should have let Arden rip me from the Judg-

ment Room. I should have fought—should have died fighting—anything but let Nyrah fend for herself in a world as harsh as this one.

"Nyrah," I screamed again, begging the gods to give me even a hint of a clue. She had to be here, but I had no idea where "here" was.

The trees rapidly thinned into a yawning darkness, and it wasn't until my feet skidded on the slippery bracken did I realize it was a cliff. The world dropped away, and I plunged into blackness. My screams died as the world slipped and slid, changing into a biting coldness that seeped into my bones.

Sharp stones dug into my hands and knees, but I couldn't see anything at all. No light, no air, no warmth.

This wasn't right. This was...

Dream walking.

I was dream walking. Done only a handful of times, I was still getting used to the feeling of being in my body and also not at the same time. But just because I was dreaming, didn't mean what I was experiencing wasn't very, very real. If I could find my sister in this space, I could find her in reality as well.

I just had to push a little farther, and I could reach her.

"Nyrah," I shouted into the nothingness, hoping for

a spark of something that would let me know where she was. "Tell me where you are!"

I used a sharp stone to cut into my palm, begging the magic beneath my skin to come forth, to shine the barest hint of light in the inky blackness.

But, still, nothing came.

No light.

No air.

No warmth.

Was she dead? Were all my worst fears coming true? Had I failed so spectacularly that all my efforts had been for nothing?

"Please," I screamed, the hot tracks of my tears the only heat in the room. "Please come back to me."

A rough arm hooked around my middle as light bloomed around me, nearly blinding as a harsh stone tunnel finally came into view. At the end of it sat a small blonde, shivering as she hugged her knees to her chest. I couldn't see her face, but I feared my sister was fighting for her very life in whatever hell this place was.

"Nyrah," I shouted yet again, my voice echoing off the walls, even as I was yanked off my feet, pulled away, my breath stuttering in my lungs. "Nyrah!"

But she didn't so much as twitch as she flickered and faded, the scene changing as Idris tore me from my sister and into whatever dream he'd concocted for *himself. Usually, we ended up in his bedroom, but not this time.*

No, this was someplace else.

Withered walls reached for the blackened sky like a giant's fingers, the roof of the building crumbling with age. A half-demolished window let in the frigid wind, whipping dead leaves and drifts of snow against the rotted benches. And as much as I wanted to ask where we were, I wanted to slap him a hell of a lot more.

Idris gripped my arm, turning me to face him. "What the fuck did you think you were doing, Vale?" His large hands cupped my jaw as his thumb wiped at something on my face. "Do you have any idea what you've done?"

I yanked my jaw from his grip, fighting off the urge to growl. I'd been so close to her. I could have reached her. "Do you? I almost had her. I could have asked where she was. I—"

"Could have fucking died. Look." He held up his hand as his golden gaze flared with his power, showing me the thick blood staining his fingertips. "You're not supposed to dream walk without me. You haven't been trained. You have no idea how dangerous it can be."

Breathing was dangerous. Being in the castle was dangerous. Every gods-be-damned thing in my life since the day I took my first squalling breath had been dangerous. I shouldn't have survived this long as it was, and after agreeing to come to this stupid broken kingdom, I'd nearly been killed a half-dozen times.

"It's not the first time I've gotten a bloody nose. I'll heal."

Pivoting on a foot, I headed for the door. I needed to get back to Nyrah. Golden power shot from his fingertips, curling around me, even as I backed away from it. It hauled me closer, lifting me off my feet, so I was forced to look him in the eye.

"Lesson number one of dream walking: If you get hurt in your dream, you get hurt in real life." He held up his hand again, the blood marred by the light of his power, but it was there all the same. "Meaning, this blood? It's on your face now. Those cuts on your feet? Your hands? You're hurt, Vale."

Didn't he understand? Didn't he know how much I'd bled for my sister already? How much I would give to see her, to have her safe, to... "Who gives a shit about a little blood? I could have figured out where she was. She was so close—"

His jaw hardened, the dark slashes of his eyebrows pulling into a scowl. "You have no idea if that was her at all. Second lesson of dream walking: Not everything you see in your dreams is what it appears to be. You have no idea how to ward your mind, how to protect yourself. That could have been your sister, sure. It also could be a dream demon or a mage in disguise, or—"

A crushing weight filled every part of my body as tears made the already-surreal world blurry. "Or it could be someone else ready and willing to kill me to keep you caged. I get it."

It was one more reason to find Nyrah before one of Idris' enemies found her, one more reason to break the curse, one more reason to shove this sham of a wedding along and just fuck whatever I wanted in the meantime.

Idris' magic got warmer, softer as he pulled me closer, the tendrils of golden power transferring me to his waiting arms. He wrapped them around me, burying his fingers in my hair as he held me tight. But as comforting as they were, as much as my body wanted to melt into him, my brain was a whole other matter.

My body was ruled by the mating bond I didn't want.

My mind, however, knew better.

"I know this isn't what you wanted to hear," he murmured, trying and failing to comfort me, "but we will find her."

The real question was: How? How would we find Nyrah when I didn't have the first clue as to where she was? How could we when she was in more danger with me than without me? When just looking for her, put a target on her back?

A hot lash of bitter anger tore through my chest, and I ripped myself out of Idris' hold. What would he know about my disappointment? He hated his brother.

"Funny," I seethed through gritted teeth. "When I agreed to marry you, you said you'd help me find her. Now, here I am about to fulfill my end of the bargain —far too soon for my liking—and I have nothing to show for it, other than a vague promise and a maybe."

"That's not fair," he growled. "We've barely had time to breathe, let alone—"

But I didn't give him a chance to lie to me. It was bad enough I'd gotten forced into this sham of a wedding, the date barreling toward me with each passing second. I didn't need false promises on top of it.

Focusing all my energy, I yanked myself from the dream world, forcing myself to wake from this brand-new prison.

Before I even opened my eyes, the pain registered. Lightning streaked across my brain as a familiar voice rumbled his displeasure.

"You're bleeding again, my Queen," Rune growled through our mental connection, setting off a spike of

agony as I tried to get my bearings. *"I believe we've had this discussion before."*

Rune himself was the whole reason I was here, wasn't he? Had Idris not been cursed—separated from his dragon—Rune wouldn't exist.

"Yeah, yeah. Staying alive is paramount. Tell that to my wandering subconscious. I didn't ask to dream walk, you know."

Yes, I had used far too much magic to seek Nyrah out. The problem was that I hadn't even consciously done it. And worse? I didn't know how to stop it, or even if I wanted to. All this had started because I'd been defending my little sister. The power I'd hidden for so long bubbled to the surface as I'd made sure she was safe, signing my own death warrant in the process.

But I hadn't died that day. Kian and Xavier had saved me, taken me from the *Perder Lucem*, stole me from the mountain—the only home I'd ever known—and thrust me into a world of kings and queens, dragons and magic.

And death.

Lots and lots of death.

"You have been too lax on your magic studies. You are a Luxa. It is high time you figured out what that means."

But being a Luxa had only been a death sentence for as long as I'd had this wretched power, and learning about it wouldn't change how many people wanted me dead because of it. Being a light-wielding, "supposed" curse breaker wouldn't stop the assassination attempts or the impending nuptials to a man I could barely stand or the odd fateborn mate bond I had with not one but three dragons.

It would only keep me alive.

In theory.

That was if it didn't kill me first.

Peeling my eyelids open, I was faced with a pair of angry dragon shifters staring at me like I had just taken out a blade and stabbed them in their hearts. Kian's amber eyes blazed with wrath as he clenched his jaw, while Xavier's cool blue ones were tight with worry. Neither of them wore a shirt, and what could only be my blood was smeared across their skin, like I'd tried to bleed out at some point.

I probably had.

It wouldn't be the first time for that, either.

Searching the recesses of my mind, I vaguely remembered falling asleep on Kian's chest the night before while Xavier played with my braid. I had barely recovered from the last assassination attempt, so the lecture I was about to receive would be one for the history books.

"Don't," I croaked, trying to ward off stern reprimands and urges to remember that I was a frail little Luxa with no grasp of the severity of my actions. Gods, I'd heard it enough over the last few days. "Please, just don't."

It wasn't my fault that people were trying to kill me. It wasn't my fault that to save myself and them, I'd been forced to overextend my power. And it wasn't my fault that I'd accidentally dream walked into what could have been a trap.

Kian's gaze softened as he knelt at the side of the bed. "You scared us to death, little witch. I don't know how much my old heart can take."

I reached for his hand, threading my fingers through his. "I didn't do it on purpose."

Xavier circled his fingers around my ankle, his jaw still tight, his gaze still sad. At the cliffs when I'd nearly fallen to my death, he'd sworn that he couldn't survive the god of death taking another person he cared about. I had yet to ask him about it after everything, but something about his expression made me want to know who had put it there.

It made me want to know everything—all his secrets, his past, his dreams.

"You never do," Xavier murmured, his thumb rubbing sweeping arches over my skin.

The doors to the bedchamber flew open in a blast of golden power, and Idris prowled into the room, his golden gaze alight with wrath. I had no idea why he was here, but his presence was supremely unwelcome. I'd managed to avoid him for the last twenty-four hours while I got my head around our impending nuptials, and I wasn't too keen on speaking to him now.

It was bad enough that he invaded my dreams and prevented me from finding Nyrah. Now, he was winding up to give me a lecture I absolutely did not need.

Again.

Then he stalked closer, and I noticed the blood staining his nostrils and shirt.

Alarm had me sitting up, ignoring the ache in my bones and the tearing in my joints. *"Rune? Why is he bleeding?"*

"You ventured where you should never go, my Queen. Dream walking is a nasty business."

Maybe I did need that lecture.

But it wasn't until he reached the frame of the bed and pointed a finger at me with that burning fury smoldering in his eyes that I grasped just how dangerous what I'd done really was.

"This is the last night you're sleeping anywhere but in my bed, Vale. If you can't control where you dream walk, the only place you're dreaming is next to me."

It was a command.

An order.

A royal fucking decree.

It would be stupid to say no.

But when had that ever stopped me?

CHAPTER 2
IDRIS

My future bride was gearing up for the mother of all fights, and I was here for it.

Her brilliant green eyes flashed with her ire as she shakily climbed out of bed, and I had to fight every instinct I had not to fall at her feet and beg her to listen to me. For the last week, I'd watched her bleed far more than I ever cared to, and this shit was stopping here and now.

It was one thing for a complete stranger I didn't give two fucks about to try and break this bullshit curse. It was quite another to watch someone I cared about—maybe even loved—get hurt over and over again because of it.

It didn't matter if she had two mates right beside her to back her up.

It wouldn't matter if she had a whole damn army.

Vale would be sleeping in my bed before the night was over.

"What gives you the right to burst in here and tell me where I lay my head?" she growled, the nearly sheer nightgown clinging to her growing curves as she straightened her spine. "And what good is sleeping next to you going to do? I will still sleep, I'll still dream."

If I wasn't so pissed off that she'd put herself in danger again, the ire in her voice and the way the fabric highlighted every line of her body would have me giving in to the ache in my cock.

Gods, how could a woman be that beautiful and that infuriating at the same time?

"I'm fairly certain the crown I inherited and have kept for three hundred fucking years is what gives me that right. But let me remind you: in less than a week, I will be your husband. I will be damned if you decide to keel over before you can walk down that aisle because you're too stubborn to understand that there are limits to what your body can handle."

It was a cold, hard truth that she needed to learn before she accidentally killed herself.

"In case you weren't aware, the closer we are together, the better our connection is. If I'm next to you, I can sense when you're going too far. I can keep you safe."

Her jaw firmed as golden light illuminated her skin, flashing like lightning underneath her flesh. I doubted anyone else could see it but me, but I knew that if I gave her enough time to wind herself up, she would expend far too much of her power only to prove my point.

"Don't even think about it," I growled, warning her off before she could thrash me with it. "You have no idea how far away you were or how stretched thin your poor body was. You continue time and time again to overuse the wealth of power under your skin, and it is *killing* you."

Couldn't she see that? Didn't she realize how cold this world would be without her?

"How many times are you going to drain Xavier dry as he floods life back into you?" I whispered, trying to make her see sense. "How many times is your body going to go through all of this before it just gives out? No one is saying that you aren't powerful because you are—"

"No, you're saying my body is too fucking weak to

handle it. Trust me," she growled as she wiped at her bloody nose. "I got that message."

But did she?

Did she know how tied we were to each other already, even without completing the bond? That every time she hurt herself, it was like a lance to my heart? That her mind infiltrated every corner of my brain until she was all I could think about, all I saw? That every lash of pain, every sorrow, was a brand on my soul?

I really fucking doubted it.

"You claim to care about them," I said, nodding in the direction of my two oldest friends, "but can't you see what you're doing? Every time you overexert yourself, you remind them of a life without you. You remind them they will live forever without their mate, without the woman that they love, in agony if you die. If you're not going to be smart about using your power for yourself, why not for them?"

Her full lips parted, and she staggered back on a foot as if I'd just struck her. "That's not fair."

"You, of all people, should know that life isn't fair. You want to learn how to use your power? Fine, I'll teach you myself. You want to learn how to dream walk? I'll teach you that, too. But you can't keep using your magic like that. It will kill you."

Pain ravaged her face before she wiped it clean, but I could hear her mind. Nyrah was her first priority. She needed to find her sister—needed to know she was alive and well—but she had no idea how close she had come to losing her life.

"Fuck the curse, little witch. Who will be there for that sister you care so much about if you die trying to find her?"

Vale's gaze landed on the blood-smeared sheets, and it was as if the fight in her died.

"It wasn't on purpose. I had no idea when I fell asleep that I would dream of Nyrah or of trying to get to her. But once I was in it, I couldn't stop. And then I saw the blonde at the end of the tunnel, and I knew I had to get to her. She was cold and alone in the dark. What if—"

Kian threaded his fingers through hers, pulling her into his side. "They don't have her, remember? If they did, Fenwick would have said so to torture you. They have no idea where she is, and that makes Nyrah as safe as she can be."

Vale shook her head, pulling out of his hold. "You weren't there. There was no light, no air, no breath. It's what I imagine meeting Orrus would be like. It was so dark my light couldn't penetrate. I—"

"You were dying," Xavier rumbled, his whole

body vibrating with barely contained rage. "Your heart slowed to almost nothing, your breaths barely able to move your chest. You were so cold, so still."

He pressed the heels of his palms against his eyes as if he were trying to wipe the images away. Vale molded to his side, wrapping her thin arms around his middle like she was reassuring him of her presence. And as much as I hated sharing her, as much as I loathed that she loved them and not me, I was so grateful that they were in this room backing me up.

"But I didn't," she murmured, trying to reassure him. "I'm still here. I'm still breathing."

Xavier dropped his hands to stare at our mate. "For how long? You have been targeted by attempt after attempt on your life. What happens if one of us isn't there the next time? What happens if even Rune can't save you? As much as I hate taking away your choices, Idris is right."

Vale clenched her jaw, pulling away from him, too. "You can't be serious. It was an accident. I didn't mean to. I—" She snapped her mouth shut, shaking her head.

"If you really didn't mean to, then you *really* can't sleep anywhere else but beside me," I murmured, pinching my brow.

Her power was volatile, dangerous—more to her

than anyone else. In some ways, that was the most glorious gift we could have been given. Vale was a way to break a centuries-long curse that was killing this continent. In others, her power reminded me so much of Zamarra, it was scary.

But as powerful as she was, I still didn't know if she actually could break the curse that separated me from Rune. We knew so little about the spell weaved into my skin, taking away my hold on the source of my power. Something told me the bond would do little to help, and still, it seemed like the only option we had.

"I'll only go if Xavier and Kian can come with me," she countered, crossing her arms over her chest in a move of defiance that belayed her small frame.

So, my future bride was making demands, was she? I fought off the urge to grin in triumph. "Is this you negotiating?"

That single raised eyebrow of hers could bring me to my knees. "No, this is me telling you how it will be."

"Tomato, to-mah-to," I murmured, prowling closer to her. "Anything else you wish to ask for before you inevitably give in?"

The images flashing in her mind had my cock throbbing in my leathers. As much as I didn't like sharing, the way Vale's imagination framed it made me think it would definitely be worth trying. The scent wafting off her skin had me swallowing down a growl and fighting the urge to make her imaginings come true.

She seemed to shake herself before shoving her lustful thoughts away, her heavy-lidded eyes widening as she took a healthy step backward. If Kian's smirk and Xavier's hungry expression were anything to go by, she had just broadcasted the image of us sharing her to all three of us.

Vale swallowed hard, her thoughts taking a sharp left turn as she seemed to think about what she actually desired, aside from the three of us taking her until she couldn't walk straight.

"I want complete access to all of Fenwick's journals, scrolls, and records. That bastard couldn't have burned up the only scroll about breaking the curse. It's been two hundred years. He had to have some notes somewhere."

It made sense she wanted to see Fenwick's musings. The fucker had been hiding in plain sight, killing off Luxa under our very noses. Vale had been the only one to survive him, but it had nearly cost her life.

"Of course. Freya, Xavier, and I have been

pouring over them, but you can search the library for anything that we've missed, and you can look at what we have. Anything else?"

She rolled her eyes, seeming to fortify herself and her mind. "You still haven't agreed to the first bit."

"I told you when you agreed to marry me that I wouldn't separate you," I said, refusing to say the quiet part out loud.

The fact that I hated to share was known far and wide. It was why I was in this mess in the first fucking place. Unfortunately, my mate wasn't mine alone, and if I were to marry Vale, I would have to learn that despite my crown, I would never fully possess all of her.

And maybe that was a good thing.

Vale was like the sun: volatile and steady all at the same time. It would be stupid to think she would ever be mine alone.

"What you say and what you do are rarely ever similar. Usually, 'protection' doesn't involve a marriage proposal. Now your 'protection' has me in your bed. I'm not falling for that shit twice. I want your word," she commanded, her thoughts louder than my own. *"The last time I slept without them, I nearly died. I'd rather not have a repeat."*

No, the last time I'd been stupid enough to think a

full guard was enough to stop the assassins after her, she actually *had* died. I remembered the burning ache in my chest that nearly ripped me in two when her heart had stopped beating. Remembered how much energy she'd needed, how much blood, how close she was to never coming back.

Only this time her impending doom was at her own hands, not my stupidity. At least I had that going for me.

"I have never—not once—failed to keep my word with you." But she had a point. *"And I won't fail this time, either. They can be with you, but you're sleeping next to me. I might just need a bigger fucking bed."*

"It doesn't matter how big the bed is. The only thing it'll be used for is sleeping."

Eventually, I'd have to convince her otherwise to complete the bond, but tonight just wasn't the night to start trying. Then again, with those errant flashes of the three of us sharing her flooding her mind, I figured convincing her wouldn't be as difficult as I'd originally thought.

After Vale got cleaned up, all four of us moved down the short hallway to my bedchamber. Following the attack on the mountain, we'd sequestered ourselves to my wing, thinking that the closeness would prevent any future attacks. Little did we know, Vale would attack herself from within.

As soon as I opened my bedchamber door, I noticed the mound of pillows and extra blankets piled on the mattress. It seemed my lifelong steward was meddling again. Briar had been with my family for centuries, and she'd fallen in love with Vale almost instantly—not that I could blame her.

I supposed this was her seal of approval of this new arrangement.

By the time we'd done the awkward dance of figuring out where everyone would sleep, Vale ended up at the center of the bed with Kian on one side, me on the other, and Xavier sprawled at the foot of the bed. Naturally, Kian had wrapped around her like a serpent, curling her into his body while Xavier latched onto her ankle like a barnacle.

And me?

I stared at the ceiling, trying to ignore that Kian was already dead to the world, Xavier was close behind him, and Vale had her eyes pinched shut, pretending to be asleep like a child hiding from her parents. She could pretend all she wanted to, but I could hear her mind buzzing like a hive of bees.

I wouldn't be getting any sleep at this rate—not that I would at all with her so close. I envied Kian.

The man could sleep in a ditch if he had to, but more, he rested in the knowledge that he was in between the door and the woman he loved. It also didn't escape my notice that Xavier positioned himself between the glass doors of the balcony and Vale, either.

They surrounded her, protecting her with their bodies, and all I could do was lay there and envy them both.

"Want me to tell you a bedtime story? Because you and I both know you aren't sleeping."

She opened a single green eye, but that one eye was cutting all on its own. Still, she didn't open her mouth once.

"Is that a no? I'm going to need you to use your words, little Luxa."

The second eye opened, and her gaze was practically smoldering with her ire. *"I'm not a child. I do not need a bedtime story. Maybe if you didn't treat me like a brain-dead idiot who couldn't take care of herself, I wouldn't hate you so much."*

"You want to hate me, but you don't. The sooner you figure out why, the better off we'll all be." As much as it irked me *why* she wasn't speaking out loud, it was a small comfort to remember how tied we were that we

could talk this way. *"What if I were to tell you how the Luxa got their power—how they were created? It's not a widely known tale, only told to members of the family. It might not even be in any of the books in the library."*

I knew I had her at her raised eyebrows. Vale loved knowledge—she thirsted for it. I suspected a part of her hated that she didn't know more about what she was. That it was her resistance that had kept her in the dark for so long. I shouldn't have known that little tidbit, but the longer she remained close to me, the more and more I learned about my soon-to-be wife.

"Fine. But it better be a good story." She settled in, her assessing gaze like a physical touch. *"Or else."*

I couldn't help but curl my lip into a ghost of a smile. *"You know the curse on me affects the whole kingdom, but do you know why?"*

She shook her head. *"It is the Ashbourne line. We are integral to the flow of magic because we are the conduits of all magic in this realm. The first Ashbourne, Orin, was the revered keeper of this river of magic, the source of all power in the realm, but he was consumed by the bitter ache of loneliness, the weight of his burden almost too much for him to bear alone. He desired an equal—someone who did not draw from him or his magic, who did not rely on his power but had their own.*

"Night after night, day after day, he searched far and wide for such a being, but none came. Centuries he looked, but he found none his equal. Over the years, he married and had children, and the loneliness fell away. When his queen died, he began his search anew, exploring far and wide to ease the pain in his soul.

In the pit of his despair, he cast himself into the dreaming world, praying that he could find a companion. But this world was distorted and cruel, only showing him his failures as it trapped him in its clutches. And still, each night he returned, hoping against hope that his prayers would be answered. One such night, deep in a troubled dreamscape, a luminous figure of pure light came to him, casting away his fears and loneliness, easing the aching bitterness of his poor heart."

A faint trace of a smile lifted the edges of her lips. It was a story my mother had told Arden and me as children. He'd always loved this story, while I had hated it, knowing it would be me one day—stuck in the endless necessity of holding up the mantle of my crown. But Arden loved the pain of it all, the heartbreak. I should have known then just how twisted my brother would end up.

"Lirael was not like any being he had ever encountered, not from the waking world at all, but existing solely in the Dreaming Realm. A being of timeless magic and incredible power, he knew he had found someone who would not drain him but would heal his soul. Reluctantly, he returned to the waking world, but each night, he sought her out in this timeless space. She welcomed him as a companion, and they shared their highest hopes and deepest desires as they explored the Dreaming together.

"But the longer Orin spent in the Dreaming, the more he craved it—the more he craved her—and the bond forged in dreams began to grow. In the waking world, the king's body withered, the power used to find his love draining him near unto death. His family pleaded for him to stay with them, begged him not to go back to that far-off realm and leave them behind. But he could not resist her pull, and the magic of the world threatened to die with him."

Sorrow filled her expression, and I wished I would have thought of a better story to tell her. Vale's life had always been one of sacrifice. Maybe it was how she was made, but I still hated that for her.

"In a moment of desperation, Orin begged Lirael to come with him to the waking world and become his queen, but she could not, finally revealing a bitter truth.

Lirael was the keeper of the Dreaming, a goddess, and no matter how much he wished it, she could not leave that realm. Orin became despondent and pleaded with her to keep him with her, but she knew that if he lost his life in the waking world, the magic of Credour would die with him.

"Heartbroken, she knew the pull of her world was too much for him, and she thrust Orin from the Dreaming, barring him from entering ever again. But though she banished him, she did not leave him without a gift. Lirael spun the threads of the first Luxa witches, weaving them from her love of Orin and the pieces of her very soul. These witches would possess the light of the Dreaming, free to walk between the two realms. Using nearly all of her power, she thrust them into the waking world, breathing her life into them.

"But this gift came at a steep price. While Luxa are beings of light and magic, they are also more bound to the Dreaming Realm than any other, the pieces of Lirael calling them deeper and deeper into the Dreaming. If they stray too long, the realm will call them home, back to the breast of Lirael, never to leave again."

Tears fell into the valley of the bridge of her nose before dropping to the pillow under her head. *"That was horrible. They never had their happily ever after. It was just pain and sorrow. Why would you think that was something I needed to know?"*

As much as I hated to upset her, I also loved that she hated that story as much as I did. *"Because Luxa are born from the Dreaming, but more, they are called to the deepest parts of it. And because they are called so deep, they must tread carefully, or else they will be lost to it. I've never met a Luxa as tied to the Dreaming as you are, Vale. Never."*

And that worried me far more than even the attempts on her life.

A lot more.

CHAPTER 3
VALE

In the days under the mountain, I longed for the comforts of the ruling class more than anything. I'd wanted decent food and a soft bed and chairs with cushions. It wasn't until I was remanded to this singular set of rooms did I realize just how much I hated being cooped up.

Tying the laces of my boots, I contemplated the history lesson Idris had provided the night before. The scary part of it was, I knew he wasn't lying—that the lore of the Luxa was based on a very real truth. That realm was a problem I hadn't realized I had until it nearly killed me.

Again.

A part of me absolutely hated that I might have been that close to Nyrah and left without her. The other part of me knew just how sinister the dreaming world could be—just how violent, how dangerous. Had the *Lumentium* under the mountain kept me safe from the Dreaming? Had it blocked the Dreaming from calling me home? Or was I grasping at straws, trying to find reasons to go back to that prison of the guild to find my sister?

"You have got to be joking," Rune rumbled into my brain. *"There's no way you're going back there. You know it isn't safe."*

So the overgrown pigeon was speaking to me again? After our spat last night and his demands that I learn what being a Luxa meant, he'd refused to actually explain what the fuck he'd been talking about.

"Mind your business. It was an errant thought, not a plan. I'm fairly certain the execution attempt negated all travel to the Perder Lucem *for the foreseeable future."*

I'd need more than just determination to infiltrate the guild. I'd need a whole damn army and way more power than what I had. Grumbling, I pulled the laces of the scaled corset, cinching it tight over my torso. It had managed to keep me alive during the second trial, and I had no intention of leaving this room without it. It fit nicely under the emerald-green dress I'd chosen for the day, which I'd paired with a set of jeweled daggers at my belt.

"Sure. And your desire to find your sister didn't nearly kill you last night. That must have been some other Luxa."

Rolling my eyes like he could see me, I shoved out of the dressing room. *"And like I said last night, it was an accident. I—"*

"Didn't mean to," he growled, cutting me off like the jerk he was. *"Funny, that didn't stop you from nearly taking away everything. It didn't stop you from nearly leaving me to this life—alone—forever. It's like you want to die. When are you going to figure out that if you die, I'm stuck like this?"*

In the grand scheme, it sounded a little like bullshit. I wasn't the only Luxa alive, now, was I? There was a whole damn line of us, right? Plenty of them could still be born, plenty of them—

"Are you insinuating that I am the last Luxa? Because you and I both know that's not true. Nyrah is alive, and though I don't want her to go through any of this—" Just the thought of her being in my shoes made me want to smash something.

"Forget I said anything. It doesn't matter," he grumbled, and then it was as if he fled from my mind. Since Rune started speaking to me, he had been

there, just lurking in the recesses of my brain, waiting to give his opinion. Now, he was just gone.

Mentally, I searched for him, reached for him, and though I felt as if I could find him, it was as if he had thrown up a wall between us. *"Excuse you. You do not get to drop that little nugget of truth and then run away. What are you talking about?"*

I waited for him to answer me, but all I got was a mind full of silence. "Hello?" I shouted, not bothering to try and speak inside his head. "You cannot say something like that and then shut me out. What is going on?"

Freya raised her eyebrows, staring at me like I was losing what was left of my mind. I didn't bother explaining. If Rune wanted to be silent mind to mind, then I would just walk down those stupidly steep stairs and talk to him face-to-face. Even though just thinking about the damned things made my stomach lurch, he was keeping something from me, and I was tired of being in the dark.

Yanking my cloak off the arm of a settee, I threw it over my shoulders as I marched toward the door.

"Where do you think you're going?" Freya asked, appearing at my side as if she materialized from nothing. "You have an appointment for a dress fitting in a few hours. Considering too many people in this kingdom are trying to kill you, you're grounded, little witch."

Forcing myself not to jump, I shot her a glare. "Rune is being a stingy little shit with some key details, and I'm going down to that gods-forsaken cavern and talking to the overgrown pigeon face-to-face. Is that a problem?"

Freya knocked the fiery braid off her shoulder. "*Yes*," she said like I was a complete idiot. "It's a huge problem. You have survived not one, not two, but at least five assassination attempts—especially if we include your little mage debacle on the way here. If you honestly believe you're going anywhere, you, my tiny friend, are dreaming."

As if dreaming hadn't gotten me into this mess.

This felt similar to when Xavier and Kian decided I was getting on a boat to abscond off the continent for my own safety. I was tempted to do now what I should have done then and tell her to go fuck herself. I highly doubted Freya would think that was particularly cute.

She'd likely threaten to bite me.

"Am I a prisoner, Freya?" I asked, gauging just how best to play this.

I swear, that single raised eyebrow could flay someone alive. "No, if you were a prisoner, you'd be in the dungeons above Rune's hidey-hole. You are in the king's chambers with every luxury in the kingdom."

As if that made it any less of a prison. "But I must stay in these rooms and go nowhere else, is that correct?"

Freya's features hardened as she moved between me and the door. "You were up on that mountain. You saw exactly what our enemy is capable of. Do you honestly think outside of these rooms is safe for you? After what we saw?"

Freya didn't understand—none of them did. I'd lived a long life of fearing death with every step, every errant move. But those poor Luxa had died to break this curse—they'd lost their lives thinking they were doing the right thing. And if Rune wasn't talking out of his giant ass, I might be the last one—the last chance, the last of my kind.

Then again, he could just be a stingy, fact-hiding asshole. Gods, I was tired of this shit already.

"Not particularly, no. I also don't really care for being told what to do—especially when I'm going to be a queen in a week. You do understand that, right?" I shifted to the left, trying to get around her, but she blocked me in earnest. "Would you enjoy being remanded to a set of rooms and told that you were too weak, too fragile, to defend yourself in the castle you were supposed to call home? Would you take kindly to someone stealing the very last bit of your freedom under the banner of keeping you 'safe' when not only is that a foreign concept, but it just plain isn't true."

She blinked as if I'd just slapped her, but then that mouth of hers firmed into a hard line.

"I've never been safe—not one day in my life. I won't be safe here, in that hallway, or in the middle of the *Perder Lucem*. I *will* be safe next to Rune, and I need to know what he knows because I'm the only one who can speak to him and get an answer."

She pursed her mouth as she planted her hands on her hips, seeming to contemplate my existence for a hot second. "You have a point. I would hate it just as much as you do. Unfortunately, I can defend myself without the risk of imminent death, and well, you can't." She gently but firmly took the cloak from my shoulders and tossed it back on the settee. "I'm handling business and can't babysit you, so you're staying here."

Then she guided me to a chair and pushed me backward until I planted my ass on it. Then she waved her hand at the door, and a web of magic revealed itself. Xavier might not have been able to teach me very much in the way of magic, but I did understand that she was unlocking a ward on this very room.

"You're really going to leave me here?"

"Like I said, I have things to do, and they need to get done before your dress fitting. After that, I'll take you downstairs to see Rune, but not before."

I watched the intricate pattern of the ward breaking as she unlocked the magic to let herself out. Then Freya reached for the door handle, seeming to pause for a second. "I'm not trying to be an asshole. This is just how it has to be."

"I understand," I whispered, casting my gaze downward. Disappointment washed through me, and I figured that was probably enough to disguise my scent so she wouldn't suspect anything.

Because as soon as she closed that door, I would figure a way out of this room.

"I'm sorry," she said, and then she closed the door behind her, the bright magic of the ward weaving itself back together as it locked down every part of Idris' chambers.

She was sorry, huh? Funny, no one seemed very sorry to hide me away in a gods-forsaken tower, waiting around for something to happen. No one seemed sorry that I was being sequestered waiting for my wedding day, acting like I was too young, too stupid, too naïve to learn about the kingdom around me. Well, I needed answers, and if I sat on my hands, I wouldn't find out anything.

I waited two, maybe three minutes before I did something that Freya could never do—something Xavier didn't understand, and Idris couldn't explain. I didn't need to pick the lock on the ward.

I could cut right through it.

Letting the heat of my power wash through me, I formed a blade of light in my hand. I'd been working on summoning my power without cutting myself. It was a work in progress, but this small blade of magic was just what I needed. In one swift swipe, the glowing ward keeping me from the rest of the castle frayed, allowing me to reach for the doorknob. The cold metal was a welcome sensation as I quickly twisted the handle and walked right through that bastard of a door that had been keeping me captive.

"I hope you heard that, you dick. I'm coming to you, and there's not a damn thing you can do about it. You'd better warm up your mental vocal cords because you're going to sing, dammit."

But Rune didn't say a word. He didn't so much as rumble in my mind, and his silence was starting to freak me out. Sticking to the edges of the corridors, I tried to remember the way to the throne room. Close to those intricately carved double doors lay a small alcove where I'd once argued with Idris. Not ten feet from that alcove sat the doors to the catacombs and that gods-forsaken stone staircase that led to the blackness of the cavern.

Three left turns and two harrowing staircases later, I knew I was in the right place. But something had me checking in on Idris. I knew he was in that throne room doing something kingly, but what if the meeting was almost over? He'd catch me trying to talk to Rune, and then it would be a whole ordeal with his impossibly sexy frown and stupidly hot, high-handed ways.

"And you'd better not give me shit for that, you asshole. It's bad enough I'm even admitting that to myself."

Luckily, Rune was still quiet as a mouse. Then again, him not talking to me wasn't a good thing. Not at all.

Sticking to the shadows, I closed my eyes and tried to search Idris out. He'd been right when he'd said our proximity helped the bond between our minds. I could feel him in the back of my brain, much like I felt Rune and, to a lesser extent, Kian and Xavier. Since the mountain, I could sense him more clearly, his thoughts not quite clear all the time, but getting there.

For the first time ever, I pushed—seeking him out, reaching for him.

Staggering into the wall, I hung on for dear life as the throne room overtook my vision. I hadn't just peeked into Idris' mind, I was seeing through his eyes. Nausea weighed down my tongue as a spike of pain lanced through my head. But for whatever reason, I couldn't drop the link.

What remained of the council sat across from Idris, concern and cowardice stamped all over them as his voice thundered through the circular room.

"I didn't stutter, did I? Or did you forget that five councilmembers attempted a coup less than forty-eight hours ago? They threatened my life, my kingdom, my bride. And you think I'll let their kin live? They call me a beast for a reason, Dorian."

"But, Your Majesty, their families could be innocent. There is no reason to murder them—can't you see that?"

"I see the guild's influence has threaded its blackened fingers through my kingdom, touching everything. I see there are very few I can trust. I see that those men showed me just how far they were willing to go for their cause. I want their bloodlines eradi-

cated down to the very last drop—do you understand me?"

I yanked my consciousness from his mind so fast, it was as if I had been scalded by Rune's flames. Covering my mouth with a shaking hand, I swallowed bile. Idris had just ordered the deaths of men, women, and children.

Was this why he didn't want me to see how this kingdom was run?

Was this why I'd been sequestered to his rooms?

Was this Freya's business she had to attend to?

A lash of fury boiled through my veins, and my feet moved before consulting my brain.

"Don't, my Queen. It won't solve anything."

So, the overgrown pigeon was talking to me again? Well, it was too little, too late.

This time, it was me who shoved him out, cutting Rune off from every thought, every feeling as I rounded the corner. Guards stood outside the throne room doors, their crossed spears barring my way. Power sizzled down my arms, bursting from my fingertips as I knocked them away from the doors.

A split second later, those doors were ash, exploding in a hail of debris as I strode into the throne room, staring down the man who would be my husband in a few short days.

If either of us lived that long.

CHAPTER 4
IDRIS

Her rage hit me square in the chest mere moments before the doors to the throne room blew apart. My ancestor, Orin, carved the wood of those doors by hand, refusing to use an ounce of magic to create them. In doing so, he inadvertently imbued them with his very essence. Before Vale destroyed them with her magic, they had hung in every Ashbourne castle since the dawn of time.

And my future Queen had just blown them apart like tissue paper.

I didn't know if I should be frightened or turned the fuck on.

Both.

Probably both.

As the dust cleared, I met those gorgeous green eyes, the fury in them boiling over as brilliant magic sparked from her fingertips. Tendrils of her hair floated about her head as the heat of her power sizzled through the room, touching nearly everything with her light.

Was this how Orin felt when he gazed upon Lirael the first time? If so, it was no wonder he was willing to risk it all to be with her. Vale was fucking magnificent, and I was starting not to give a fuck that she'd blown a hole in my carefully crafted ruse.

Her dress fluttered around her legs as if she were caught in a tempestuous storm, and that light of hers got brighter, hotter, bigger, threatening to consume all of us with it.

"If you think I survived that fucking mountain to sit idly by while you kill innocent people, you've got another thing coming," she growled through gritted teeth. "Not only will I not marry you, but you can kiss me breaking your curse goodbye. I'd have sacrificed damn near anything for the man I thought I knew, but I'll be damned if I save a monster."

I was right: she was magnificent. More than that, she was nothing like Zamarra. With that one statement, she proved to be exactly who I thought she was —exactly who Rune would choose, who Kian and

Xavier would fall for, who I would be damn lucky to rule beside.

But she had it all wrong. This was just one big game of chicken, and I needed to see who would blink first.

Gently, I reached with my mind, but all I got was a blistering wall of her power shutting me out. A trickle of blood dripped from my nose as I staggered backward, the force of her rage more than I antici-pated. She had shut me out—this little slip of a woman barely into her power had all but slapped me across the face with it.

"Vale, my Queen, you—" Xavier started, but when her eyes landed on him, he, too, staggered backward.

Tears filled her eyes as a lash of her magic turned the room from warm to sweltering, the stone under her feet blackening with the heat of it.

"I expected more from you, Xavier. Him? I never trusted. But you? How could you just sit there and say nothing? Do nothing?"

Xavier forced himself to his feet as he wiped the blood from his nose with the back of his hand. "Please, little witch. If you would just let us in, we could explain."

The laugh that spilled from her mouth chilled me

to the bone. She might be nothing like Zamarra, but her power was just as strong. A shockwave of it rocked the room, knocking men from their seats as chairs toppled to the ground. Tapestries fell from their fastenings and the candelabras blew out, their iron holders crashing to the stone floor.

"Don't you dare call me that. What he's proposing is genocide." Her piercing gaze returned to me, and the heat of it was a punch to the gut. "That makes him no better than the guild. The same guild that sentenced me to death, who killed my parents, who murdered my people."

Two hundred years ago, I'd faced down a witch in this very room, clinging to life—to my magic with all the strength I had. To see Vale here with her power so great, her rage so acute, it was as if I had traveled back in time. Back then it was I who had been betrayed by the woman I loved. Now I realized Vale thought it was I who had done the betraying.

All because she believed the lie.

"Is this why you keep me locked up? Why you refuse to tell me anything? Why you dodge every question?" Twin tracks of tears fell down her cheeks before the heat of her dried them.

Those tears opened up a pit in my stomach,

making me forget the council, my crown, my purpose.

"No, Vale," I whispered, realizing just how wrong I'd been. "We only wanted to protect you. Please, if you'd just let me explain."

I should have kept her close, taught her about Credour, told her... well, *everything*. She should have been part of this plan from the start. I'd been wrong, so wrong, and I didn't know how to fix it.

Violently, she shook her head. "I watched you say it. I watched you order their deaths. 'Down to the last drop,' you said. There is no explaining it away."

She'd burn herself out if she kept going like this. Gritting my teeth, I allowed my volatile magic to rise, letting it consume every boundary and ward that kept it stable. The ache of it filled my bones, but the golden power filled the room, the tendrils of it surrounding Vale in a cocoon of energy.

Searing agony slammed into me, but I breeched her shield, curling around her much like I had in her dream. Only then could I find a crack in her mental wards.

"There you are," I murmured in her mind, relief a fleeting memory.

"Get out of my head. You're a monster."

"I love that you think so, but I'm really not. All this

is a ruse, Vale. A trick meant to flush out those in league with the guild."

Blood dripped from her nose, and she let out an angry growl as she tried to shove me from her mind.

"I don't believe you," she hissed, her voice cracking. Her attention left me for a moment, her betrayal and blind fury not waning for a second as she met Xavier's pleading gaze.

"Give me two minutes to flush a traitor out, and if you still don't believe me, I'll let you walk right out of my kingdom. I won't even stop you," I begged, hoping against hope that my plan would play out like I wanted it to.

"I swear it on Rune's life—my life."

Those brilliant green eyes finally landed on me, and it was as if the sun had returned after a long winter.

"I'll play along this time, but I'm holding you to those two minutes. If I don't believe you after that, then I don't care what I promised, I will never break your curse—do you understand?"

Didn't she understand that I didn't give a fuck about the curse—not if it meant losing her? Didn't she know by now that I would give anything for her to see me the way she saw Kian and Xavier?

That I would sacrifice anything?

That I cared less and less about a kingdom that had never once appreciated my sacrifice? About a council that was dead set on seeing magic die?

Of course not. Why would she?

I'd been the one to keep her in the dark. I'd been the one so scared someone would take her and torture her that I'd given her nothing—no knowledge, no preparation, nothing. If she stayed, she would be my queen in a few short days, and she knew she was wildly unprepared for the role.

Her lack of faith in me was my fault and mine alone.

"I swear I'm not lying, Vale. If you believe nothing else, please believe that I would never harm innocent people to save my own ass."

Her face twisted into a grimace, but her light slowly dimmed, the wall of power flickering as she pulled it back into herself. She didn't believe me—hell, she didn't even trust me—but she would give me just enough rope to hang myself with.

"You really think this is the only way to protect me—killing whole families?" she growled.

A twinge of relief hit the back of my throat as I nodded, playing along. "They conspired with the guild to kill you. They've been right under our noses all along. We have to flush the rot from the kingdom."

And while what I was saying had a grain of truth, genocide would never be on my list of options. Arden, however, had never stopped there, now, had he? He and Zamarra had been a team, and still he murdered her kin—Vale's kin. Granted, not being my brother was a low bar, but I'd fucking clear it.

"And if it means saving your life," I added, telling her the absolute truth, "then I'll kill whoever I need to make sure you stay breathing."

"Very well." Her shoulders slumped as she bowed her head, selling it far better than I ever thought possible. "I won't stand in your way. Do what you must."

The five remaining members of the council peered at her over the debris, but it wasn't until one seemed to shimmer from the ether did I realize just how close the danger was. Before I could warn her, Vale was caught in his snare.

I now remembered exactly why I'd kept her in the dark. Because the danger was everywhere—it was everyone—even in someone I trusted.

Ithran brought his blade to her throat, putting her small body in front of his as his magic crackled through the air. The High Lord ruled the Fae, his power rivaling most in the kingdom. As one of my closest advisers, outside of Xavier, he had been the least of my worries, and yet, here he was trying to take my world from me.

"What do you think you're doing, Ithran? Let her go," I thundered, readying my magic as Xavier drew his sword. "If you have a problem with me, I'm right here."

"Oh, so now you pay attention," he hissed, his midnight eyes flashing with his magic. Tendrils of darkness pooled at his feet, curling like ropes around Vale's legs. "But only when I have what you want." The Fae Lord tilted his head as he ran his thin, pale nose up the side of Vale's neck. "Pretty little Luxa has too much power. She should share. You surely don't."

"Vale, don't move. I'll get you out of this." It was a stupid platitude, and yet, I couldn't stop myself from promising her something I didn't know if I could deliver.

She let out a mirthless little laugh that had Ithran digging his metal-tipped fingers into the tender flesh of her middle. Vale hissed in pain as blood darkened her emerald dress.

Too much blood.

"Two hundred years living off of scraps of power, and this little whisp of a woman waltzes in here with a boatload of it, shining like a beacon in the dark. Call me crazy, but why would we let her waste all her magic saving you, when we could tap her neck like a keg and drain her dry instead? Cut out the middle-man, so to speak."

"I can get out of this," Vale whispered in my mind. *"I'm not dead yet, remember?"*

I fought the urge to shake my head. The last thing I needed was Ithran realizing she was armed with more than her magic. *"Don't. He's too powerful. Stay still and maybe I can talk him around."*

He brought those metal-tipped fingers to his lips, licking the blood from the razor-sharp edge. Ithran closed his eyes in bliss as he tasted her, and I couldn't stop my magic from rocking the very castle underneath our feet.

I didn't care if I brought the whole fucking thing down on our heads as long as she got out of this alive.

"Your brother makes promises he can't deliver. You dawdle breaking your curse, following the rules when your kingdom is dying. No wonder everyone around you is gunning for your bride," Ithran mused. "And fuck if she doesn't smell good enough to eat. I wonder why you haven't claimed her. I would have the first night."

He ground his pelvis against her backside, and Vale's pale cheeks reddened, her rage getting the better of her. Any other time I'd welcome it, but this time, I was helpless as she ripped the blade from her belt. Flipping the dagger in her hand, she jammed it into Ithran's thigh, twisting away from the one at her throat.

But just like when Arden had her up on that mountain, she failed to protect her middle.

I watched in horror as Ithran's blade went into her side. Vale staggered back, covering the wound with her hand, her legs crumbling beneath her almost instantly.

Xavier darted forward, but I was frozen for the longest second of my life. The roar that came out of me might as well have been my death knell. Power exploded from my skin, tearing through the room as Ithran staggered backward.

My golden magic and Xavier's blue fire met a wall of Ithran's shadows, jabbing like spears against the High Lord's defenses.

And then it was as if everything just froze.

My magic.

Xavier's flames.

Ithran's shadows.

Sounds died, the wind stopped, the fight immobilized as a sword of light appeared in the middle of Ithran's chest. He clawed at the blade for what seemed like far too long before glowing veins of magic snaked up his throat, filling his eyes, burning them out from the inside.

Then that blade hooked left, cutting through him like butter. The High Lord fell in pieces to the ground, revealing a bloody-but-very-alive Vale, the ripped bodice of her dress gaping to reveal the black scales of her armor. My knees hit the ground as relief weakened every limb.

Ithran hadn't taken her from me.

Vale was alive.

She was alive.

She staggered, but before I could reach for her, Xavier had her in his arms, holding her up as he healed her middle. She wilted into him, relief hitting her face as she rested her head on his chest.

Her smile was wry, but she was looking at me without contempt for once.

"I don't know how to tell you this, but you have an internal problem. You might want to get on with fixing it before it kills me."

My laugh was mirthless as I took stock of the room around us.

"Tell me something I don't know."

CHAPTER 5
XAVIER

Even with Vale in my arms, I still felt as if someone would steal her from me at any moment. Idris was on his knees in the middle of this room staring at the body of his enemy, and still, I would rather clutch Vale to me than fulfill my duty to him.

I knew it was wrong, and still, I couldn't make myself move.

She never should have been here. She never should have been without a guard. And under no circumstances should she have been anywhere near the traitors in our midst.

And yet, with all the wards and protections, I'd nearly lost her in a split second.

Again.

I knew my grip on her middle was too tight. I knew the way I was holding her was completely inappropriate in our mixed company. All it would take was Idris' wounded pride to shatter everything. All it would take was a councilmember making a fuss, or Kian to waltz in, or Freya to start on her bullshit, and everything would go pear-shaped.

And still... I couldn't let her go.

Dorian, and what was left of the council, murmured their disbelief at Ithran's actions, but I just couldn't bother to give that first fuck. I didn't care about anything but the woman in my arms, and the fact that she was breathing.

Everything else was irrelevant.

My animal warred with the blind panic in my gut for dominance, ripping me apart as my gaze roamed her body, looking for more wounds to heal. Ithran had practically tried to disembowel her, and for what? Power? Power he would get if he just waited a week? The bond would break the curse and then all this would be over.

But a part of me didn't believe that, and I seriously doubted anyone else did, either.

How many times had we been here with her hurt and me praying this wasn't the last breath, the last heartbeat, the last time I'd see those brilliant green eyes staring at me?

"I'm fine," she whispered, her small hand covering mine at her middle where I had just healed her. Her words were meant to reassure me, but all they did was spark a fury that had no outlet—not here.

"You're fine, huh?" I seethed, desperately trying not to yell in the middle of this gods-forsaken room. "The only reason you're breathing is because you had the stroke of genius to put on armor—armor you shouldn't need in this castle, and yet"—I toyed with the rip in her dress—"here we are."

Guilt flitted across her face for a split second before she wiped it clean. "I know you're angry, but I never meant for this to happen."

"And just like I said last night: you never do." Clenching my jaw, I made my first smart decision of the day and shut the fuck up. If I uttered another word, it would spark an argument that would burn this whole castle to the ground.

"That's not fair," she whispered inside my mind. *"I had no intention of coming here and every intention of seeing Rune. Had I not overheard your false plot, I wouldn't be in this room at all. How was I to know Idris*

was lying? And why did you keep this from me? Why do you insist on keeping everything from me?"

As much as she was right, she was wrong, too. And why was she going to see Rune? Why was she by herself? Why—

"You're not where I left you," Freya drawled as she sauntered over, plucking debris from her copper braid. "I could have sworn I warded you up nice and tight in the king's chambers. Want to tell me how you got out? I thought I told you to stay put."

The blistering heat of fury in my gut doubled as scales rippled over my flesh and up my neck. Fangs lengthened in my mouth as my animal reached for the surface. And it wasn't just my anger flooding my veins, it was Vale's—her anger, her fear, her betrayal —none of it had dissipated.

Not one bit.

"And I told you that I needed to talk to Rune," Vale replied, casting a worried glance at my scales as she worked to unclench her jaw. "I haven't had a mommy in a very long time, Freya, and trust me, you aren't her." As Vale pushed from my arms and onto her feet, the scathing glare she sent Freya could have melted iron.

Didn't she understand just how dangerous every-where was for her?

Didn't she care?

The rumble of a growl vibrated my chest as I tried to swallow down my rage. How could she have been so reckless? Couldn't she see?

Talons erupted from my fingertips, the hold on my animal slipping inch by inch. Vale gripped my hand, hiding my lack of restraint in the folds of her skirt as she pulled me from the room. I barely had the control to follow her, but we didn't make it very far.

Without consulting my brain, my feet carried us into a hidden alcove, the dark shadow of the corridor hiding us from view. I crowded her, pressing her against the wall as I breathed her in, taking her scent into my nose to remind myself that she was alive.

"Xavier? Tell me what's wrong."

Wrong? Everything. Absolutely everything was wrong.

Fighting off the urge to mark her with my fangs, I clutched her to me tight as I refused to think about Ithran's metal claws in her belly—his dagger at her throat. The scent of her blood still filled my nose over everything, and I swore I could feel his blade tearing through her dress, plunging into her side.

One little garment had been between life and death.

One decision had meant I would live without her, or I wouldn't.

I couldn't take it.

"You could have died. I would have lost you. Again and again, you keep landing in danger, and I don't know how to breathe anymore. Every second we're apart, I think I'll come back to the worst."

Lifting her off her feet, I clutched her closer, burying my nose in the crook of her neck, breathing her in as her legs wrapped around me.

Fuck, that feels good.

"I'm alive. I'm safe."

But for how long? How long did we have until someone else tried to take her from us? It was like I'd forgotten how to breathe without her—forgotten how to live. I wasn't sure I could if she was gone.

"At night I dream I'm too late. I get to that room after you'd been attacked, and I can't save you. Your blood cools on my hands, and I watch you leave this world without me. Over and over—it's all I see."

She pulled backward, clutching my cheeks as she stared into my eyes. "I won't leave you, Xavier. I'll never leave you."

It was an empty promise—one she couldn't keep even if she wanted to. I was a dragon, and she was a

Luxa. Luxa didn't have a good track record of staying alive in our company.

"You can't promise that."

Gently, she brushed her soft lips against mine, and the need in my veins turned to ravenous hunger, sparking a desire so acute, I ached. I readily deepened the kiss, tasting her tongue with mine, drinking her down as I pressed her against the cold stone wall. The heat of her center did nothing to quell the ache in my cock, did nothing but make me mindless.

I needed her.

I needed her right there and right then.

We were in the middle of a barely hidden alcove. Anyone could've walked by and discovered us, and still, I couldn't make myself move one single inch—especially once her slim fingers reached inside my leathers and circled my cock.

"I need you, Vale. I need you so bad I can't think."

My eyes rolled into the back of my head as she ran her hand from base to tip. *"Fuck. If you don't stop that I'll take you right here. Is that what you want?"*

Vale squirmed against me as I raked my fangs against the tender skin of her neck, her low moan of need echoing mine. *"Yes. I want that. I want you. I need you."*

Lust, need, desire, it multiplied inside us, the emotions feeding off of each other until the pair of us were nearly mindless. She tore at the laces of my leathers as I reached up the skirts of her dress. The heat of her was like a beacon for my fingers, calling me home. I stroked her over her underwear before my impatience got the better of me. A second later, the scrap of lace was in ribbons as I tore it from her body.

My fingers found heaven as I plunged them inside her tight heat, loving the flutter of her pussy rippling around them. She was so wet, so ready, so hungry for me.

"Gods, I need you, Xavier. Please."

Fuck, if I didn't love it when she begged.

"You have to be quiet, understand? Not one sound or I'll stop—leave you aching and needy until you can't stand it anymore. I'll make sure it's hours until you come."

Her moan of frustration was my reward as I pulled my fingers from her and brought my cock to her opening. It got louder as I hovered just outside her entrance, and I pulled back.

"I thought you were going to be a good girl. Good girls get fucked, bad girls have to wait. Which one are you going to be?"

I was so close I could feel her slick heat wetting

the head of my cock, and yet, I had her exactly where I wanted her. The flush of her arousal crawled up her neck as those brilliant eyes grew heavy-lidded.

"I'll be good. Please."

I knew exactly how good she could be, but I liked her bad most of all.

Slowly, I pressed inside, and I had to grit my teeth, so I didn't turn into a ravenous beast and pound into her. I wanted to. Gods, how I wanted to, but I used every bit of restraint I had to sink inside her inch by inch.

And she needed the time. She was so tight, so hot, so fucking wet. The scent of her had my mouth watering so much I wished I would have gotten a taste before we got started.

Later. I'd taste her later.

"More. *Gods*, more," she moaned as she tightened her legs around my hips, pulling me in, holding me tight as she tried to take me deeper.

Vale's brow puckered as she sucked in a whimpering gasp when I pulled all the way out. *"Quiet, little witch, or you get nothing."*

Nodding, she covered her mouth with her hand. It wouldn't help even a little, but I did love her enthusiasm.

"So fucking greedy. Have I told you how much I love how greedy you are?"

A second later, I was back inside, and already, I was close to losing control. Her hot hands on my skin, her shuddering breaths, gods, I would unman myself if she didn't quit. For self-preservation's sake, I held her wrists in one hand, pinning them to the wall.

It was equally the smartest thing I could have done and the dumbest. Smart because she couldn't drive me crazy with her touch, and complete idiocy because Vale really liked being restrained, and the whimper that came out of her nearly had me losing my mind.

Driving into her, I relished every moan, every cry, every flutter of her pussy. Vale couldn't be quiet, and I couldn't stop. If I stopped, I'd explode. Covering her mouth with mine, I fucked into her like the beast I was.

I was too close to losing it, too close to forgetting my carefully crafted control.

"Starting the party without me?" Kian drawled, his presence both a shock and not all at the same time. His abilities made sneaking up on people his favorite hobby, and sometime over the last two centuries, I stopped reacting.

Plus, I was busy.

Vale's breaths hitched as Kian drew closer, her pussy tightening around my cock as he enveloped us behind his veil of power. His illusion magic meant Vale could be as loud as she wanted, and no one could hear her scream.

"Gods, look at you, little witch," he murmured, nibbling at her neck, taking her wrists from me so I could fuck her harder. "All flushed and needy. You're going to come soon, aren't you?"

Moaning, she nodded, and not once did I stop. Not when Kian dipped his finger into her bodice and pulled, exposing a perfect breast, not when he sucked her pink nipple into his mouth. Fuck, it was as if her pussy had gotten hotter, searing me all the way down to my soul.

"Touch her clit," I ordered, needing her to come more than I needed air. "She's so close, I can feel it coming. She's going to scream."

Kian raked his fangs against the tender skin of her neck. "Is that what you want?" he taunted. "You want to come?"

Her blunted teeth sank into her bottom lip as a fine sheen of sweat dotted her brow. *"Pleasepleaseplease. I'll do anything. Please just let me come."*

"*Fuck*. You should hear her begging," I groaned, my balls tightening at just the thought of her pleas.

"Oh, I can. I'm sure Idris can hear you, too. Is he whispering in your mind, little Luxa?" Kian asked, nipping at her ear. "Is he describing how we'll spread you out and take turns fucking you? Maybe we'll fill all your holes at once? Take your mouth and pussy and ass at the same time. Fuck you until you can't think. I bet he is."

Her breath hitched as she nodded. "H-he's telling me to take my f-fucking like a good g-girl."

"What else is he telling you?" I asked, needing her to keep talking. Every time we pushed her boundaries, she squeezed me so tight.

Her eyes rolled into the back of her head when Kian found where we were joined by feel alone, the call of Vale's sex like a beacon. As soon as he touched her, it was as if she were kindling waiting for the first spark. She thrashed in my arms as her moans got louder, stronger, her release right at the surface just waiting to break free.

"Look at me," I ordered, my talons gripping her flesh but not breaking it. "What. Else. Is. He. Telling. You?"

She shook her head as she tried to pull me closer with her legs, but neither of us would let her get very far. My thrusts slowed, and Kian removed his hand. "Tell me or we won't let you come."

Vale whimpered. "Okay, okay. H-he said n-next time he wants to w-watch me c-come."

There were a million reasons that was a bad idea, and a million more why I'd make sure that happened as soon as possible.

"Let's not keep the king waiting, then. Come for me. Let all of us feel you falling apart."

My thrusts turned brutal, punishing, and then her orgasm sizzled through the bond. Invading my senses, she took over every thought, every breath, every part of me, enveloping me in her bliss and taking me down with her.

Kian thrummed her clit as he took her mouth, quieting her screams as I filled her with my seed, her golden light wrapping around us like a cloak. As soon as I came down, I stole her from Kian, taking her lips for my own. Sweeping my tongue into her mouth, I swallowed another moan as I reluctantly pulled my cock from her depths.

Fuck, I missed her already.

And other than a really good orgasm, we'd solved absolutely nothing.

Gently, I set Vale on her feet, keeping her steady as she got her bearings.

Kian's gaze landed on her middle where there were five slashes showing her bare skin. The fabric sections of her corset were no match for Ithran's metal claws. We'd need to get her a new one with full dragon scales from top to bottom instead of just at the sternum and ribs.

"Someone had better be dead." His nostrils flared as his irises lengthened to the slits of his dragon. Blackened scales rippled up his neck.

"I took care of it," Vale murmured, covering the slashes with her hand.

His attention moved to her ribs and the rip in her bodice. His eyes were full-on glowing now, but he kept his hold on his control. "Come on, little witch, let's get you cleaned up before you meet the new council."

I nearly staggered back on a foot, aching to rip her out of his arms. "What? No. Not after what just happened. We can't trust them."

The plan had been for the new council to get here much later, for Freya to do a bleed and read of the older members and the new to make sure they weren't with the guild. Until that happened, Vale wouldn't be safe.

I doubted she would be safe regardless.

"We can't keep her in the dark, Xavier. We'll lose her

if we do."

Kian's voice in my head outside of his dragon form was a brand-new development. And while it was likely tied to us mating the same woman, it didn't make me like his words one bit.

I tightened my hold on her. "The only way she's walking in that room is with armor, you understand me?"

Vale whipped her head up to stare at me. "You're not going to stop me?"

There was no stopping her—not really. And Kian was right. If we stood in her way, she'd find a way to leave us. I saw her in that throne room. Another betrayal, and she would never trust us again.

I was caught between protecting her body or her heart. At least if she had armor on, it would make one of those jobs easier.

"Haven't you figured it out yet, little witch? There is no stopping you."

I just hoped not standing in her way didn't end up killing her.

CHAPTER 6
VALE

Hell was real, and it was alive and well in Idris' bedroom.

"Is this necessary?" I whined, hanging onto a post of Idris' bed as Kian cinched my new corset.

The additional armor was on the outside of thick fighting leathers that fit me like a second skin. The leathers themselves were scaled at all major arteries, but the corset covered my entire middle from collarbone to hips. Magically crafted, the blood-red scales could have only come from one dragon—a dragon that was still not speaking to me.

"Asshole. If you'd just talk to me, I could tell you thank you, you turd."

I could barely breathe in the thing, but Kian still

trussed me up like a turkey, making the already-snug fit even tighter. I didn't know when they'd started crafting it, but the detail was exquisite. And just like so many garments, it had simply appeared in Idris' room for me to find.

"I want you to take a look at the dress I peeled off of you and ask that shit again," Kian growled, his hot breath on the sliver of exposed skin of my neck.

Fighting off a shiver, I ignored the pulse in my sex as I glanced at the pile of rags that used to be my dress. Kian had cut it off me as he checked my whole body for further injury. I had a feeling his inspection had more to do with him destroying a reminder of how close I'd come to death rather than the highly erotic foreplay it had turned into—foreplay that wouldn't see me satisfied until this meeting was over.

"Fine. The armor is necessary." Given how I'd nearly gotten gutted by a creepy Fae Lord, I couldn't exactly blame him for his caution, but... "Can you tell me why you insist on teasing me, then?"

Kian wrapped his fist in my braid and pulled my head back as he yanked me flush against him. Even through his leathers, his hard cock pressing against the small of my back was a stark reminder that he hadn't gotten any relief in that alcove.

Yep, he was torturing the both of us on purpose.

While I'd offered to help him in that area, Kian had declined, and now I was aching again.

"Punishment, little witch. You don't listen to begging, you thoroughly enjoy spankings, and I will never cut into your pretty skin with anything other than my fangs. Denying you is all I have. Maybe if I make you so horny you can't see straight, then you'll stick with one of us long enough to get through this."

No wonder he was a general. The man was fucking diabolical. "And it makes no difference to you that none of this is my fault?"

His teeth raked against my neck as he turned us to the one spot in the room I was ignoring like my life depended on it. "Is it your fault that you sliced through the ward of this room like it was nothing?"

I closed my eyes to try and ignore it, but I could still hear the water running, and my brain had supplied all it needed to picture what was happening in the bathing chamber.

"Open your eyes and watch. It's no fun if you don't watch."

My belly dipped as I did as I was told—for once. The door to the bathing chamber was wide open. Positioned exactly so I could see him was a very naked Xavier, his fiery blue eyes on me as bubbles cascaded down his torso. His hand was wrapped around his thick cock, the slow strokes making me squirm.

"Is it your fault that you explored the castle unattended?"

Yep, this was Hell, and I was burning in the flames of mindless desire. I'd bet if Kian deigned to touch my clit, I would combust right there and then.

"Is it your fault that you consistently and pathologically ignore the advice of everyone around you, even though we are centuries your senior?"

Kian nipped at the lobe of my ear, his sultry voice touching every inch of my skin as I watched Xavier's erotic show. Gods, he was evil—they both were. And dammit if he didn't have a point.

"Is there any chance I could get you to consider my side of things before you tease us all into oblivion?"

His low chuckle in my ear was pure evil. "You don't have to tell me your reasons because, had I been in your shoes, I likely would have done the same thing. You left this room because we were keeping you in the dark. You went through the castle because you thought Rune was lying to you. And you ignored our advice because you thought we didn't trust you to be able to handle it."

If he knew all of this, why was he being a stingy prick?

My thoughts must have been loud because he answered me in that low, sexy growl that had my clit pulsing and my core aching for him.

"I'm denying you as much as I'm denying myself. Time and time again, we forget this lesson, and if we don't quit, we'll lose you. If we are to trust you to be our mate, we need to tell you what you're up against. If you are to trust us as *your* mate, then you need to listen to our advice. Both sides are failing miserably, little witch—none of us are right."

Turning in his arms, I latched onto his leathers and brought him down to my level. It wasn't lost on me that he wouldn't bend unless he wanted to, but I still felt the power of his kiss curling my toes. The flames of blind need sizzled down my spine as the kiss went from sweet to carnal in the span of a single second. Kian lifted me off my feet, and I locked my ankles behind his back.

We'd just be a little late, right?

"Do not make me come up there," Idris growled into my mind, the threat just as intoxicating as Xavier and Kian's teasing, reminding me of his voice in my head as Xavier pounded into me, as Kian whispered

in my ear, as pleasure washed through me so acute I thought I might die from it.

I hadn't thought him in my mind would be something I almost needed, but in that alcove with Xavier inside me and Kian surrounding me, and Idris fanning mindless pleasure through our link, I realized he and I were a lot closer than I'd thought.

Something had changed after he made his promise. It was almost like trust—the walls around my heart crumbling just a fraction.

"I have a demolished throne room to deal with in the middle of a brand-new council bleed and read, and your desire is so strong, I'm considering telling the entire continent to go fuck themselves so I can watch you come."

Gods, these three were going to kill me. Fuck our enemies, this brand of torture would do me in for sure.

"Now be a good little Luxa and get your delicious ass down here. You have a council to swear in."

That had me straightening, pulling away from Kian's mouth as the room around me practically disappeared. My focus was only on Idris. *"I knew I'd be in the throne room, and I knew I'd meet them, but I had no idea I would be swearing anyone in. Are you serious?"*

A teeny trill of pride hit me right in the chest—Idris' pride, not mine. *"You wanted to be part of this kingdom. It's time I trusted you to be my queen. No more secrets, right?"*

"What is it?" Kian murmured, setting me on my feet.

I blinked away my surprised tears, the emotion hitting me out of nowhere. "Idris wants me to help swear the new council in."

For the first time, it wasn't like I was just some witch they'd found to use for their own gain. It wasn't like I was a tool to be wielded or a bargaining chip. For the first time, I was taking part of what would be the rest of my life. And while I had never dreamed I would actually be a queen of this kingdom, the fact I was actually participating filled me with such a sense of purpose that I almost didn't know what to do with myself.

I hadn't been here for very long, but every single moment had felt like I was a pawn in a game I had never wanted to play. This felt different.

The water shut off and Xavier strode into the room, a fluffy white towel around his hips. "Please tell me something else hasn't gone wrong."

"No," I whispered, a true smile hitting my mouth for maybe the first time all day. "Just the opposite."

* * *

The throne room was still in shambles, a fact that did not make me feel at all proud of myself. My rage had done permanent damage, had possibly hurt Idris' reputation, and had the potential to affect how these people saw me. According to Xavier and Kian, we needed their support to help quell the unrest in the continent—that having these factions behind us would ensure the kingdom thrived after Idris' curse was broken.

Not that I knew how to break the curse or if I was even capable of it.

"You are," Rune murmured, his voice welcome, even if he was a little shit. *"You are the key. Now quit doubting yourself and pick your head up. You will be Queen soon. Act like it."*

The bite of tears hit my eyes for a second before I swallowed them down. *"Glad you're talking to me again. I missed you. Please don't shut me out anymore. I hated it."*

I could practically feel his eyes rolling. *"I had no intention of shutting you out the first time. There are rules to this curse, my Queen. Rules I cannot tell you, but ones I must abide by. I nearly broke one of them. I'm sorry, I didn't mean to cause you distress."*

"You could have just said 'I can't tell you.' I'm

starting to learn with this curse, the more someone knows, the less they can say."

Now that Fenwick's scroll had been destroyed, I wasn't sure how I was supposed to figure out what to do to even begin breaking Idris' curse. The few people who had the knowledge of how the damn thing was created couldn't say a word about it.

"Pay attention, my Queen. This is not the room to lose focus."

I blinked back into the room, my wary gaze landing on the group of magic-wielders kneeling at Idris' feet. They seemed nothing like the council that had once stared at me with contempt. Half of them looked scared out of their minds. The other half seemed ready to finish what Ithran had started.

Considering the state of the room, I didn't blame them. While I'd been busy donning armor, Freya had drunk from each new and old member—or at least the ones who hadn't run screaming after Ithran's death. Her abilities as an ancient vampire made it so she could see the intentions of anyone she drank from—good or bad—but I didn't trust it. While she'd deemed each of them free of death magic and without ill intent, I had my doubts. People had a way of hiding the truth here.

The scent of Ithran's blood still filled my nose as I tried to forget cutting him in two.

Who in their right mind would want to be here? A Fae had just died not ten feet from where I was standing, and I'd been the one to take his life. They probably thought of me like an agent of Orrus, ready to take them to their end.

And that was if they didn't want to tap my veins for power.

A few of them shifted uncomfortably, the weight of this room's recent past lingering in the air. My gaze flitted from one new face to another. This wasn't the first cutthroat situation I'd ever been in, but it was far less predictable. At least under the mountain, all anyone wanted was *Lumentium* in exchange for food.

Here, everyone's motivations were suspect, more mercurial than magic itself.

"It has been two hundred years since I have sworn in a new member to this council," Idris began, his gaze assessing each person like they were a personal threat. "Today, we welcome nine new members. You may ask yourself why we are inducting so many. I'm sure you've heard the rumors buzzing through the villages of the attempted coup on this throne."

The silence of the room had the icy finger of fear raking down my spine. Despite the heat of my leathers, I nearly shivered under the weight of the council's stares, wondering which one of them would try to kill me next.

"A coup that was thwarted by your future Queen. She secured this kingdom with her blood and power, and without her, we would have fallen to the guild. A silent war has been raging, one that steals magic, hoards it away, draining the very life from this continent."

A thread of power thrummed just below the surface of his words, touching each of us.

"I ask of you to swear your allegiance to the Crown, to stand with us in our war against the guild that threatens to steal the very breath from your lungs, the very blood from your veins."

As one, the council recited a credo I did not understand. *"De meo sanguine. In vitae mi. In acie mea."*

"It means 'on my blood, on my life, on my line,'" Idris supplied, nearly startling me out of my skin. *"They will swear to the Crown, to the continent, and to us. Then it's your turn. You ready?"*

Shakily, I nodded, barely noticing the slight lift to his lips as he continued with his speech.

"I ask of you to swear your allegiance to the continent, to stand for the very land under your feet."

Again, the council recited their promise. *"De meo sanguine. In vitae mi. In acie mea."*

"I ask of you to swear your allegiance to the rightful heir to the Crown and to my future wife and fateborn mate."

A shocked murmur filled the room as council members—both old and new—shared furtive glances like they knew something I didn't. After a tense moment, they repeated the oath. *"De meo sanguine. In vitae mi. In acie mea."*

I wanted to ask why everyone was freaking out, but it wasn't the time. Idris glanced back at me, a subtle nod signaling that it was my turn. Stepping forward, I was now even with him, standing as a united front.

My eyes slid closed as I called upon the magic that had once meant execution and death—that could still mean death if I didn't play my cards right. Reaching deep, I pulled at the thread of power, and all at once, light bloomed from my skin. Swelling from my body in a crackling dome of energy, it engulfed each member of the council, holding them tight in the circle of my protection.

"A Luxa took everything from you—took your

magic, your way of life," I began, my voice trembling, but I pushed forward. "A Luxa cursed your king. But a Luxa will set this kingdom free."

"What are you doing, Vale?" Idris demanded, real fear in his eyes.

He didn't understand just how horrible it was to live with uncertainty, to worry no one cared if you lived or died. I couldn't be a good leader if I didn't honor the vow they'd just given me.

"Making them a promise."

"You swear your allegiances to me, but what do you get in return?"

My gaze flitted from one member to another, showing them that I wouldn't hide, wouldn't falter. They needed strength, they needed power, and they needed someone they could trust.

"On my blood, on my life, and on my power, I promise that I will break this curse and return your kingdom to its former glory."

Idris threaded his fingers through mine, golden power dancing over his flesh. "We stand as one against those that would rip us apart, that would turn families against each other. Let this council be a beacon for our people in our darkest times and let none of us forget the price of treachery."

The council rose as one, and while I could detect apprehension from some, a few seemed ready for this new chapter.

If only I could trust them.

CHAPTER 7

KIAN

Vale was far too close to the new council for my liking.

Considering how many times she had nearly died at one of their hands, I wasn't too keen on having her any farther from me than she was right then, and even that was out of my comfort zone. For the sake of propriety, I was forced to stand behind her and Idris, watching and waiting for someone to make a move.

Xavier and Freya stood at my side, both of them twitching toward their weapons as we waited for an attack. Just like me, neither of them trusted this new council. After the last two days, I wasn't sure I would trust anyone outside of my inner circle ever again.

I'd spent those last two days garnering support

throughout the kingdom, selecting new members from all twelve factions. Not all of them sent representatives, but most had. After Freya's bleed and read, I thought I'd feel some measure of comfort that Vale and Idris were safe, that we could move forward. Still, even with their promises, even with the spell weaved into the very words of their oath, I did not feel any better.

Arden didn't want the curse broken. He wanted Idris separated from Rune, amputated from the bulk of his magic, and weakened to the point of distraction. If the fucker wasn't just as cut off from his magic as Idris was, this war would have exploded across the continent ages ago.

But I'd gotten complacent, comfortable in my role, not realizing that the danger lived in my fucking house. It wouldn't happen a second time—not with Vale's life on the line.

Idris dismissed the council, allowing them to leave if they wished. Save those who ran from the room as if the executioner's axe was pointing at their necks, a few remained either to talk amongst themselves or to bask in the fact they hadn't been killed on sight. One stood taller than the rest, his interested gaze on Vale as if he were sizing her up.

His short, dark hair seemed to transform in the

light, flowing from the deepest of purples to the lightest of grays and back again. The strands seemed to dance in a breeze only he could feel, floating about his head in a nimbus cloud. His approach was almost soundless, his magic cushioning each step, his eyes latched onto Vale as if she were a beacon.

I'd almost forgotten how much I hated Elementals, and air ones most of all. Talek was a staunch reminder that the last Elemental we'd had on the council was the same asshole to nearly put a blade through my neck.

Not-so-patiently, he waited his turn, his gaze never once leaving my mate as he inched closer. Something about him grated on my nerves, and I couldn't figure out what it was until he plucked her hand up and pressed his lips to her smooth skin.

My blade was at his throat before I thought better of it.

"How about you don't touch her again, and I won't take your head where you stand." Iridescent blood dripped from the wound at his neck, but he paid it no mind. "Let her go. Now."

Talek raised his hands in surrender, dropping Vale's fingers as if they were on fire. "My apologies, I thought the fateborn mate bullshit was just that. I had no idea she was actually spoken for."

Idris gripped my shoulder, staying my blade as the urge to take Talek's head almost overtook me. "Let's all calm down, shall we? There's no reason for violence. Talek here was simply introducing himself."

Growling, I reluctantly removed my blade from his skin. "No offense, but too many people have put their hands on our future Queen in the last few days, and none of them have meant her goodwill. You'll have to excuse me."

Talek's smile was good-natured enough to make me worried about his intentions, but I couldn't take his head without cause. Reluctantly, I stepped backward and let Vale take care of herself.

Vale's spine stiffened as Talek's gaze lingered on the mating mark that should be invisible to his kind, but she didn't flinch or step back. Instead, she lifted her chin in quiet defiance, one that reminded me why she was Queen—even if she didn't feel like one yet.

"To save yourself some unfortunate misunderstandings and a boatload of hurt, please understand, I am utterly and completely spoken for. I have not one but three mates, and they're very protective, so maybe a no-touching rule should be in place?" Vale offered, her smile gentle but her voice firm.

"Fair enough," Talek muttered with a smile, his body bending in half in an elaborate bow. "I simply wanted to meet the woman that had claimed our king's heart. You are just as exquisite as I thought you would be, though I am surprised you have more than one mate. Doesn't seem very fair. Fateborn mates have been a thing of myth for two centuries, and now you have three? It might just be the jealousy talking, but it seems very greedy of you."

Vale seemed charmed by the Elemental, her smile genuine, even though he still seemed to be sizing her up. "Well, just like with all aspects of life, I don't get to argue with Fate. She seems to decide my path more than I do."

Talek's gaze landed on her shoulder again. "Are you sure you can't make room for one more? I'm a very attentive lover."

Freya grabbed my sword hand before I could take his head. "I suggest you get to the point of whatever gambit you're spinning before I let the general go and he eats you for dinner. Trust me, no Elemental power will save you from an angry dragon, let alone three."

Talek's genial smile landed on her as he lifted his shoulder in a halfhearted shrug. "Can't blame a guy for trying. At this point, most people would kill for a fateborn mate. To be that connected to someone—it's something that's been missing in these lands for a very long time."

His gaze swept over Vale, his attention settling on the scales at her pulse points and covering her middle.

"Is there something you needed to discuss, or was accosting my bride your main goal?" Idris asked, his smile wide in the same way Rune's was right before he ate someone.

Talek's form seemed to flicker a bit, his smile dimming. "While I'm grateful for the dispatching of my predecessor, I noticed a few council seats were missing. Coup or not, a few factions seem to fear lending you support."

Idris' jaw clenched. "And you agree with them?"

Talek placed a hand on his chest, feigning shock. "Of course not. But I am a simple man with nominal power in comparison to some. It does not matter whether I join your cause or bow out, there will always be someone to take my place. No, the problem lies in not how many are missing, but who. We have the Fae Lords and the mages, the vampires and the lower shifters, the banshees and the wizards, the witches and the djinns and the shapeshifters. But someone is missing, and her absence is a blow."

My growl rumbled through my chest, but it was Idris who had finally lost his patience. "Your point?"

Talek's stormy gaze met mine for an instant

before he returned his attention to Idris, and I instantly realized just who his allegiance resided with. "Lady Selene's influence extends far beyond the boundaries of Everhold. She controls the waters, the sea, and if you cannot convince her to back your side, your brother might take it as an invitation."

I'd rather chew my own arm off than admit it out loud, but he was right. Of all the delegations I'd contacted, I hadn't been able to reach Selene. Considering the amount of power she'd amassed in the last few centuries, not having her at our back was precarious at best.

Everhold wasn't just a province—it was the lifeblood of Credour's trade and defense. Selene controlled the shipping lanes, the naval fleets, and the flow of goods between continents. Without her, we might as well hand Arden the keys to the kingdom.

At worst, she was the final nail in a coffin that had been closing for two hundred years.

"I don't want to tell you how to do your job," Talek continued, "but Everhold is a key component of the continent. I wouldn't be doing my due diligence as a member of this council if I didn't remind you of this. If at all possible, I would suggest you remedy that relationship. And fast."

I had to give it to him, he was taking his role seriously, and damn if it wasn't good advice. Still, I didn't trust him. If there was anything Elementals were known for, it was looking out for their own interests above all else. Traveling to Everhold could be a trap.

"We'll take it under advisement," Idris replied, his posture just as rigid as mine and Xavier's. "I appreciate you giving your position such commitment."

Talek's smile seemed bitter until his gaze landed on Vale. "It was an honor to meet you, Vale. I look forward to serving the Crown—especially with you sharing the helm."

He gave them a fluid bow as only an Elemental could and swept from the throne room, his feet never once disturbing the debris in his path.

By the time the dregs of the council left, my stomach was in knots and my animal was itching to come out of my skin. The faint traces of Vale's thoughts churned in my brain, our bond allowing me to glean her opinion on the matter.

"Please tell me none of you are considering this," Freya grumbled as she perched on the arm of a half-demolished chair, her gaze on me.

Idris might be King, but I was his general. I'd been watching his back for two hundred years, and sniffing out traps was my specialty. Everhold could be our biggest political foothold or utter failure, and there was no way to know which it was without sacrificing something.

I fought off the urge to yank my hair out by the roots. "Not considering it could be a death sentence."

Freya pinched her brow like I was giving her a headache. "There's a reason we don't trust Elementals, Kian. Just look at what happened with Evrin. I do recall he tried to put a spear through your jugular a few days ago."

"We're going," Idris rumbled, his gaze never once leaving Vale's.

Their mental connection was the strongest out of all of us. While I couldn't hear their conversation, I knew Vale had a hand in changing his mind.

"Are you insane?" Xavier snarled, pulling Vale away from Idris. "You want to go to Everhold? Now? In case you forgot, you two are getting married in a few days and this kingdom is on the brink of war. And you want to take a vacation to what is essentially shark-infested waters?"

Xavier's voice cracked, just slightly, as he pulled Vale closer. "We almost lost her. Too many times to count. And now you want to march her into another fight? How many times do you expect her to come back to us in one piece?"

Vale placed a quelling hand on Xavier's arm. "What good is a wedding going to be if the kingdom falls in a week? You heard Talek. Selene is a major player. I'm assuming someone who controls the sea is not someone we want Arden getting his hooks into."

"She's right," I murmured, the truth of Vale's words hitting me like a spear in the chest. "If we don't get Selene on our side, it won't matter if the curse is broken or not. Even if she doesn't back Arden, too many will defect, fearing we can't protect them."

Xavier's shoulders slumped as betrayal colored his expression. "And what happens if it is a trap?"

I didn't have a good answer for him.

We'd just have to cross that bridge when we came to it.

"Rethinking your decision?"

Yes, I might have been staring at Rune's scales as if they held all the answers in the universe.

Yes, I was rethinking every single decision I had ever made in my life—especially the one that would soon have me riding a dragon across the fucking continent.

Would I tell Idris that?

Of course not.

A girl had to have her pride, right?

For some reason when I considered traveling to Everhold, not once did it cross my mind that it would involve flying. The last time I'd rode on Rune's back I'd damn near died. In fact, two out of the three times

I'd ridden with a dragon, I'd been on Orrus' doorstep ready to hop on over to the afterlife.

But if what Talek said was true—*and that was a big if*—Selene could be the key to me maybe *not* marrying a complete stranger in seven days. A few hours ago, I thought I was ready for this, but now?

How could I help convince anyone I would be able to break the curse if I didn't believe it myself? I'd bitten off far more than I could chew, and I'd finally remembered who I was.

I wasn't a queen.

I was a dirt-poor miner from Direveil.

I was a slave to the guild, clinging to the last scrap of hope that I wouldn't fall to my death and leave Nyrah on her own.

Not so long ago, I'd been starving and near death, trying to find any way possible to keep my sister alive. I wasn't prepared to act as an ambassador to a crumbling nation. But with the kingdom in disarray, and war at the front gate, it seemed like if we had a major player at our back, maybe Arden would settle down. Just like his son, he was a coward—preying on the weak, the scared, the hopeless.

Why else would he withhold food in exchange for *Lumentium*?

But something about that had always irritated

me. As a child, I'd asked my mother why the guild needed it, only to be met with a sharp reprimand and a sore cheek. Now that I was free, all the questions of my youth bubbled up to the surface.

What was he using it for other than weapons? I'd been mining all my life. There couldn't be a use for that much *Lumentium*—not unless he planned on arming the entire continent ten times over.

But I didn't have answers for any of it and had run out of people to ask.

Finally, I blinked back into reality to meet Idris' golden gaze. "No. I'm just wondering if it's necessary for me to go with you."

So far, I'd managed to piss off nearly every council member, survived a handful of assassination attempts, and jumped off a cliff. Did I really need to risk falling off Rune's back into a watery abyss? That seemed a little foolish on my part.

"You know better than that, my Queen. I wouldn't let you fall," Rune promised, his oath less than comforting. *"There are too many monsters in the water. They'd gobble you whole and then I'd be stuck like this forever."*

I also hadn't considered what was in the water I could be falling into. Fantastic.

"Somehow, you managed to make it worse. How is that even possible?"

Then the damn dragon chuckled, his huff of laughter echoing through my brain like a gong.

"It's a gift."

I'd been paying so much attention to Rune's banter, that I missed the second Idris lost his patience. One second, he was three feet away, his mouth curved into a teasing line, and the next, he was in my space, backing me into his dragon's side.

"Do you honestly think I would travel across the continent without my Queen by my side?"

But I wasn't his Queen—not yet.

I had maybe less than a week before I was bound to Idris. Half of me resisted—the thought of marrying anyone at all so foreign that it was almost laughable. I had no clue how to break his curse let alone how to be a queen. I'd had a taste of it in that throne room, and all it had gotten me was a mind full of doubt.

The other half of me wondered what bonding to Idris would be like. How I could possibly share myself with not one, but three men. My core clenched at the memory of his voice in my head, begging to watch me come. Of the pleasure he could give me without laying a single finger on my skin.

But as much as my body seemed to want him, a part of me warned that this marriage was closer to a death trap rather than wedded bliss.

Idris dipped his head, staring into my eyes so intently, I could almost feel him rooting around my mind.

"If you're not my Queen, then that must have been some other Luxa at my side a few hours ago, promising my council her very life to break the curse." He tilted his head to the side, his irises glowing with his magic. "My mistake."

Squinting, I fought off the urge to kick him in the shin. "Stop filching through my brain, you snoop. I didn't say that out loud."

"Where's the fiery woman who shredded magically infused wood like it was tissue paper? Where's the confident Luxa who stood tall in my throne room defying me in front of the very kingdom she refuses? Where is the witch who waited for no one and saved herself?"

Unshed tears stung my nose as I peeled my gaze from his. Was that how he saw me—a confident woman prepared to go to battle for a kingdom she barely knew? Or was I still that frail girl under the mountain just scraping by?

"She got told she had to ride hours on dragonback to Everhold, and she's feeling a little out of her depth."

That wasn't quite it, but it was about as good as I could explain it.

"Says the girl who roared at a dragon like she was one. What if I promise I won't let you go the entire way there? Not once."

The plan had been for me to ride with Xavier and Idris to ride with Rune. Since I'd done it before, the plan made sense, but I'd barely survived the first ride with Xavier without puking and the second hadn't been much better.

But I didn't know if Idris was doing this to be kind or if this was just another manipulation, another bargaining chip up his sleeve, and I hated that I didn't know better. I also hated that even if it was manipulation, it was working.

"Are you sure we can't take a boat?" I'd never ridden in one of those either, but at least it was closer to the ground. Then again, it wasn't like I could swim.

Idris banded an arm around my back, drawing me away from the safety of Rune's side. "I'm sure. And as luck would have it, I *do* know how to swim. I won't let you fall, my brave one. I promise."

His promise echoed Rune's so much it reminded me that they had once shared a mind. "Quit snooping."

"It's not snooping if you're practically yelling at me."

He had a point. My thoughts were loud even to me.

"Plus, I swore to you that you wouldn't dream alone. I'm not leaving you to fend for yourself. That time in your life is over."

Gritting my teeth, I ignored the way that statement made my insides ache. I ignored my welling tears, and the thread of comfort his heat brought me as the winter chill seeped into my bones. We were still on the ground, and I was already freezing. What would flying be like?

"I'll keep you warm," he murmured, unclasping the cloak at his neck and throwing it around my shoulders.

Shit.

It was getting harder and harder to dislike Idris—especially when he kept doing crap like this. How was I supposed to keep my wits about me when he was turning up the charm?

Nyrah.

Swallowing down my tears, I remembered my

little sister. She was how I would stay grounded. She was how I wouldn't get caught up in my feelings for Idris—how I wouldn't fall so hard for all of them that I got distracted from my purpose. The sooner the curse was broken, the sooner I could find her—the sooner I could bring her home.

Wherever that is.

Idris clasped the cloak at my neck, his pensive expression telling me he'd heard every word in my mind. Footsteps echoed from the wide tunnel at our left as Kian and Xavier emerged into the frozen courtyard. Barely covered in cloaks, the pair of them were mostly naked, their clothing and weapons stowed in the bags they'd dropped in the snow at their feet.

Xavier's mouth was drawn in a firm line, his jaw clenching and unclenching as he scanned the cloak around my shoulders. He'd been against this plan from the beginning and changing before we even left was not helping matters at all.

But the thought of riding by myself made me want to crawl out of my skin.

Nodding, Xavier unclasped the fastening at his neck. "Will Rune's saddle fit you both?"

"Yes," Idris murmured, "it will. I'll keep her safe, old friend."

His blue eyes flashed with unspent ire. "Yes, you will."

That simple statement was more threat than agreement, but I figured that was about as good as we were going to get.

"Freya gave the council their marching orders," Kian interjected, his amber gaze flicking from me to Idris to Xavier. "They will reconvene here in three days' time. Hopefully, we'll have some good news for them."

Three days.

We had three days to convince the leader of Everhold that we were worth a damn. Three days to convince her to back us and not my parents' murderer. Three days to hopefully turn the tide.

I hoped everyone assumed it was the cold rather than my nerves that had my teeth chattering.

Glad no one made a mention of it, I watched as Kian and Xavier shifted into their beasts. Now that I wasn't shocked anymore, I got to admire the way the weak sunlight shimmered off of Xavier's scales, the way their pale iridescent color matched his long tresses.

And where Xavier was light, Kian was pure darkness, his body made of shadow. Those amber eyes latched onto me as he approached, his looming figure coming so close, I could feel the heat of him in the air.

I hadn't seen Kian's dragon since we'd bonded, and it seemed the beastly side of him was very interested in my scent. His giant nostrils fluttered as he took me in, his gaze not breaking from me once as he inched closer.

"I love the way you smell, oroum di vita. My mating mark looks good on you."

How he could see it while I was fully clothed was still a mystery, but that part didn't exactly matter right then. Slowly, I started backing away to the safety of Rune's side, the red dragon shaking his body as he began to stand. The glow from his throat did not spell good things. Idris moved in front of me, much to the displeasure of the black dragon.

"His animal is drawn to you, my Queen," Rune murmured, positioning himself for a fight. *"You might need to move away from him. But do it slowly. He will see you as prey if you run."*

Yes, I'd gathered that. What mattered more was if he planned on trying any funny business. I was open to new things in the bedroom, but fucking an actual dragon was not on my list of things to try.

Xavier's tail struck Kian, breaking him from his trance, and Kian slowly blinked, coming back to himself. While he was still stunned, I crawled up Rune's back, figuring I was safer on the back of a dragon instead of being pursued by one. The wide leather saddle was fitted with two pommels, the pair almost like a steering mechanism of sorts.

A few seconds later, Idris was at my back, his strong arm curling around my middle as he tugged me into the cradle of his thighs. I couldn't miss the bulge pressing into the small of my back or the way his nose raked up the exposed skin of my neck as he placed a leather strap over my thighs. My heart was beating out of my chest, and I couldn't tell if it was Kian's pursuit, our impending trip, or the king at my back.

"He's right, you know," he rumbled in my ear, "you do smell wonderful. I wonder what you'll smell like after I put my mark on you."

Ignoring the way his voice tightened my nipples, I turned to stare at Idris. He didn't meet my penetrating gaze, too focused on the buckle at my hip sinching us together. "You could hear him?"

The corner of his mouth lifted, and those gold irises met mine. "Like I said, your mind is a very loud place to be. Now, hang onto the pommels, brave one. Rune is known to be the fastest dragon on the continent."

Eyes widening, I whipped back around as I latched onto the pommels with my gloved hands, a nervous sweat breaking across my brow despite the cold. Idris tightened his hold on my middle, and not a second later, we were airborne, the ground falling away from us so fast my stomach felt like it had been left behind.

Fighting off the urge to scream, I barely got a glimpse of Kian and Xavier trailing us before I squeezed my eyes shut, tremors of fear taking root. Freezing wind lashed at my face, the cold needling my very bones as I tried not to lose what was left of my sanity. Riding Xavier was nothing compared to the breakneck speed of Rune, his body knifing through the air faster than any arrow.

Idris clutched me closer, his warm breath barely making a dent, the frigid gusts carrying them away before they could ever hit my skin.

"Tell me about Nyrah," he demanded, his voice in my head the only thing keeping me sane as I tried not to think about how far we were from the ground.

I shook my head, my braid nearly whipping me in the face as I tried to hang onto my sanity. Rune wouldn't let me fall. He'd caught me before. I was strapped in, hanging on. I was safe.

When Nyrah would have nightmares, I'd stroke

her hair and tell her she was safe over and over again. I would remind her that I would always be there, that I would keep her safe.

What a liar I turned out to be. She wasn't safe and neither was I.

"Come on. You can do this. Tell me about your little sister. She's why you're doing all of this, right? Teach me about the person you're fighting for."

I didn't know where to start—she was too precious, too special. She was a fragile flower blooming in the midst of Hell. How did I quantify my baby sister into terms he would understand?

"Tell me about when Nyrah was born. You were ten, yes?"

I managed a nod, and then the details spilled from my mind. Everything from the first time my mother placed her in my arms to the time I'd snatched her off the stone steps before she could fall like so many others. How she'd hated being tethered to me, but it had been the only way to keep her from wandering the caves.

I told him about her defiance, her strength, her sense of justice, and all the while, I kept my eyes closed, leaning back into his chest as I tried to forget where we were. I focused on his heat, his hold on my middle, the way he never let me go.

Before I knew it, Rune was dropping, the air warming around us, as the salty scent of the sea filled my nose. Squinting, I peeled my eyes open, revealing the sun falling behind a monstrous castle, the spires reaching like fingers into the sky.

Streaking over the brilliant blue water, Rune dropped lower, his talons just breaking the surface before he rose again. He climbed higher, over the trees and walls, circling the castle before picking a large courtyard to land in.

Dotted with impossibly large trees, we coasted into the open space, just missing a giant fountain that nearly rivaled Rune in size. At the center was an incredibly beautiful woman, her face tilted toward the sun as she held an iridescent orb close to her chest. Water bubbled from the orb, falling down her dress, her dainty feet playing just over the surface.

I was so mesmerized by the statue, that I didn't notice the danger until it was already upon us. Idris stiffened at my back, clutching me tighter as Rune let out a bellow of a roar, the sound so loud I let go of the pommels to cover my ears.

Only then did I notice the figures that seemed to melt into the shadows of the trees, their forms wavering like ripples of the surface of a pond.

The fading light glinted off the wickedly sharp

spears in their hands as Kian and Xavier landed on either side of us. Their minds were begging for us to flee, to run.

Because Xavier and Freya had been right all along.

This was a trap.

And we were surrounded.

This wasn't the first time I had been stuck between a rock and a hard place. Hell, this wasn't even the first time that I'd been stuck in the middle of a snare in the last week. But as the guards emerged from the trees, I realized just how precarious our situation was.

"*There's a chance we could leave,*" Rune murmured, his voice almost a whisper as if he was trying not to be overheard.

"*What do you mean a chance? Can't you just zoom into the sky? Because if that's an option, we should definitely do that.*"

Was I a frantic mess to even suggest flying off? Absolutely.

But I'd been the one to convince Idris this was a

smart plan. It had been our mental conversation that had turned the tide to come here. If this was what got my men killed, I'd never forgive myself. My heart pounded in my chest at the thought of any of them getting hurt because I'd been too stupid to see the obvious trap in our midst.

"There's too much magic. We were allowed to land. It felt off as soon as I reached the tree canopy. When I say 'chance,' I mean a slim one."

Fuck.

Freya and Xavier had told us this was a horrible idea, that Talek's warning about Selene was a carefully crafted trap that we had just waltzed right into. And someone had to have told them we were coming. With Kian's illusion magic, no one would have been able to see us, even if they'd been looking right at us.

No, this was worse than the mountaintop. At least on the mountain, Rune hadn't been caught with me —he could have saved Kian and Xavier and Idris.

He didn't, but he could have.

"Plus, we need to be here," Rune hissed, his conviction rattling inside my chest. *"If Arden wins the continent, we are beyond saving. The continent will fall to the guild. We have to get Selene on our side."*

The guards raised their spears, inching closer as

Kian and Xavier moved to defend Rune, and by exten-sion, Idris and I. *"Sort of looks like she's already chosen her side, Rune, otherwise, we wouldn't be met with a trap."*

"You don't know her like we do. What you see as a trap, she sees as a clever welcoming party. Granted, it could turn into a trap later, but sirens are known for their games. She has just informed us that she wants to play—whether we like it or not."

Fantastic. I always wanted to mind-game my way to survival.

It was my favorite.

A sleek figure approached, prowling through the courtyard like she owned it. I supposed she did. Her white hair was arranged into an intricate braid that swung down her back, the sparkling jewels and iridescent pearls threaded through the strands winking in the setting sun.

That said nothing of her dress.

It was as thin as gossamer while also managing to cover her most important parts. She moved as if she were gliding through water, the set of her shoulders so effortlessly commanding, even on the back of a dragon I felt inferior. Her skin was nearly as pale as her hair, highlighting the sheen of blue scales dotting her neck and collarbone. Sea-green eyes glowed with her magic, the swirling depths of them nearly calling me to her.

Selene was a force to be reckoned with, of that, I was certain.

"How good of you to visit," she cooed, her innocent expression belaying the pull of her voice. It was melodic, intoxicating, but there was a thread of danger there that had me gripping the pommels for reassurance.

She was good, I had to give her that, but I would not be swayed.

"She's using her siren power, right?" I asked Rune, but all I got back was a disgruntled growl.

I took that as a yes.

"How good of you to welcome us with such *tight* security," Idris growled from behind me, his hold not leaving me once. "And here I thought we were friends."

Selene's smile showed off her sharp fangs, the move likely intentional. "You came to my home with three dragons unannounced. *I* thought *we* were friends. If I waltzed into your home with`an army, you'd take it as the threat it is. And I'm painted as the bad guy here? Doesn't seem fair."

The lady did have a point.

Or at least she had one until she snapped her fingers.

Sea-green magic flooded from her hands, wrapping around Kian and Xavier before either of them could move. The sharp crack of bones snapping had me flinching, my fingers reaching for the daggers at my belt before I thought better of it. Their grunts mingled with moans of agony as they began to shrink, their bodies reforming into their human shapes.

As soon as I heard their pain, I yanked a blade free of its sheath.

If she thought she could snap her fingers and hurt my mates, I'd make sure she wouldn't have any fingers left to snap.

A snarl erupted from my throat as my power bloomed from my skin, the golden glow expanding into a dome of magic, knocking the closest guards backward. Slicing through the belt at my hips, I slid off Rune, the dragon almost frozen as he, too, seemed caught in Selene's snare.

Oh, no, she did not.

The grass at my feet blackened with each step as my power swelled to encompass Rune and Idris before blanketing over Xavier and then Kian. Gasping, they clung to the charred ground, their eyes dazed as Selene's magic hung onto their minds, even behind my shield.

"Release them," I ordered, rage roiling in my gut. Fire filled my lungs as fury boiled my blood. I ripped Idris' cloak from my shoulders as I drew another dagger. "We meant to come in peace. But if you don't stop fucking with them, you'll see what happens when I stop trying to be nice."

Selene squinted, her eyes glowing brighter as the green of her spell stabbed at my shield. Tiny pricks of pain dotted behind my eyes as if she were trying to penetrate my mind.

That bitch.

"That's cute, but now all you've done is piss me off."

Growling, I crossed my arms at the wrists and shoved, my magic exploding outward. The shield doubled in size, its border sending guards sailing off their feet into the courtyard wall as the rocks beneath me cracked from the heat. The pretty fountain I'd admired wobbled as the ground pitched, the water boiling on contact with my power.

"So much power for such a young little thing. Will you burn out, too, little Luxa, like all the rest? Or will you show me what you're made of?"

Rune had been right. This was all a game—one I

not only didn't want to play, but one that might kill me no matter what I did.

A welcome presence at my back nearly had me sagging in relief. I hadn't started bleeding yet, but I didn't have too much left in me before I lost face. Idris curled his arm around my middle, his magic mingling with mine as my body started to tire, reinforcing my ward.

"*Stop*, Selene," he growled, his voice thundering through the courtyard. "Or it won't just be my future Queen you'll have to deal with. I may not be the king I once was, but do not forget where your power comes from."

Her smile was simpering yet a little disappointed. "She doesn't seem so tough. I just wanted to test her a little. How could I be sure she'd be able to break your curse if she couldn't withstand a little *prodding*?"

Idris let out a dark chuckle, the sound so sinister, it made me remember all the stories of just how evil the beast of a king was rumored to be. "She's already killed one person today. Let's not make it two."

"Don't back down, my brave one. She'll see it as a sign of weakness."

For the first time since we'd breached the canopy, Idris spoke inside my head. As relieved as I was to hear it, he honestly should have saved it for a less obvious statement. Selene still hadn't backed down an inch, and I could almost feel Kian's pain, Xavier's agony, the helplessness of them being lost to her magic.

I wasn't just pissed off, now I was made of pure fury.

Closing my eyes, I imagined spikes forming at the edges of my shield, stabbing into her power just enough to make her listen. At her guttural hiss, my eyes flashed open, and I watched with glee as blackened blood oozed from a cut on her cheek.

Okay, so I might not have been as conservative as I'd intended.

Oops?

Her form flickered, the glamour she'd projected melting as the planes of her face got sharper, leaner. Her magic softened her features, but now her pale skin was less white and more on the gray side, her eyes now missing a pupil, her lips less full, revealing a double set of sharp fangs and razor-like incisors.

"I believe my mate told you to stop," I hissed. "I suggest you heed his warning."

The green of her magic receded almost instantly as her eyes went wide. "Mate? You should have said so in the beginning." She bowed her head, her knees hitting the stone pathway in respect. *"Aevír ni thrystun ef vátta ek henne var skuld til þú."*

I had no idea what she'd said but Idris seemed to relax. *"Vér eru ei skuld enn. Vér bíðum nótt vígs. Enn hvert hótun við hana er hótun við mik."*

"I would love it if someone spoke in a language I understood," I groused, squeezing Idris' hand at my waist.

He squeezed my middle, but it was Xavier—my sweet Xavier—who spoke to me inside my mind. *"She was apologizing for attacking the king's bonded mate. He explained that you two were waiting for the wedding, but she should treat you as if you were his queen already."*

I fought off the urge to fall to my knees in relief as Xavier and Kian began to come back to themselves. Xavier remained on his knees, his labored breaths making my heart ache for him. Kian managed to get to his feet, standing at our side as if he was prepared for battle. Naked as the day he was born, his skin glistened with sweat as steam seemed to rise from his body.

"She doesn't know that you have more than one mate, and you should keep that to yourself. Fateborn mates are rare. Rarer? More than one."

I fought off the urge to nod. Personally, I thought

Idris probably should have kept our lack of a bond to himself. But who was I to advise in matters of diplomacy? So far, I'd been of the camp of burn first, ask questions later. I had no interest in stirring the pot any more than it already was.

Xavier and Kian seemed to be of the same bent.

"You can drop the shield, little witch," Kian croaked, his glowing amber irises still in the slit of his dragon. "Selene is smarter than she looks. Attacking the fateborn mate of her king is an act of war." His head slowly turned to the siren queen. "Isn't it, Selene? You do remember how much I love war, don't you?"

As I dropped my shield, Selene's glamour seemed to settle back into place, the hard planes of her features smoothing to her own definition of beauty.

"I recall you enjoying more than most, General." She said it with a seductive purr that made my hackles rise.

While Kian was the first man I'd ever made love to, I knew I had no such claim on him. Somewhere inside, my heart was tearing itself in two as bitter bile raced up my throat. Instinct had my face blank as parchment, but inside I was screaming.

"Do not tell me you've bedded that woman, Kian. Don't you dare."

Kian's gaze flashed to me before returning to Selene. "Don't flatter yourself, siren."

He had. He'd fucked that woman, and now I was supposed to play nice while she tried to flaunt it in my face.

"Don't let her see weakness, my brave one. She'll exploit it."

Again, Idris telling me something I didn't need to be told. I'd grown up in the guild. I knew a predator when I saw one.

Forcing myself not to react, I returned my daggers to their sheaths, settling back into Idris' hold.

Somehow, I doubted the games were over.

No, I had a feeling they were just beginning.

CHAPTER 10

VALE

My hands never once left the hilts of my daggers as I followed Idris and Selene through the entrance of the grand castle. The stone was completely white just like Selene's hair, the giant archway reflecting the dying light of the day.

Guards stood on either side of the arch, their spears at the ready. Both were shirtless, their multi-colored scales mingling with their tanned flesh under a boned breastplate, decorated with spined shells. Instead of pants, they wore patterned kilts, the fabric only reaching to the middle of their calves, and just like Selene, they were barefoot. It seemed like at any moment, they would be ready to jump into the warm waters to do battle, or maybe drag a ship to its end.

Inside the castle was just as luxurious as the outside. Midnight-blue walls faded into an aqua ceiling, where magic had water dancing as schools of fish raced through a multicolored reef. It was as if we were upside down, watching as the ocean illuminated with golden sea creatures playing hide-and-seek.

Kian bumped into my back before steadying me, pulling me along so I didn't get left behind. A part of me wanted to slap him, and the other part completely understood. If you couldn't see past Selene's glamour, she was drop-dead gorgeous. Coupled with her siren abilities, if she wanted him, it would be almost impossible to refuse her.

"Come on, little witch. You don't want to be left behind, now, do you?"

I was leaning closer to that "slap" option.

No, I didn't want to be left behind, but I also didn't want to feel inferior to an evil she-beast. Dropping his hand, I marched forward, refusing to be mesmerized by this new place. Considering how much magic was being used, I doubted anything was real anymore. Even Selene's face was an illusion.

"I suppose I should give you a good place to sleep, considering your journey," she said, her gaze flicking to the still mostly nude Kian and Xavier. What *had* to be a pleasured shiver worked its way over her body as she pinned her gaze to Kian's bulge, like she was fondly remembering just what he could do with his cock.

"Don't let her get under your skin," Idris reminded me. *"She can only affect you if you let her."*

"No shit."

I wasn't an idiot. I knew exactly what she was doing. I just didn't understand how I could possibly not gut her like the fish she was when that was all I wanted to do. My fist clenched the hilt of the blade at my hip, but I forced myself to let it go.

Gutting her wouldn't solve anything. In fact, it was the exact opposite of what we were meant to do here. As much as it would make me feel better, politically, we'd be fucked.

Up a grueling flight of stairs and down an impossibly long hallway, Selene led us to a suite of rooms fit for a king. It was almost as if she'd known we were coming the entire time. While Talek was on my shit list, I would almost welcome a bath and a nap before we got into whatever torture she had in store for us.

"We had these rooms prepared especially for you, my King. Your retinue can stay close by, and we can have our discussion of my support at dinner." She curled her fingers into the crook of his arm. "I suggest your *entourage* stay here for just a little bit while you and I discuss some matters of State."

It was no surprise that both hands found their way to the hilts of my daggers. What *was* surprising? Idris actually agreed with her.

"Of course. I need to discuss a few things with you as well before dinner."

Betrayal latched its putrid fingers onto my heart and refused to let it go. His golden eyes met mine before flicking down to the weapons in my fists. "Get cleaned up. I'll be there in a minute."

"Don't do anything crazy. She's testing you. Stay calm."

Calm? He wanted me to be calm? How exactly did he expect me to be calm when one of my mate's former lovers was dangling innuendo in front of my face while she took another one of my mates away from me?

Calm didn't quite seem to be in the cards for me.

Xavier hooked his arm around one of mine, gently loosening my fingers around the hilt as he pulled me into the opulent room.

"Dinner is in a few hours," Selene informed us, her fake smile twisted into something resembling glee. "*Do* get cleaned up. You smell like dragon. And considering I doubt you have anything suitable to wear in that duffel you call luggage, there should be some dresses in the wardrobe that will fit you. *Well*," She dropped her gaze to my somewhat-lacking chest, "if you can fill them out."

There weren't very many women under the mountain—too many of us had starved and died long before our male counterparts. I wasn't exactly versed in dealing with snide, catty bitches who wanted to claim something that didn't belong to them.

That didn't mean I wouldn't give it my best.

"I'd rather smell like dragon and wear fighting leathers than dress like a manipulative cunt, pining after men who don't want her. That said, I'm sure I can find something suitable—even if I have to take it in."

And then because I was more focused on landing a punch to her stomach rather than doing the job we'd been sent here to do—I blew her a kiss and gave her a little finger wave before gliding into the suite as if I owned it.

I would be damned if she thought she could get under my skin.

"That's it, my brave one. Hit her where it hurts. I'll be back as soon as I can."

But Idris' voice in my mind did nothing to stop the images of her and Kian curled around each other.

Did nothing to stop my brain from supplying the noises he made when he was so close to coming, when his moans became desperate.

"I've been aching to hear all about your troubles, Idris," Selene cooed, her lyrical voice like thorns in my ears. "I'm completely at your disposal. I'd be happy to get you *all* sorted out."

Whipping around, I caught her smile as she guided Idris away, the green of her magic swirling around her ankles as she glided down the hallway. And even though I could practically *feel* her in my mind, supplying all the building blocks of my rage, I still couldn't shove her out.

How had she gotten in? How—

"Take a deep breath, Vale," Kian suggested, but I was three seconds away from losing it. If that door didn't shut fast enough, I'd sprint down that corridor, shove my blades through her jugular, and rip her fucking head off.

By the time they closed, I had already pulled the blades free from their sheaths. But it wasn't until Xavier stood in my way, preventing me from completing the task at hand, did I even marginally come back to myself.

"There's no need for that. Just because you've met someone we've bedded, doesn't mean you get to lose it now. We have a job to do, and that doesn't involve you getting jealous."

And then my sanity took a vacation.

"*We've* bedded?" I growled through gritted teeth. "Who is *we*?" A golden glow raced through my veins, aching to erupt from my skin as I forced myself to sheathe my blades.

Kian cut his amber gaze to Xavier. "Way to go, man. I haven't even dug myself out of this hole yet, and you went ahead and jumped right into it with me." He held up his hands in surrender. "It was centuries ago—before the curse, before everything. You weren't even born then."

Somehow that did not make it better.

Because now, instead of just Kian's moans and pleas in my head, Xavier's had joined in. I could almost see them wrapped around each other. But it made an awful sort of sense, too. Kian and Xavier had been so eager to share me at the inn—so in sync with their movements. They'd done that before—shared a woman before.

Bile rose in my throat. "Did you share her like you shared me?" I whispered, tears filling my eyes.

Was that ripping sensation just under my ribs my heart breaking?

Was it the death of the last special thing I had?

Was I just another game to them, another woman to bed?

I'd never experienced anything like this—this jealousy.

Xavier moved closer, trying to take my hand in his, but even though I didn't have my daggers in my grip, I still wanted to stab and slash and rend. The golden glow of my magic was growing, expanding, and it hurt so bad I thought I'd die from it.

Kian moved closer, his hands still raised, but his gaze was so open, so transparent, that I couldn't help but stare into those amber depths. "She's wormed her way in. Get her out of your head, little witch. Selene is twisting everything you think, everything you know."

My body was on fire as rage ached to burst free from my skin. "You know what's in my head?" I snarled, my magic flickering as it expanded. "The sounds you make, the words you whisper in my ear, the way you kiss me—only it's not with me. It's with her."

It just kept getting louder, overtaking everything I was, everything I would be. Clutching my head, I tried to get it to stop, tried to clear my mind, but it was too strong. It was visions of her with them all, stealing them away, ripping them from me.

And why wouldn't they go?

Of course they would. I'd kept them all at a distance, barely giving them any indication that this situation hadn't just been thrust upon me. I was still trying to find ways to get out of the wedding, to leave, to hide. It made sense that they would choose her. So what if our minds were linked?

I couldn't break the curse.

I couldn't control my power.

I knew nothing about running a kingdom.

I couldn't save my sister.

It was all a mistake. I was the wrong woman. They didn't want me.

"No, my sweet girl," Xavier whispered, but his voice set my teeth on edge. "We're with you. Always with you. No one can take your place. You're our mate, Vale."

Shaking, I backed away as the images were nearly all I could see. "You didn't choose me—you're stuck with me," I whispered as the heat of the golden light filled every part of my body. Blistering my skin, my eyes, my very mind, I felt the trickle from my nose as it began to bleed. "You're—"

My words died in my throat as Xavier's blue flames hit my shield, shoving me backward. Startled, my magic flickered and died, my hold on it slipping as the pictures got stronger. Without my shield, they got louder, digging into my memories, into the bond we shared.

Selene's magic ripped it, shredded it, made me scream with the agony of my magic pulling away from me. Red tinted my vision as blood flowed from my nose, my lungs burned, and all the while I prayed for death. Someone hooked me around my middle, their steady hold not once leaving me as ice-cold water cut into my flesh.

Two pairs of hands peeled my leathers away, freeing my skin as more water cooled my overheated body. My lungs expanded, and I took my first unencumbered breath in hours. The images in my head faded bit by bit as fingers buried themselves in my hair, stroked my skin, whispers filled my ears.

"That's it, little witch. Breathe deep," Kian reminded me, his touch pulling the ache from my very bones. "Let us help you."

"She doesn't control you, my love. Remember who you are to us," Xavier whispered, his voice so much different now that I didn't feel like I was dying.

I was draped over a solid chest, my cheek resting on a shoulder as two sets of hands roamed my skin. The pain from Selene's spell eased a bit, but it wasn't gone. "What's happening to me?"

Kian's warm lips landed on the mating mark on my shoulder, sending a bolt of heat through my core. "The effects from a nasty spell, *oroum di vita*. I don't know how she got in, but we've seen this before. We can help you if you let us."

Xavier curled around me, his biting kisses waking something I could have sworn died mere moments before. "We want to fix it. Let us, my love."

His rough hands stroked down my body as the water pelted my skin, and like a cat, I arched into his touch, craving more. "H-how do you fix it? Wh—"

Xavier's mouth dropped to the mating mark, and I bit my lip to keep from moaning. The sensitive flesh seemed to have a direct line to my core, ramping up my desire tenfold.

"Wh-what's happening?" I repeated, but I mostly didn't care. I just didn't want them to stop. I feared if they stopped, I might die.

"Sel—*she*—breached your mind somehow and hit you with a jealousy and inferiority working. *Veythara*. It's a foul bit of magic meant to make the affected hurt themselves until it is lifted."

Kian adjusted me until I was straddling him, my overheated body suddenly keenly aware of every millimeter of his skin. "With as much power as you have, it could make you burn out or worse. If it doesn't kill you, the only way out is with your mate's help."

Xavier fisted his hand in my hair, the gentle squeeze of his fingers pulling my head back, exposing my throat to Kian's waiting mouth. "What she doesn't know, is you have three mates who will do anything to keep you breathing." His warm breath caressed my lips, his mouth brushing mine. "Want to know how we heal you?"

The amount of effort it took to focus on his words instead of Kian's mouth on my neck, on the anticipation of his kiss, on the new fire growing within me, was almost too much to bear.

"Y-yes."

"To break the working, we have to show you what you mean to us," he murmured against my lips, his hand wrapping around my throat as Kian's kisses drifted to my breasts. "We have to show you how much we worship you."

Did I want their worship?

Yes, I did.

Kian's mouth closed around my nipple, his tongue flicking against the tight bud before he raked a fang over the sensitive flesh. "And we want to worship you, little witch. We want to watch you come over and over again." He tightened his hold on my hips, my center rubbing against the hard ridge of his cock. "Would you like that?"

"Like" wasn't the right word. I *needed* it—more than air, more than light.

I needed *them*.

Answering with a moan, my hips bucked as my lips crashed into Xavier's, my tongue sweeping into his mouth. He took over the kiss immediately, devouring me as Kian rocked me against his length.

Pleasure sizzled down my spine as he put the perfect pressure on my clit, but as good as it felt, I was still empty.

Desperation had me whimpering, needing something I couldn't articulate.

"She needs more," Xavier growled, lifting me off of Kian, pulling me into his arms. "She doesn't just want to be worshipped, do you? You want us to fuck every hole, fill you up so full you can't breathe, is that it?"

A soft mattress hit my back before I could answer, but Xavier didn't need me to. My need so acute, I had no doubt my mind was screaming with my hunger for them. Legs splayed wide, Xavier held my knees apart as he knelt between them, his gaze almost like a physical touch.

"*Fuck*, your scent," he growled, his crystalline eyes flashing between human and his dragon. "Every time I smell you, I want to bury my face between your legs and drink you down."

He yanked me to the edge of the bed, and a moment later, his hot breath feathered over my sensitive skin. "Already dripping, my love? Tell me how much you want my mouth on you."

"I need it," I whispered, the order loosening my tongue. "*Please*."

"Gods, I love it when you beg, little witch," Kian rumbled, capturing my wrists in his hold and stretching them over my head.

My back bowed as I stared into his amber irises. His lids went heavy as I let out a desperate moan when Xavier gave my sex that first lick. Kian's mouth landed on mine, his dizzying kisses like a drug as Xavier wound me up, his touch so gentle it was practically a tease.

I let out a needy whimper, my hips squirming, even under both of their holds.

"Do you hear that?" Xavier rumbled, his voice like the thickest honey over shattered glass. "It sounds like she needs more. What do you want, my love?"

My mind went to the last time they shared me, my desire nearly burning me alive as I remembered the way they moaned as I swallowed their cocks. That power? I needed that as much as I needed the pleasure.

"I know what she needs," Kian growled, letting my wrists go as he turned me, setting me on my hands and knees. "She needs a cock in her mouth while you fuck her with your tongue. Is that it, little witch?"

Kian fisted his cock, letting out a nearly inaudible groan. A drop of seed pearled on the dark-pink head, and I couldn't stop myself from licking it. Kian wrapped his fist in my braid, the bite of pain so at odds with the pleasure coursing through the bond.

I could feel him again—in my skin, in my mind. Moaning, I took him into my mouth, the flare of desire nearly consuming me as I swallowed him down. My moans got louder when Xavier thrust two fingers inside me, his ministrations not stopping for one moment as he spun me into a frenzy. But I needed something else —something besides his finger and tongue.

I needed him.

"*More*," Kian panted, his husky plea making me melt. "She needs more. She needs both of our cocks inside her. Can't you feel her begging for it?"

My core clenched at the thought of his cock in my mouth and Xavier's in my pussy.

"Fuck, she's squeezing my fingers like a vise. Gods, baby. You need it bad, don't you?"

I clenched around his fingers again, my sex sucking at them like my mouth on Kian's cock.

A second later, I whimpered when those fingers were gone, and Xavier replaced them with his thick cock. I moaned around Kian's length as Xavier pushed inside me, the walls of my sex fluttering as they tried and failed to clench around him.

Kian's fist tightened in my hair. "Relax your throat, baby," he rasped, his breath rougher, darker. "I'm going to fuck your pretty mouth while Xavier fucks your dripping cunt. And you're going to take us both like the good girl you are. Yes?"

I couldn't nod, I couldn't move, but I could reach out with my mind. Kian's eyes rolled into the back of his head as the images of the three of us wrapped around each other filled it.

"Fuck, you've got some good ideas. But first..." He trailed off before thrusting into my waiting mouth.

At the same time, Xavier pulled out before filling me so full, about all I could do was moan and hold on to the bedclothes for dear life.

Xavier's desire reached for my mind, mingling with Kian's—with mine. It was overwhelming, bearing down on me, and I was drowning beneath it all.

"That's my good girl," Kian groaned as I reflexively swallowed, my throat contracting around him before he pulled out and thrust again. "Do it again. Swallow me whole. Fuck, you take our cocks so good."

As if my body lived to obey him, I swallowed

again, and his hold tightened. "You're too fucking good at that. Gods, your mouth is heaven."

Gasping around him, my climax reached for me, their pleasure bombarding my senses. But I wasn't ready.

It would be too big, too much. It was a tidal wave threatening to pull me under and never let me go.

Then Xavier's giant hands spanned the entirety of my hips, his thumbs spreading me wide. He massaged my virgin hole, the puckered ring of muscle accepting him as my lust threatened to consume me.

Gods, I couldn't fight it off.

"Not yet," Xavier growled in my ear, his big body curled over mine as he slowed his thrusts. "You're not allowed to come until I say. Remember?"

My eyes rolled into the back of my head as his thumb continued to torment me, my orgasm loosening its hold, even as the pleasure began anew.

"You want to be full, little witch?" Kian asked, his husky voice mingling with the essence of his desire filling my mind.

I wanted it—wanted it more than I could say, but I didn't know if I could take it. They were so big, and I was so small.

Kian pulled from my mouth, his thumb raking

over my swollen lips. "Don't worry, baby. You can take it."

He moved from the bed only to return a moment later with a vial. Yanking out the stopper with his teeth, the warm, slick liquid hit my backside. Xavier's thumb slipped inside just a little before the ring of muscle loosened, letting him glide in.

"Gods, look at your greedy hole," Kian murmured in my ear, his fingers strumming my clit as Xavier's thrusts picked up speed. "I bet you've been thinking about this, haven't you? Of Xavier in your ass, and me in your cunt, fucking you together until you can't see straight. That's what you want, isn't it?"

My arms collapsed underneath me as Xavier removed his thumb, replacing it with two fingers. He fucked my pussy and my ass, his thrusts picking up speed, but both soft, teasing. I thought I might die from the ache of it.

Sweat broke out all over my skin, my words failing.

"Yes. Please yes."

Kian and Xavier gave me what I wanted. Before I knew it, I was draped over Kian's lap as he sat on the edge of the bed. I inched down his length, the walls of my sex fluttering signaling how close my release was. Then the warm head of Xavier's cock pressed against the tight ring of muscle, the slick liquid helping him ease in inch by inch.

I'd thought I was full, but then Xavier just kept going, filling me oh, so completely. I clung to Kian, my head lolling on my neck until it hit Xavier's shoulder. My ragged pants turned to moans as my body relaxed, the urge to move almost overwhelming.

"That's it, little witch," Xavier growled in my ear as my hips bucked. "Fuck, you take us so well."

I moaned at the praise, my orgasm threatening at the edges of my consciousness. It would consume me, and I didn't care anymore. I was desperate for it—for how close it brought us, how connected I felt to my mates.

"Fuck, she's so tight, so hot," Kian moaned, his rough fingers strumming my clit in teasing strokes as Xavier raked his fangs down my neck. "Gods, you're perfect. So fucking perfect."

"Please let me come," I begged, my voice gone. *"I need it."*

They moved in tandem, one filling as the other retreated, the pleasure so extreme my chest threatened to cave in.

This was worship.

This was connection.

This was love.

Their minds mixed and mingled with mine, and all I felt was the truth—I was not their burden. I was their peace. Their freedom. Their home.

And in that moment, I knew they were all those things for me, too.

Home. Peace. Freedom. Love.

The last threads of the siren's spell lifted, and a presence filled my thoughts, welcome and warm, his desire making me whimper.

"There you are, my brave one." Idris' voice in my head had my core clenching, my mind buzzing. *"I thought I told you I wanted to watch you come. Don't tell me I missed it."*

"Please, tell them to let me come. I'll be so good, please."

His dark chuckle sent shivers down my spine. *"Oh, no, my brave one. Not until I can watch you fall. I've felt it, but I know watching it will be magnificent. Let me?"*

Did I want him to watch me come? It didn't even take a second for me to think about it. *"Yes."*

Idris' pleasure reached me, growing by the second as if he were getting closer. My hips bucked harder, answering Kian and Xavier's thrusts. The sound of a door opening barely reached my ears, but I knew I'd managed to call Idris to me.

I needed him, too. I needed him so bad, I couldn't breathe—didn't want to breathe.

Opening my eyes, I met his golden ones. Still in his leathers, he stalked toward us, the scent of his desire filling my nose. Or maybe I was just so deep in their minds that I could sense it. Either way, where there could have been jealousy, all that was left was lust, need, and an ache to touch me.

This was how it was supposed to be.

"Gods," he murmured, his fists clenching at his sides. "I was right. You look magnificent."

I reached for him as Kian's and Xavier's thrusts turned deliciously rougher, but he didn't take my hand. "Not this time. This time is for you, not for me. I can wait."

"Kiss me?" I begged, wanting to touch him somehow, the need so intense it burned through every limb, every pore.

He towered over us as he moved closer, his golden eyes flashing with unspent magic and desire.

Then he gently raked a roughened fingertip down my cheek.

"If I kiss you now, I'll end up marking you. Is that what you want?"

The thought of his mark on me had my sex clenching as much as it could being so full. Groaning,

Xavier moved his hands to my breasts, lifting them like an offering as Kian dipped his head to take a nipple into his mouth. His fangs nearly pierced the flesh as Xavier's raked against my throat.

"Yes. Please. I need it. Kiss me."

Idris dropped his mouth to mine, his tongue claiming every part of it as Kian and Xavier struck, their fangs slicing into me as my climax slammed into us all. Their releases washed over me, drawing out the high so long I almost hoped it would never end. Moaning into Idris' mouth, I relished his shudder as my desire threatened to pull him down with us.

Before I could take a breath, Idris' razor-like incisors latched onto my shoulder right over the mark my other mates had made the first time we'd bonded.

A second orgasm overtook me, drowning me in pleasure so acute it was as if I'd been struck by lightning. A scream broke free of my throat, quieted only by Idris' punishing kiss as golden power mixed and mingled with mine, with Xavier's, with Kian's, showering us all in magic.

I felt tied to them in a way I hadn't previously, the bond so obvious to me where it had only been a tendril before.

Safety.

Warmth.

Home.

They're my home.

And I would do anything to protect my home. Even make nice with a siren who wanted to take everything from me.

I just had to not fuck up and kill her first.

Piece of cake.

CHAPTER 12

KIAN

While running my fingertips over the raised white scars marring Vale's perfect skin, I plotted Selene's demise. I knew I wasn't the only one contemplating the siren queen's end, but my revenge would be the most permanent.

It would endure for decades until she begged for death.

And when I finally granted it, she would be sent to Orrus screaming.

Few deserved the fury of a curse such as *Veythara*, and certainly not Vale. My chest ached with the memory of her pain, of her tears, her fear. Every drop of blood and every mark she'd made on her skin was etched into my soul.

Too many times had someone tried to take her from us.

Too many times had someone threatened to steal my world, my life, my heart.

I swore it on Orrus himself that if another being hurt my woman, I would take their fucking head.

Just like the man who'd given her these scars.

He would die screaming, too.

I'd make sure of it.

My gaze shifted from Vale's back to Xavier's slitted pupils. His focus was on the raised flesh under my touch, and every few seconds, the muscle in his jaw would jump. Out of all of us, he'd been with her each time she'd nearly been taken from us, his mind, his soul twining with hers each time he'd healed her.

He likely knew more about Vale than she knew about herself.

And each bruise on her soul was engraved onto his heart.

Vale dozed across Idris' chest while he twirled the soaked strands of her hair around his index finger. I had to admire the man's restraint. If I had a naked Vale laying on me, there wouldn't be a protocol in the world other than her lack of willingness that would stop me from taking her over and over again.

It didn't make sense to me why he wanted to wait

for their union before he bonded with her. But then again, there would probably never be a recognized marriage between she and I.

No ceremony.

No fanfare.

I wasn't a king, and multiple mates were unheard of. The only people who would know about what Vale meant to me—to us—would be a select few.

Vale reached backward, her fingers opening and closing as if she were asking for my hand. Readily, I gave it to her, and she yanked me closer as she curled tighter into Idris.

"Why are you sad?" she murmured, rubbing her cheek on Idris' chest.

Vale was barely conscious, and I couldn't blame her. After Selene's torment and how we had to break her spell, Vale was floating on a cloud. Xavier and I helped her wash up, her legs refusing to hold her in the opulent shower. She was blissed-out and dreamy, and she deserved to be.

"I'm not. Just thinking," I replied, pressing a kiss to her shoulder.

"Bad thoughts—all three of you." She lifted her head and raked the wet strands out of her eyes. "You all helped me through mine. Why won't you let me help you through yours?"

Because she'd gone through enough—more than enough. She didn't need our explanations or our begging for forgiveness. She didn't need our plans for vengeance, either.

"It's nothing, little witch. Rest. We have enough to deal with tonight without me adding to it."

Pulling from Idris' arms, she turned to me. Her loose black hair curled around her breasts, and I ached to forget why we were here. Ached to hold her, kiss her, to take her over and over again until she could never forget our touch, our love.

But there was also a creeping bit of misery there, too. I'd bedded someone who tried to kill her. Yes, my vengeance would be far-reaching, but she needed to know that what I—what we had with Selene was nothing compared to what Vale shared with us.

"Guilt?" Vale whispered, her brow puckering. "Is that guilt I sense? For bedding a woman ages ago? You know that was the spell talking, right?"

Veythara didn't work like that. "Not completely. That particular spell can only exacerbate what is already there. Insecurities, fears, self-loathing, regrets —anything you feel about yourself—it takes it and twists it."

I met Idris' golden gaze, and though he was completely still, the flames of rage nearly melted the side of my face. He hadn't known just how close we'd been to losing Vale—just how close we'd come to an eternity of loss and pain.

How close she'd come to burning out.

All because Selene was a vindictive bitch who couldn't best her on her own.

Vale dipped her head, allowing her hair to fall forward and shield her eyes. "So I was a little insecure."

The pitiful shrug that accompanied that lie made the whole of my chest ache.

"I know it's not rational to be upset you had sex with another woman. She's beautiful and powerful. It makes sense why you would want her. You said it was a long time ago, right? Then I can't be upset with you —with either of you—about it. I can't even be mad you shared her."

"Yes, you can," Xavier said, squeezing her ankle. "You're allowed to feel however you feel."

Of course he'd be the one to say all the right things. "Yes, it was a long time ago, and yes, we did share her." I shot a glance at Xavier, my jaw tightening as I remembered the encounter. Telling Vale the truth about that night would only make it worse, but lying was off the table. She'd been lied to enough.

"I wouldn't call the experience particularly memorable. It was at a party where everyone had consumed far too much Fae wine, and I don't recall much of it."

Not a lie. I wouldn't tell her the part where that wine had been drugged and we'd been seduced by a woman too powerful to realize that not all of her partners were willing. Then again, why else would she have drugged us? Maybe she thirsted for more power still, and that was why she'd hurt Vale.

Just because she could.

Xavier moved closer, blue flames dancing on his fingertips as he ran them up and down Vale's calf. It was his tell. If he used his magic and wouldn't look anyone in the eye, he was bluffing his ass off. It was a distraction, a gimmick, a way to misdirect without lying outright.

"I remember very little from that night. The only good thing to come out of it was that it changed our bond as friends. It helped Kian and I understand that when we found a mate—*if* we found a mate—if Fate was kind, we would get to share."

Vale's gaze sharpened on the both of us, her green eyes glowing with a bit of her magic. She could feel the bluffs, the disguised truths, the veiled horrors.

She deserved more than that.

"When we were children, we were orphaned," I explained, trying to make sure she understood. "Though, I suppose that isn't the right term for it. Abandoned is closer to the truth. I was surrendered to a cruel orphanage when I was maybe eight years old. Xavier came along a few years after that. All we've ever had was each other."

Vale's parents hadn't left her of their own free will. Even as poor and starving and overworked as they'd been, she'd been wanted. I wondered what it would be like to have a family like that.

I fought off the tremble of my lips, my jaw firming into granite. It was an old wound—one of many—but she needed to know who her mates were. "In our species, a mother can tell if her offspring is too weak to thrive. She deemed me unworthy of my animal as a baby. A dragon's first shift typically happens between five and seven years of age. By the time I turned eight, she'd decided I was too weak—that I wouldn't be able to shift. I went back after I joined the King's Guard—after I had finally been able to shift, finally got my abilities. But by the time I got there, they were all gone."

Xavier's hand stilled on her calf, his story worse

than mine. I'd always known my family hadn't wanted me. He'd had the rug pulled out from beneath him.

"I had my healing abilities long before I learned to shift. But in a family full of dragons, healing isn't exactly necessary. My family deemed my gifts worthless, and when I didn't shift by the age of twelve, they were done with me. It was like night and day. One minute I was wanted, and the next I wasn't. And unlike Kian's family, mine stayed right where they were. When the curse hit Idris, some of the oldest of the dragons couldn't withstand the lack of power. Some died without their magic, many willingly met Orrus. Those of us who were considered too weak, stayed to live and breathe another day."

I'd remembered that time. Xavier had been nearly driven mad with grief. His parents, his siblings— nearly all of them had chosen death. I'd always had a feeling that maybe mine had done the same, but I couldn't prove it. It had been our weakness that had turned into a strength. Our weakness that had kept us breathing.

Until Vale, I'd considered us all cursed.

Until her, I'd thought we were the unfortunate ones—staying alive while the world burned around us. That at least Xavier's family had understood when to cut and run.

Xavier's smile turned bitter for a moment before he wiped it clean. "When I thought just Kian and Idris were your mates, it hurt so bad because I thought that not only would I never have you, but I would lose the life I'd always envisioned for myself. I would lose my best friend, my partner, the only real family I'd ever known—the only family I have left."

His fingers sparked again, and I knew it was to avoid the real meat of the issue.

He couldn't fool me. Xavier still felt that way. It was only so obvious because I'd known him so long. He worried one day he would wake up and it would all be a dream. That somehow, he would always be on the outside, always be looking in, always abandoned.

Just like me.

"But you do have me," she whispered, covering the blue flames dancing across his fingertips. "I promised you wouldn't lose me."

We knew better.

People could promise a lot of things. They could promise you their hearts, their souls. They could promise their loyalty, but people like us never really believed in promises.

It was why we never made any we thought we couldn't keep.

I hooked a finger under her chin, drawing her gaze. "Then promise us we won't lose you over this, either. Trust me, if we knew then what we know now, we wouldn't have stepped one toe in this place, let alone—"

Vale's grin turned wry. "Fucked her stupid? Yeah, I gathered. I can't say that I will never feel insecure around her but," She tapped her sternum, "I know better. In here. I won't let her back in my head."

Idris' hand flexed on her hip. "I doubt you let her in the first time. She used our connection," he growled, his fury lancing through my mind as if I were the one mated to him and not Vale. "She used our bond to hurt you through me."

This hadn't been the first time and I doubted it would be the last unless...

"Please tell me we get to instruct her how to treat our future Queen," I asked, the list of Selene's punishments growing by the second.

"No," Vale chided. "We need her alive. We need her behind us. Or else all of this pain—all of this bullshit—was for nothing. I'm going to put on a damn dress and smile like she didn't just try to kill me, and we will hash out whatever we need to. We didn't come all this way for her to weasel out of helping us now. You three need to calm down."

I knew my mate was being incredibly mature and sensible.

I also knew I didn't give that first fuck.

Apparently, Idris was of the same mind. He sat up, his hand capturing her chin as he made her look at him. "Selene doesn't get to do what she did to you and walk away without consequences. I told her who you were to me. She spelled you knowing that you were my mate, knowing that you were her future Queen, knowing what it would do to me and what it would mean to the continent if you'd died. There is no such thing as calm when it comes to people hurting you."

"So far, she has attacked all of us," Xavier noted. "The only reason you're still alive is because we were here with you. Our King is correct. There is no walking away from this—not after what she's done."

I was glad I wasn't alone in this. "No one touches you and lives, little witch. No one. She's breathing borrowed air on borrowed time. I want you to know that."

Vale's eyes filled with tears before she blinked them away. She dipped her head, that curtain of dark hair covering her face once more. But I still felt pleasure coursing through her body at the three of us being ready and willing to protect her in any way, shape, or form necessary to keep her breathing.

We came here for an ally, but Selene had made an enemy.

She was about to find out *exactly* what that looked like.

CHAPTER 13

IDRIS

Vale's gorgeous green eyes met mine as Xavier lovingly laced up her corset. While she gripped the bedpost, he would drop kisses to her shoulder with each pull. Every hitch of her breath and secret smile sent a bolt of lightning down my spine, straight to my cock.

I'd thought sharing her would kill me. That first day when I'd scented them on her skin, I'd thought I would murder my closest friends, spill their blood all over my hands, and scare her away forever. It turned out, I not only didn't mind sharing Vale, but I was beginning to crave it.

Watching her come apart between them had nearly driven me to claim her right then and there. The kiss we shared had almost broken my resolve, but I'd held onto my restraint by the finest of margins. When she'd reached for me, I'd almost forgotten everything.

My gaze trailed down the column of her throat to the pale-blue sleeve that was playing peek-a-boo with the mating mark at the crown of her shoulder. The magic had changed the teeth marks into a faint, sweeping, golden design embedded into her skin like our tattoos. It was delicate just like she was, and it would darken into its permanent form once we completed our bond.

Just looking at it made me hard.

"I can't focus when you're looking at me like that," Vale murmured as a shiver seemed to work its way down her spine. "How am I supposed to keep my wits about me if you're staring at me like you want to eat me up?"

Lifting my lips into a smirk, I dodged her questions. "But you look good enough to eat. Are you sure you don't want to be our meal instead?"

"The sooner we do this, the sooner we can go home," she taunted, the images in her head enough to make me come in my leathers if I let myself.

"Oh, I plan on wrapping this up as soon as possible just so I can watch you come over and over again. I have plans for you, Vale. Many, many plans."

I didn't know when her walls had crumbled, but I loved being on the other side of them. Her heart was warm and fierce, and I never wanted a single breath on this earth without it.

But the scent of her rising desire hadn't just hit my nose. It was driving Xavier crazy as well. He'd stopped his lacing and seemed mere moments away from bending her over the bed and burying himself in her tight, wet heat.

If we were ever going to make it out of this room, we needed to focus. I just didn't know how I would begin to do that with the flush of desire working its way up her throat.

When Kian waltzed through the bedroom door, it was almost a relief. He'd made sure we had safe passage through the castle with no obvious traps. We were late, but that didn't matter.

What mattered was that we would catch Selene off guard.

"Sweet gods," he growled, his pupils elongating into the slit of his dragon. "Are you sure we need to go to this thing?"

His words were almost a plea for mercy, but it had to be done.

"You mean, do we have to parade our mate in front of the bitch who tried to kill her? Do we have to inform Selene that she failed so spectacularly that she's a walking, talking dead woman? Afraid so."

Kian's irises burned bright as his jaw turned to stone. "Right."

Xavier curled his arm around Vale's waist, tucking her into his side. "She won't touch you, my love."

Vale's laugh tightened its hold on my heart. "Oh, I'm not worried about me. I'm more worried about what happens when you kill a siren queen on her own turf. Rune says that this plan is ill-advised, but he would love the chance to eat a few guards. He says he thinks they'll taste like squid."

I agreed with my dragon. This plan was shaky at best, but it was what we had. Rising from the bed, I held out my hand for Vale. "As always, Rune is wiser than all of us."

Pulling her close, I curled her fingers around my forearm. She would never be farther from me tonight than right there.

Kian took point, exiting the room first with Xavier at our backs, the illusion of the corridor sweeping around us as we headed to Selene's private dining chambers. I'd known coming here wasn't the smartest idea I'd ever had, but *not* coming here was a risk I couldn't take. The continent was on the tipping point.

One move in the wrong direction could bring the whole thing down on our heads.

We'd barely survived the last coup. The last thing we needed was to waltz into another one. Had I realized Selene would try to hurt Vale—try to kill her—I would have brought more guards, more weapons.

Just... *more*.

As with every other room in this gods-forsaken castle, Selene's private dining chamber was made of magic and falsehoods. Sirens were gifted magic-weavers, their illusion work powerful enough few could break through. Kian was the only illusionist I knew of who could sense each spell, each falsehood, each lie for what it was.

Selene hated him the most for that. She loathed that he would always have the truth of a situation, which was why she'd perpetually chosen other methods of subduing him. Vale, however, was another animal entirely, and now that the *Veythara* had failed, she would try to hurt her over and over again.

The siren queen did not like to fail—of that, I knew for certain.

Striding into the room, I enjoyed the gentle graying of Selene's face as she recognized my mate was not only alive and well, but my mark was on her exposed shoulder.

The Herald snapped to attention, his gaze falling to Vale's mark and back to his mistress. No one had expected Vale to survive Selene's little trick—not even the man who announced us.

"Presenting His Majesty, King Idris Ashbourne of Credour, and Her Grace, Duchess Isolde Vale Tenebris."

The room stood simply to bow, Selene's reluctance less than a surprise. I couldn't say I'd been a particularly good king. The lengthy list of my failures could paper the continent, of that I was absolutely sure.

I'd failed to recognize Zamarra for what she was. I'd failed to see that my brother had lost his heart to a madwoman. I'd failed to kill him when I should have. My people suffered while I tried and failed to find a cure for the curse that stunted their power, withered their lives, poisoned my kingdom.

The only thing I'd ever done right was to fall for the beauty at my side.

And I would protect her.

Vale's eye barely twitched at the use of her sovereign name, but her mind buzzed akin to a hive of bees.

"Just one more thing to hate her for," she mused,

her attention never wavering as she stared the siren queen down. *"It's bad enough I know she did something to the guys, and I still don't know what it is. Did she have to full-name me? Bitch."*

There was one thing about Vale that I absolutely adored and hated all at the same time. She knew the second she was being lied to. While Kian and Xavier hadn't lied outright, they still knew enough about that night to tell Vale the truth.

Then again, if they had, Selene would be fish food the second Vale saw her. A part of me wanted to see what she would do. The other part wanted to salvage as much of this night as we could before I made sure Selene never breathed another second of air.

Had Kian and Xavier not made me vow not to breathe a word of their assault to anyone, I would have killed Selene ages ago. Now that she'd hurt Vale? There would be no stopping me this time.

"And the fact that she tried to kill you makes no difference to you."

Gently, I guided Vale down the set of stairs into the bowels of this insidious room, her pale-blue confection of a dress glittering like diamonds as it fluttered about her gorgeous legs. Not an ounce of magic or glamour, and she was still the most beautiful woman I'd ever seen.

"She's not the first person to try. And she failed, remember? Spectacularly. It's not my fault she's sucks at trying to kill me."

Selene stood to the right of the head of the table, her shoulders tight as her glamour flickered, her gaze never once leaving Vale's faint golden mating mark. "So good of you to join us, my King."

That sounded awfully like a reprimand. Considering what she'd done, she was lucky she was still breathing. I opened my mouth to respond, but Vale beat me to it.

Nearly shouldering Selene out of her way, Vale took her spot at the right of the head chair, exactly where she should be.

She gave the siren queen a guileless smile. "Oh, are we late?" Vale whispered, her grin widening. "That's my fault. You know how it is when someone tries to kill you, sometimes it takes a few extra minutes to clean yourself up."

The smile slid off Vale's face as she stared Selene down. I relished the way the siren paled further when I pulled her chair out for her, seating her before the entire table. I dropped a kiss to the golden bonding mark before taking my own chair, allowing the rest of this farce of a dinner to continue.

Selene seemed at a loss when Kian let out a growl,

his eyes flashing with his dragon as he took the spot next to Vale. Cowed, she swept to the foot of the table and lowered herself onto her seat.

Awkwardly, the rest of the retinue took their places, the breach in protocol casting a pall over the evening. I didn't care that I had sat my intended before myself. If anything, it told Selene just how fucked she was without saying a word.

"Thank you for having me," I growled, my tone less than kind as I watched the vile woman paste a saccharine smile on her overly glamoured face. "So far, we have been threatened by your guard, you've breached protocol by attempting to impugn her status with me, and I won't even touch on the rest. Do we have a problem, Selene?"

Her gaze flicked around the room, guilt dulling her glamour. "O-of course not, Your Majesty. We had no idea you were coming—"

"Lie," I snarled, cutting her off. "You knew exactly when and how we were coming. You knew why, too. Even if someone in my council *didn't* inform you, you're not showing up when an emissary was requested should have been a clue that we would arrive on your very doorstep. There never should have been guards in that courtyard, and yet, there were. You attacked my Hand and highest general, you attacked my bride. Remind me, Selene—what kingdom do you serve?"

Selene took a large gulp of her wine. "Y-yours, Your Majesty."

Sitting back in my chair, I studied the siren. Shoulders hunched, she'd lost the confident, overly sexual quality to her speech, settling into the poor down-trodden damsel routine. But I wasn't fooled.

"I don't think so. I think you serve someone else. Because if you served me so loyally, as you claim, you wouldn't have tried to kill my wife. Has anyone done that and survived?"

I'd caught the slip as soon as I'd said it, but calling Vale anything else didn't feel right. She would be my wife in a few days, then she would be tied to me forever. I already considered her mine, and this woman needed to know it right before I made sure she knew nothing else.

"I-I don't think so." Selene's fingers fluttered over the table setting, gripping the opal-plated knife before setting it back down. That paltry weapon would do nothing but piss me off.

"I'll confirm it for you. *No one* has survived after taking a hand to my fateborn mate. Do you know why?"

"Because she's the key to breaking the curse?"

Pitiful tears filled her eyes as she looked up from the table.

"Good try but incorrect. While she is very important to breaking my curse, that is not why they fail to keep breathing. Those that threaten my bride, my fateborn mate, my wife, your Queen die because a threat to her is a threat to me." Shoving to my feet, the chair clattered to the ground behind me, making the siren jump.

"Do you see that mark on her shoulder? Not only is it a sign of our bond, but it is a sign of the end of the dark days of this kingdom. If the fateborn mates can rise again, then that means the curse is nigh. The power you long for is so close you can taste it. Why would you jeopardize that?"

"I—" She shook her head, her gaze flicking toward the open doors of the balcony, the sounds of the sea rolling through the room. The murals on the walls slipped and slid, their images reforming into new ones.

She waved her hand, breaking the illusion that her closest advisers were in the room with her. Even her glamour faded as the people at her sides disappeared. There was no one but Selene and us, and the siren queen stood, matching me.

"I did it to save us all," she hissed, her gaze never wavering from the mural. "You should have bonded with her. I gave you ample opportunity. Why do you delay freeing us all?"

Rage had me seeing red. Kian ripped Vale out of her chair, moving behind me as I flipped the mammoth table out of my way. A second later, Selene's scaled throat was in my hand as golden bonds wrapped around her body.

"Firstly, I don't answer to you. I told you when I would complete our bond, and under no circumstances will it be a single minute before then. I have one chance to keep my promise to her, and I will not break it—not for this kingdom, not for you, or anyone else."

Eyes bulging, her thick claws raked my skin, but I didn't care. "Then how does she live?"

"You failed to realize something in the middle of your machinations and scheming. Vale doesn't have just one mate. She has three. Your little spell couldn't follow through because she has three of us to make sure she stays breathing."

"But—" Her gaze flicked to the mural behind me, and instantly, I felt the change.

There was a mage in this room.

A Girovian one to be exact.

Selene wasn't just a bitch, she was also a traitor.

So much for playing nice.

CHAPTER 14
VALE

Broken table shards littered the floor at our feet as golden magic poured from Idris, wrapping around Selene with a blazing heat that reached my skin from across the room.

The scent of cooking meat hit my nose, turning my stomach as the reality of the situation struck me. She'd betrayed her kingdom—her King. She'd spun this scheme, and for what? Power? Why was it always power with these people? Given the illusions she'd just shattered, she already had plenty of it. Why did she need more?

But as Idris' magic sizzled against her skin, the walls of the room slipped and slid, the images on the murals churning into something else. Something sinister.

Rune's presence filled my mind, stronger than it had ever been before. He sensed what we all did—danger was coming for all of us. *You need to get out of that room, my Queen.*

I would have loved to listen to him, but it was already too late.

The silhouette of a man coalesced in the darkest shadows of the farthest painting, his hooded form solidifying as he breached the wall, pulling himself from the mural and into the room itself. Kian yanked me behind him as Xavier stepped between Idris' exposed back and the tall man, his slender figure belying the power that radiated off of him.

Fenwick had been powerful, but this man was something else altogether.

Xavier's blue flames coated the floor as Kian reached for the sword at his hip. My magic lurched to my fingertips, the blinding glow pouring from me as a bolt of light formed in my palm.

His hands were raised in surrender, but I didn't believe that for a second. Eerie violet irises glowed from beneath his cloak, and instantly I knew what that meant. I'd seen those purple eyes before when a group of Girovian mages had tried to murder me where I stood, simply for wearing a Festian emblem.

Boiling-hot rage bubbled in my chest as I remembered the arrows in Xavier's back, his blood on my hands, his agony protecting me from their death blows. Xavier seemed to remember it, too. The growl that erupted from his throat was punctuated by iridescent white scales rippling up his arms as he tried not to shift.

His mind buzzed with his betrayal, but I knew better. I'd known it the second she'd dropped her magical façade. Selene was the puppet, and we were about to meet the puppet master.

"I mean you no harm, dragon," the silky voice murmured. "I simply would like a word with your King."

A word with our King?

"Over my dead body," I barked, moving from behind Kian as the bolt of my magic lengthened into a sword.

"What are you doing?" Kian snarled, hooking his arm around my middle.

"Stop," I growled into his mind as I watched the dark swirls of death surround the mage's head and shoulders.

He didn't have the same magic as the other mages who'd tried to murder us. No, this one was close, personal friends with an evil dictator. Just like

Fenwick, this mage was using death magic. Unlike Fenwick, he was a fuck of a lot more powerful.

With his hand still wrapped around Selene's throat, Idris turned to regard the mage in our midst. "I'd known Selene was a traitor, I had no idea just how far she'd fallen. What did you promise her in exchange for killing my bride, mage? Money? Power? Prestige?"

"None of the above," I said, not taking my eyes off the cloaked figure. "Selene is just another one of Arden's puppets, isn't she?"

My gaze flicked to Selene, her claws ripping into Idris' hand as he held her off the ground by her throat. Just like the assassins sent to murder me in my sleep, she had dark magic coursing under her skin, churning around her head, clouding her mind. If I didn't hate her so much, I sure as hell would pity her.

Then again, I understood all the truths Kian and Xavier refused to say. Selene was just as much a predator as the mage, only he'd gotten the upper hand on her.

Slowly, the mage pulled the hood from his bald head, his sallow skin doing nothing to hide the swirling black magic as his cold gaze slid over Selene's squirming body. The tips of his ears came to sharp points, the tops decorated with small golden rings. His nose was sharp, pointing to a thin-lipped blackened maw of a mouth that stank of rot.

Shrugging the cape from his shoulders, he revealed his blackened fingers, the dark magic interrupted only by golden rings, and intricate cuffs on his forearms. He resembled a younger Fenwick, only less the beard, and unable to hide the grave magic swirling under his skin.

"She is not a puppet. She is a tool, a weapon—or at least she used to be. Now she's nothing more to me than expendable. Kill her if you must, she has outlived her usefulness. She can't even manage to kill a weak little Luxa like this one."

He jerked his chin in my direction before that cold gaze landed on me. Tilting his head to the side, he studied me for a moment before his attention slid back to Idris. He seemed to think that I wasn't a threat. That I hadn't taken the lives of mages just like him.

And I'd do it again.

"I-I did everything you asked, Malvor," Selene croaked, the tips of her toes scrabbling for purchase on the debris-littered floor. "I got them here. I spelled her. Let my people go."

Malvor narrowed his glowing purple eyes, his

disappointment clear. "You were supposed to kill her. She's still breathing. You didn't fulfill your end of the bargain."

"But why? Why work with Arden? Why kill innocent people? Why kill me?" This was the first one of Arden's allies that had even been marginally rational —that wasn't warped by a spell or half out of his mind. If he knew something, I wanted to know it, too.

He raised his eyebrow, astounded that I'd be the one giving him lip. "It's nothing personal. I'm sure you're a fine enough woman. It's just... *business*."

I tried to step forward, but Kian yanked me back. "Business? My life is business to you? The kingdom— all of magic—is fucking business?"

His blackened smile chilled me to the bone. "That it is. The curse can't be broken—not for any reason. Again, it's nothing personal."

"Rune?"

A dark chuckle filled my thoughts. *"Already on my way. Keep him busy."*

"You'd rather lose magic forever than break a curse? I'd love to know why," I said, trying to step forward only to get hauled back once more. "If you really plan on killing me, I won't back down without a fight. You could save yourself a lot of trouble if you help me understand. Why can't we break the curse?"

"What are you doing?" Xavier growled, his thoughts nearly splitting my skull as his rage burned through my body.

I fought off the urge to roll my eyes. *"Stalling so Rune can have a snack. Now are you going to back me up or what?"*

The mage seemed to be fighting a smile, his patronizing expression making me grind my teeth as I attempted my first stall tactic. "It's not that complicated. You tell me why and maybe I won't help him. It's not like he likes me, anyway. The only reason Selene is on his shit list is because she fucked with one of his toys."

That was a bold-faced lie, but the mage didn't need to know that.

His smile turned into a full-on grin. "Is this the part where you try to get me to divulge my evil plan, little Luxa? I'm afraid I'm not falling for your games. I know how much you care for him. It's written all over your face. I think I'd rather just..."

I didn't see him weaving the magic until it was almost too late.

Inky blackness flowed from his fingertips, knocking into Selene with a force powerful enough to rip her right out of Idris' grip. She flew backward, slamming into the wall as her icy-blue eyes clouded over. Sea-green magic rose from her skin, swirling up her legs as her arms lifted. Guttural words slipped from her lips as her power churned through the room.

I scarcely had a chance to breathe before Kian shoved me out of the way. Putrid black magic streaked across the room, crashing into the wall right where I'd been standing. Idris yelled something unintelligible as he barreled toward Selene, but we had bigger problems.

Malvor lifted his hands as the foul magic slithered through his fingers, his purple eyes glowing brighter as shards of the table lifted in the air. I'd seen this song and dance before. On instinct, I threw my shield wide, barely covering my men before the mage launched debris straight at us.

Most of the wood burned up on contact, but one of those place setting knives made it through, embedding itself into my shoulder. I barely felt the pain as I ripped the damn thing out, launching it back at him with all the fury in my blood. The throw went low but still hit true, catching him in the thigh as I formed a bolt of light in my hand.

Kian ripped me off my feet, putting himself

between me and Malvor as Xavier's magic pinned the mage to the closest pillar. Those blue flames turned to knives, cutting into his flesh, tearing him to ribbons. Blackened blood flew to the stone floor, and all the while he laughed—the dark, haunting glee pouring out of him as Selene's chants got louder.

It didn't matter that she was going blow for blow against Idris or that the inky blackness was contorting her body. The battle was far from over.

The scent of the sea filled my nose as wind began to whip through the room. The ocean roiled in the distance, but it was the ear-splitting thunder erupting from the water that chilled me to the bone. True fear took root in my belly as the castle shook beneath my feet.

Blue flames danced in the air as a bellow of pure rage turned into a dragon's roar.

The wall beside us crumbled inward. Stone crashed to the floor as the side of the castle seemed to dissolve. My stomach went into freefall as the ground beneath me fell away, my shield no match for what-ever had collided with the building. A thick arm of a great beast reached for me, its flesh sizzling against my magic but it just kept coming.

Strong arms caught me before I hit the ground, snatching me away from the beast before I went flying again. A scream caught in my throat as I met Idris' glowing gold gaze, before a white-scaled fist closed around my middle, ripping me away from him as the beast caught him instead.

"*No*," I screeched, launching a bolt of my power at the thing holding him, but even as my aim hit true, the wound was small compared to the giant creature.

Xavier's wings caught the limited air, pulling me away from the collapsed building and toward the sky as a flash of red streaked toward us.

"*Go back*," I screamed into Xavier's mind. "*Go back for him.*"

"*I can't, my love. It's too dangerous. Idris can handle himself. I have to get you the fuck away from whatever Selene unleashed.*"

"*Is that a gods-be-damned kraken?*" Kian croaked, his blackened scales streaking past us, heading straight for Idris. "*Get her the fuck out of here before it figures out it grabbed the wrong person.*"

Several arms breached the churning water, creating great waves that overtook the docks and pummeled the poor beach. And still, Selene never once broke her chant while the mage practically screamed in glee.

Rune hadn't been exaggerating when he'd said there were things in the water that could gobble me up whole, but never once did I think they would be this big. Golden magic hammered the tentacles, but Idris was still stuck.

"Rune, please. Please save him," I begged, hoping against hope that I wouldn't lose him.

A week ago, I'd hated him.

A day ago, I'd despised Idris.

An hour ago, I'd fallen in love with him.

A minute ago, I'd known I'd do anything to keep him.

I couldn't lose him now.

Rune veered to the right, growling as he went. *"Stay alive, my Queen. That's an order."*

Xavier's course changed, pulling us away from the fight. *"Don't you dare. If I can't fight that big beast, let me take on Selene."*

I hadn't been able to pull Nyrah away from her beast, but I could damn well fight this one.

I wouldn't lose Idris—I wouldn't lose any of them.

Not ever.

There was no way in hell I was taking Vale anywhere near that monster. After watching her nearly get crushed, I was fighting off the urge to haul her off the continent altogether and damn the consequences.

My heart refused to slow down, the organ was nearly beating out of my chest at the memory of Idris yanking her out of the way and throwing her to me before getting captured by that beast. I'd barely shifted in time—barely caught her in time—and still, she was far too close to danger for my comfort.

Lightning cracked far too close as a squall of a storm roiled in the sky. So it wasn't just the monster, it was all the siren queen's power rising in the air. If

Idris didn't make it out of this, I knew he'd want her to.

I couldn't let her die in this. I just couldn't.

"Please. If I can't fight that thing, I can help save him another way. Selene is controlling it somehow. Let me help him. Let me stop her."

I would give her anything—my very last breath if she needed it—but I didn't know how to give her this.

"Please, Xavier. Please don't make me watch him die when I could do something to stop it."

There was a time not so long ago when I would have pulled her from this fight completely, when I would have hidden her away, ignoring her wishes and done what I thought was best.

Unfortunately, that time was over. Now I was so in tune with her, that my heart was breaking inside my very chest.

"I swear to all the gods, if you get hurt, I will never forgive you."

She wilted in my clutches, relief threading through the bond as I changed course. Funny, less than half a day ago, she had been so fearful of being in the air, and now she was consumed with so much rage that she barely noticed the height.

And we were high—high enough that she should have been screaming her head off. But not my woman, not my mate. She was focused on the evil bitch who'd put our King in danger.

"I don't care that the mage is controlling her. If I have to kill her, I will."

That caught me by surprise, even as I sped toward the siren queen. *"What do you mean the mage is controlling her?"*

A bolt of light formed in her palm, quickly transforming into a sword. *"Can't you see it? The mage is made of death magic. It's all around him, all around her. He's manipulating Selene—likely holding her people hostage, too."*

I didn't have the time or will to feel sorry for Selene, nor did I particularly care what happened to her people. Her people stood by while Kian and I were drugged and manipulated. Her people saw what she was capable of and turned a blind eye. They'd served us up to her without a single question.

The entire island could burn for all I cared.

Selene could burn.

Actually, that wasn't a half-bad idea.

My jaw cracked as I opened my mouth wide, the biting burn of my flames aching to be set free. Selene was powerful enough that this would likely not work at all, but I had to try, even if it upset Vale. Clutching my mate to my chest, I unleashed my fire, breathing it into the smoldering rubble where Selene had been moments before.

The sound of her chants still echoed in my ears, but they were fainter, smaller.

I at least had the right direction, even if I hadn't stopped her.

Banking left, I circled back, coating the rubble in my fire before landing on the destroyed beach. Selene lay pinned by the flames that consumed what was left of the tapestries, but it wouldn't last. She'd be free of the fire soon enough.

Glamour gone, skin mottled with burns, Selene held her arms up, still chanting in that guttural language that turned my stomach. On instinct, I searched the sky for Idris and Kian, but all I saw was Rune streaking through the air, his fiery breath scorching the beast from the deep. Then golden magic exploded in the sky, the shockwave of it nearly knocking me off-kilter.

Vale took advantage of the distraction and squirmed out of my hold, racing toward the sea witch as if all our lives depended on it. In her hand was the sword made of her magic, the searingly bright blade poised to strike.

"*Vale, no,*" I roared and moved to follow her, but a tidal wave of scorching magic tore into my scaled flesh, the putrid stink of the grave clawing into my body.

Erupting in a roar, I unleashed my flames on the mage, burning through the rot and decay as I searched for Vale. Caught in the throes of battle, she stabbed and slashed at Selene, but she was unable to cut through her magic. But Selene was on defense, barely holding Vale back as she continued her chants, the grotesque monster of the deeps roaring its displeasure.

That just left the mage to me. Staggering in the rubble, Malvor tried to fend off my fire, his power a paltry shield as he tried to keep standing. Blackened blood ran from the wounds at his middle, soaking through his dark tunic.

If I could have smiled in that moment, I would have.

Admiring my handiwork, I felt my flames rise again. He couldn't hold me back for long. But as I released them once more, Malvor struck. Using my confidence against me, he snuck in a hit, his fetid magic funneling into my chest, banding around my throat, slicing through my wings. Panic filled my very bones as grave magic pulled the air from my lungs, the sight from my eyes.

Brilliant light bloomed around me, searing away

the darkness as a battle cry echoed through my thoughts.

"I will not lose them. Do you hear me, Orrus?" Vale screeched, cutting through the magic as if she were the sun, the moon, and the stars herself. As if she were a goddess in human form. Her skin glowed as her inky hair floated about her head. The delicate fabric of her dress was torn at her knees, her shins scraped to hell and back, her shoulder still pouring blood, but she'd never looked more magnificent.

Her sword sliced through the bonds at my throat, freeing my lungs from their deathly hold.

"I will not lose them to you. Not a single one of them, do you understand me? If you fucking want them, you'd better come here and get them yourself because I am not letting my mates go."

Staggering to my feet, I lashed out with my battered wings, knocking the mage to the ground as he tried to staunch the flow of blackened blood from a fresh wound at his chest. Vale lifted her sword again, cutting through a stream of blackened magic curling in the air between the mage and Selene.

With a single stroke, she cut it clean through, and another wound tore through the mage. Shock stole the remainder of the smirk on his face as he scrambled backward. At the same time, Selene cried out, her guttural chants cutting off as the blackened magic clouding her eyes dissolved.

Collapsing to the sand, she sucked in a breath before reaching out toward the sea. Vale didn't give her a chance to even think about using another spell.

Her blade was at Selene's throat before she could say a single word. "Call your dog off, or so help me, I'll take your fucking head right here and right now."

Selene's newly pale eyes regarded Vale as if she were a nuisance rather than the executioner she would likely be. "Gladly," she croaked. "I'll need my head to do it, though."

Vale's sword sizzled against Selene's neck, the promise of death clear as day.

Officially cowed, Selene bowed her head as she began to hum a soothing tone, the melody pacifying the squall in the sky as the beast calmed its thrashing. Kian and Rune circled in the air as the giant tentacles slipped beneath the surface, and the water stilled as if there had never been a battle at all.

All that was left was the mage, and I had plans for that bastard. Pain lanced through my middle as I tried to stand, my vision blurring as I peeled myself from the beach. Calling my flames forth, I spotted the fucker dragging himself through the rubble. I was down but I wasn't out yet. As my fire crawled up my throat, he reached the broken mural, the darkened landscape the same one he'd slithered out from, the image rippling as his magic touched it.

I didn't wait—couldn't.

My flames flew from my throat, coating the wreckage of the castle. But I was too late. Before my flames ever reached him, he slipped into the mural, disappearing from sight. Exhaustion had me collapsing to the sand, defeat weakening my limbs as our only lead to Arden vanished into the night.

The shift hit me like a battering ram, snapping my bones with a fresh wave of agony, the remnants of the mage's spell lingering in my flesh. Gasping, I fisted my hands in the grainy sand as I prayed for relief.

But there was none.

Not until Vale's cool touch graced my overheated skin.

"Xavier? Look at me. Please look at me."

She sounded so upset, so I forced my eyes open, taking in her perfect features. Her green eyes glowed with unspent power as she cupped my jaw, worry etched in every line.

"I-I'm okay," I croaked, forcing myself to stand, to rise, to suck in air. My lungs were on fire, my bones made of jelly, but I fucking did it.

Disappointment washed through me as all my

failures hit me one by one. I'd failed to kill the mage, failed to keep her safe, failed to protect Idris. The last thing she needed was to worry over me.

"You're bleeding," she murmured, her gentle touch sending an ache through my chest.

I cupped her cheeks, pressing a kiss to her forehead as I took her scent into my lungs. "So are you, my love."

A second later Idris pulled her from me, looking her over as if he were afraid she was an illusion. Kian and Rune crowded us, but Vale pulled from them to curl into my side like she was prepared to hold me up if she had to.

"He'll be back, you know," Selene called, drawing our attention to the fallen queen. She was bloody and broken, the burn from Vale's magic refusing to heal. "And gods know if he'll bring friends. You need to leave. Save yourselves before it's too late."

Vale tore from my arms and stalked across the beach, her rage erupting from her fingertips in streams of light. "Give me one reason I shouldn't gut you right here."

Idris caught up with Vale—not pulling her back but backing her up. She'd fully stepped into her role as Queen, and she'd never looked more magnificent.

The smirk on Selene's face elicited a growl from

Vale—one that even rivaled Kian's. "Because I have what you need."

Vale grabbed the siren queen by the throat, yanking her from the beach as if she weighed nothing. Once a frail thing, Vale was stronger than ever, stepping into her power.

"And what the fuck would you know about what I need?"

Eyes wide, skin sallow, Selene tried and failed to pull Vale's grip away. "T-the c-curse. The answers to breaking it. I know where they are."

Vale dropped Selene but looked like she was fighting off the urge to kick her. "I'm listening, though I wouldn't trust one word that comes from your mouth. Not after what you've done."

Gasping, Selene seemed to fold into herself. "I did what I had to, to keep my people safe. You would have done the same, my Queen. Either way, my information is as reliable as I can make it. You have to go to the birthplace of the Luxa. You have to go to Bonefell. There are scrolls—or at least there are supposed to be. The Girovians have been searching for weeks, and they think they have a lock on them."

The laugh that came out of Vale was as mirthless as it was chilling. "A wild goose chase if there ever was one. There are *scrolls* just floating out there in the ether, waiting to be snatched up. Sure. We'll leave you be without consequences for some mythical scrolls with the keys to the universe on them."

Even I thought Selene's "information" was thin at best.

"It's said that the scrolls were hidden decades ago by a rogue family, and no one has been able to find them since. Funny you say you know nothing about them, though, since the people who supposedly hid them share your surname—or do you not know a Rowena or Eldric Tenebris?"

If Selene had slapped her, Vale would have looked less surprised.

"What is it, my love?" I asked, but Vale shook her head.

"You're making it up," she whispered, tears filling her eyes as she backed away from the siren queen. "You're lying to me."

Selene tilted her head to the side as if she were studying her prey. "Am I? Or do you not recognize the truth just because it's hard to swallow. Your parents took the scrolls, hid them away, and now you're here. Two plus two still equals four, Vale. It's not my fault you don't want to do the math."

Vale's mind was buzzing with turmoil, but one thought kept bubbling to the surface.

The book. I have to find the book.

Selene seemed to know that she'd hit true, rising to her feet as she bowed her head in deference. "Now we're even. I might not like you, but letting the guild win was never my intention. Had Malvor not imprisoned my people, I would have warned you."

Idris' gaze cut to Selene. "Even? You think we're even? After what you've done?"

Vale put a calming hand to Idris' chest. "She makes a good point," she said before extending a hand to Selene. "I give you my thanks for the information. We can expect your support and an emissary once your problem is handled, then?"

Selene regarded her warily before taking Vale's outstretched fingers. "Of course. Everhold will always back the true leader of Credour. Idris is the source of all magic, and Arden is a spoiled child with a broken toy. No one in their right mind would follow him."

My mate nodded, let Selene's fingers go, and then with all the strength she had, she plowed her fist into the siren queen's jaw. The snap of bone echoed through the night air, and Selene dropped like a stone. Vale snatched her hair, hauling Selene's head back as she made the siren look her in the eye.

"We'll never be even, and you fucking know why.

I know what you did to my mates. I might not know all the gory details, but I know enough."

Selene's face lost what little color it had as her pale eyes went wide. "I-I—"

But Vale wasn't done. "If I ever hear a whisper about shit like that going down in your domain again, I'll gut you like the rancid fish you are in front of all your people and let the birds have you. And don't you *ever* forget it."

Vale let her go, spitting at Selene's feet, disgust evident in every line of her body.

I couldn't say I blamed her, though the world was getting mighty fuzzy.

"I expect your emissary in two days," Idris rumbled, his tone brooking no argument. "If they are late to the wedding, I will take it as an insult. Do make sure they show up on time."

Appropriately cowed, Selene dipped her head, kneeling at Idris feet. "Yes, my King."

Kian tossed my arm over his shoulder when I started to sway, but the movement pulled at a stitch in my side. I touched the overheated flesh, and my hand came away coated in thick, red blood.

The last thing I heard was Vale's scream as the world fell away, and darkness swallowed me whole.

CHAPTER 16
VALE

Xavier's blood had long since dried on my hands, but I couldn't let him go.

Idris and I had poured so much magic into him when he fell, and still, he was barely clinging to life. Unlike Selene, death magic clung to him, poisoning him, and I couldn't fix it.

Neither of us could.

Shivering, I held onto Xavier as the wind whipped my face, the jacket Idris had thrown over my shoulders a paltry barrier to the frigid air. The first rays of dawn crested the horizon, but there was no light to be had in my soul.

"We're almost there, my Queen," Rune murmured. *"He will make it. Your mates are strong. He will survive this."* His reassurance seemed forced, but he was

flying faster than I'd ever seen him fly before, so maybe there was something to it.

Then again, it seemed as if Orrus himself was breathing down our necks, threatening to take him from me. The monastery came into view after we crested the final mountain—the Order of the Ashen Veil was a group of ancient maesters known for healing the worst cases on the continent. Or at least that was the platitude Idris had given me after we climbed on Rune and bolted through the night to Bonefell.

At this point, nothing seemed real.

Not Xavier's limp body in my arms as we drew closer to the monastery, not the beautiful dawn shining its light on all of us, not anything, and especially not Idris' words of comfort swearing that Xavier would survive.

Far too slowly, Rune began his descent, his turns careful so we didn't lose our precious cargo. It had been hours, and not once did Xavier's eyelids flutter, not a single moan of pain, nothing. The only thing that kept me clinging to hope were the thready breaths wheezing through his lungs, but even those were becoming fewer and farther between.

Xavier was dying, and there wasn't a damn thing I could do about it.

Don't you do it. You can't have him—do you hear me? You can't.

By the time the red dragon landed, Xavier's breaths went from calm and still, to gasping, his body jerking as if he were barely pulling in air.

"*No, no, no*," I cried, clutching him closer. "Stay with me. Please stay with me. I love you, please."

The sound that came out of me was that of a dying animal, my wail louder than the wind, louder than my prayers, louder than my world crumbling beneath my feet.

Please, Orrus. Please don't take him. I'll do anything. Please.

The only thing louder than my wail was Rune and Kian roaring for entry, the monstrously tall gates to the sanctuary something even the dragons couldn't bypass. As soon as Idris got the leather belt tying us to Rune's saddle free, he ripped Xavier from my hold, hauled him over his shoulder, and sprinted to the opening gate.

Clumsily, I clambered off Rune, my legs barely working as I tried to follow. The sand beneath my bare feet scarcely held me up as I tried to hurry, and yet, each step seemed to swallow me up, swallow me whole, steal every ounce of energy I'd clung to and gave me nothing in return.

Just when I thought I couldn't take another step, Kian was at my side, lifting me off my feet and into his arms as he carried me through the gates. I wished I could say I saw the beautiful architecture or the stunning statues that seemed to line the grand hallways, but I couldn't. I didn't see anything but the group of robed maesters surrounding a very still Xavier.

His giant body lay across a fragile cot, his limbs hanging off the edges, and many hands went to work, cutting away his clothes, assessing his wounds. I wanted to hope, but it was too hard. Kian set me on my feet, but my legs barely held me up. I'd willed so much energy into him—so much power—and it hadn't been good enough.

Idris backed away from the huddle of healers, fresh blood coating his tunic as he put a trembling hand to his mouth, Xavier's scarlet lifeblood staining his tanned skin red. He returned to us, tucking me into the warmth of his chest.

"You're freezing," he murmured, rubbing my arms, but I didn't feel anything. I didn't care if I froze to death if it meant Xavier would be okay.

A small woman approached, her hair covered in a white kerchief. In her hands was a bundle of blue cloth—a cloak. Silently, she offered it to me, her gaze not meeting mine but catching on the dried stains on my dress. One would think someone who worked with healers would be more used to the sight of blood, but this poor girl wasn't.

"A-are you hurt, Miss?" she asked, her voice so soft I barely heard it over the clamoring of the healers.

Was I? My gaze fell to my middle where the worst of the blood was. But none of it was mine. It was all his. Dress torn and soaked through, I guessed I looked like a nightmare, but I couldn't make myself care. I'd failed to shield him. I'd forced him to let me stay in the fight and look where that had gotten him.

Once again, he'd put himself in danger because of me.

Once again, he'd taken hits meant for me.

And once again, he was bleeding because of me.

I didn't need a cloak. I didn't need a gods-be-damned thing except for Xavier to open his icy-blue eyes and tell me he was going to be okay.

Kian took the fabric from her, but his gaze didn't waiver from Xavier, either.

One of the maesters broke away from the rest, his face a grim mask as he approached us. He dipped his head in Idris' direction before settling his gaze on me.

"He carries the scent of a mate. I take it that is

you, yes?" His impassively cool blue eyes seemed to stare right through me as if he could see all the way down to my soul.

"Yes," I whispered, unable to force even the slightest bit of air into my lungs.

"You are Luxa, correct? Not a dragon. Your kind is so rare I forget what you smell like. The bond you share, while complete, it is not as strong as it would be if you were a shifter. I take it you tried to save him?"

I nodded, but Idris answered.

"We both did. His body took some of our power, but—" Idris' voice cracked, cutting off his words.

But Xavier's body wouldn't absorb it. It'd taken almost everything I had just to slow the bleeding, and it hadn't been enough.

"As you know, wounds created by grave magic are difficult to heal. We will do all we can, but your mate's condition is grim."

Fury ignited in my bones, filling my whole body with the flames of pure rage. A familiar sword of light formed in my hand, and I lifted it to his throat.

That answer wasn't good enough.

His impassivity wasn't good enough.

His lack of faith wasn't good enough.

We didn't fly hours to this hole-in-the-wall

monastery to get told no. We didn't risk his life—risk everything—to come here for them to throw up their hands in defeat. My eye twitched as the world continued to churn around us, but this little bubble was nice and still.

"Do you value your life?" I whispered, hot tears filling my eyes as I tried to make him understand just how far I'd go to keep Xavier breathing.

Alarm threaded through his expression before he locked it down. "Yes, I do. I—"

"Good. That's very good. I want you to value *his* life just as much as you value yours," I ground out through gritted teeth as tears spilled down my cheeks. "Because if he leaves this earth without me, you will follow him. I don't care what you have to do, you save him, understand?"

Idris curled his fingers around my wrist, gently guiding the blade away from the maester's throat.

"I understand," the maester murmured, "but I want you to be prepared. Our magic—it's dying. *We're* dying. We will do all we can, but if I gave you false hope, that would be so much worse than if I just told you the truth."

My light flickered and died as my heart wrenched in my chest.

"May I suggest you rest in the royal quarters. We will—"

Violently, I shook my head. "I'm not leaving him. I swore I wouldn't leave him."

Kian curled his arm around my middle, and I nearly lost my hold on the last shred of my sanity.

"Easy, little witch." His voice cracked in the middle, his pain compounding on my own, drowning me under its weight. "Let's get you cleaned up."

I tried to dig my feet in, but he swept me up in his arms once again, carrying me when I refused to move. I could have fought him, but I knew Kian would never let me go.

"I'll stay here," Idris murmured, his worried gaze meeting mine. "I won't leave him."

And as reassuring as that statement was supposed to be, I feared Xavier would leave this world and I wouldn't be there. He wouldn't know how much I loved him. He would never know how much I wished it were me instead of him.

Gritting my teeth, I held in a sob as I clung to Kian's shoulders. I tasted blood by the time we arrived in a grand suite that I hated on sight. I wanted to be strong. I wanted to be a rock. I wanted to stand on my own. But one of my mates was dying in a healer's bed, and I was too far away from him to do anything about it.

As soon as the doors closed, I broke, the sobs stealing my breath as they shattered me into a million pieces. I barely noticed when Kian slid to the bathing chamber floor. All I knew was his warm embrace as the ache in my heart took me over. We clung to each other, holding tight to ride out the storm of emotions that threatened to drown us.

Because it wasn't just my heart that was breaking. It was Kian's, it was Idris', it was Rune's. Their emotions echoed in my chest, drowning me in their fear, their regret, their sadness. I could barely breathe under the weight of it. But worst of all? It was my own thoughts, my own fear, my own agony that tied the anchor to my ankle and dragged me down.

"I-is Xavier going to die because I'm not a shifter?" I asked the question before I thought better of it. "Is it my fault that he's here?"

My brain replayed the maester's words. I wasn't a shifter or even a powerful enough Luxa to save him. I couldn't give him what he needed. I wasn't good enough.

Kian gripped my chin, pulling my face to meet his. In his eyes was sadness, yes, but more it was pure fury. "Don't you ever say that again. Xavier is here because he would rather take the hit a thousand times over than watch you take one for him. Because he would rather save you—save any of us—than stand by when he could have done something. If the roles were reversed, would you want him blaming himself?"

No, but that wasn't really the issue, now, was it?

"He got hurt because I refused to leave the fight. He's here right now because I wouldn't leave the battle, because I wouldn't let you and Idris go it alone. He's still hurt because I'm not powerful enough to save him, because I don't have enough magic, because I don't know how to use it, because I've spent my entire life denying what I was." I sucked in a shuddering breath. "Xavier is hurt because I was too scared to read a stupid fucking book that would tell me everything I needed to know."

Kian's amber irises glowed with fury, and it made sense. I'd been the one to fuck up. If there were anyone he should be mad at, it should be me.

"You know that's not right. This war was set into motion long before you took your first breath. None of this is your fault. None of it. I don't want to hear you take the blame for so much as a fucking papercut in this war, do you hear me? You might be the cure, but you have never been the cause."

It didn't matter how much I wanted those words to be true, they just weren't. And it didn't matter how much I wanted to change it, I couldn't.

The only thing I could do was pick myself up off this floor, get cleaned up, and be at Xavier's side for whatever happened. It wasn't much, but—

"Stop it," Kian growled, his grip tight on my waist as he clutched me to his chest. "Stop walling yourself off, stop denying the truth, just fucking stop it." His lip trembled before he hardened his jaw. "I need you to be in this with me—with us. I can't—"

He sucked in a breath that made me want to start sobbing all over again. "I can't do this without you. I need you with me—your emotions, your thoughts, your presence. I have to feel you. Please, I—"

My mouth was on his before he could say another word. I couldn't comfort him any other way, but I could kiss him. I could channel all my love, all my hope into him in the only way I had left. Kian's tongue dueled with mine as he clutched me to his chest tighter, stealing all my breath as he yanked the jacket from my arms.

His talons sliced through the tattered remnants of my dress, shredding the fabric as he had done the day before. Only, this time, it wasn't my blood he was trying to get rid of but Xavier's. I ripped at his leathers, freeing him from his pants and positioned his hard cock against my opening.

Kian's teeth raked the skin of my neck, his touch rougher than it had ever been, but I needed it. His fingers fisted in my hair, pulling my head back as he entered me in a single hard thrust. My breath left me as pleasure stole all sense of reason, all my guilt, every thought, every worry. I knew they'd come back, but for this one shining moment, there was no pain, only love.

Any other time, I'd need to get used to his size, but right then, I welcomed the bite of pain mixed with the ache of need coiling in my belly.

"Gods, you feel so fucking good," he growled into my skin, the rake of his fangs punctuated by another hard thrust.

I cried out with each one, the pleasure so intense, I wasn't in control of my body anymore. Somehow Kian twisted, pressing my back to the cold floor as he continued to pound into me. My teeth found the skin of his shoulder, my nails found the skin of his back, and with both, I tore at him as I wrapped my legs around him and hung on.

He groaned into my skin, his teeth cutting into my flesh, and yet, I couldn't get enough.

It was rough. It was wild. We were two injured

animals fighting for dominance, and yet, when my release slammed into me, it took me by surprise.

"That's it, little witch. Come for me. Give me everything."

Power surged through my limbs as golden light exploded in the room. Glass shattered, stone hissed and cracked, but I couldn't stop—not until it ran its course. Pleasure stole my breath, and when his orgasm raced down his spine, curled his toes, and pulled him under with me, it was as if I could feel it in my own body.

Every slide of his skin, every flex of his muscles, every ragged breath in his lungs, it was as if our bodies had merged. There was no him, there was no me.

There was only us.

But the bliss didn't last as long as I'd wanted it to. The second his mind switched back to the darkness weighing us down, I felt it. Kian slipped from my sex before plucking me from the cold floor.

I avoided looking around, but my destruction was plain as day. The mirror and windows were shattered, the stone floor cracked, the cast iron tub itself was twisted into something unrecognizable.

Kian said nothing as he turned on the water, and together, we showered while I tried very hard not to think about why the water washing down the drain was pink or why my abilities destroyed every breakable thing in this room.

It was only once he'd started drying himself off, did I realize just how drained Kian was. After back-to-back shifts, hours of flying, and a battle, he was just as tired, just as hurt as I was.

He needed food, he needed rest.

But we wouldn't get that.

After he rounded me up a dress from somewhere and he a set of leathers, we returned to Xavier. Idris paced the small alcove, Kian passed me to him, and Idris held me tight, burying his face in my wet hair as we settled in to wait.

What seemed like an eternity later, the same maester I'd threatened summoned us to his bedside. They'd done all they could, and now it was just another waiting game.

They brought us chairs, and Idris took me with him, settling me on his lap and refusing to let me go. I couldn't say I blamed him, though, if I didn't think it would hurt him more, I would have tucked myself in Xavier's bed.

Exhaustion pulled at every limb, every pore. I didn't even recall falling asleep.

But when I opened my eyes, I knew I was in a world of hurt.

Because I was now in that dark, desolate place again.

There was no light.

No warmth.

No air.

And this time, I didn't know if there would be a way out.

CHAPTER 17

VALE

I shouldn't be here.

Darkness seemed to swallow me whole as I felt for the rocks that I knew would gouge my palms. The damp stones cut into my flesh just like I thought they would, the sting of my skin breaking telling me everything about this prison.

But even though I knew exactly where I was, I still didn't know anything at all.

"Nyrah," I called, the ache in my chest threatening to break me.

A part of me really wanted Nyrah to be at the end of this tunnel, to have one good thing to happen today, but I knew better. If I called her name, there was no way on this earth or any other that my baby sister would ignore me.

This place wasn't right—never had been. I'd just been too blind to see it. As much as I wanted to find my sister, I did not feel her—not even a little.

No light.

No warmth.

No air.

Idris was too tired to come save me. I had to make myself leave. I had to do this myself.

Closing my eyes, I pictured the burned-out church Idris pulled me to the last time I'd been stuck in this gods-forsaken place. I visualized the skeleton of the building reaching for the sky like a giant's hand, the pews knocked over and scattered, the sanctuary in disarray.

I yanked myself from that darkness, pulling myself away from the vile things that called me forth, and the world around me faded. Shimmering in the waning sunlight, the church melted into existence exactly like I'd pictured it.

It was just as broken and burned out as I remembered, but this time, it was somehow different. When I'd been here with Idris, it hadn't seemed as sinister. Maybe it was just because I'd been so mad at him then. Maybe it was just his powerful presence that reassured me. But now I felt like the not-so-brave girl I'd always been under the mountain.

Somehow, I'd returned to the coward, the weakling, where nothing seemed within my grasp.

The funny thing was, I shouldn't be here, either. I was dream walking alone—something I not only should not do but, had not so long ago, nearly killed me. I had no idea what being here meant or why my dreams pulled me into the darkest places, but my mates had enough to deal with without me fucking up again.

A high-pitched female giggle echoed all around me. It was as if the owner was right next to me and everywhere at the same time. Whipping my head this way and that, I searched for the source of the sound, but there was no one. It wasn't until I got a glimpse of blonde hair out of the corner of my eye that I realized just how fucked I was.

I should be alone. In this dream, in this place, I should be all by myself unless Idris came to find me. Whoever was with me shouldn't be here.

I fought off the urge to go looking, ignored the insistent pit in my gut that told me it was Nyrah. The one that screamed my baby sister was simply playing hide-and-seek with me.

What had Idris said? Not everything you see in your dreams is what it appears to be.

I knew enough of liars and cheats to know that if

someone was offering me my greatest wish it would always, always be a trap. This was a trick.

"If you're not my sister, please leave me alone," I begged, unable to crush the last bit of hope flickering in my chest. "I don't want your tricks, and I am not going to fall for your lies. Please, I'm begging you, just leave me be."

And still, my feet disobeyed me, sluggishly striding forward as if to follow the tantalizing sound of my greatest wish. In my wildest dreams, Nyrah was safe and warm in a bed.

Not in rags, not starving, not prey.

In my fantasies, she wasn't touched by the guild, or a bargaining chip to hoard away. She was free, she was cared for, she was safe.

Intellectually, I knew whatever I found here wouldn't be the truth. It wasn't as if I had brought myself to this damned place. Whatever resided here was meant to hurt me, to stall me, to drain my power—what little of it there was. But even though my rational mind knew without a sliver of a doubt that I had to get out of here step by step, bit by bit, I still followed that voice.

A hard, warm hand closed around my bicep, and instantly I breathed a sigh of relief.

Idris.

Whirling on a foot, I met those glowing golden eyes, the rage in them familiar, but behind all the anger was pain—pain I knew well. My relief got the better of me, and I jumped into his arms, clutching him close to my chest as the knot in my lungs loosened.

Not everything you see in your dreams is what it appears to be.

He himself had said that, right?

How could I know it was really him?

How could I be sure?

Slowly I let him go, backing away as a new fear took root. "How do I know it's you? How do I know anyone is who they say they are?"

His expression softened, the rage in his eyes melting ever so slightly as understanding replaced his anger. "At least you took one thing from our lessons. You don't, my brave one. You can never really be sure, but what does your heart tell you?"

My lip trembled, and for the first time, I let myself be vulnerable just this once. "That it's you. That you're here with me. That you didn't leave me by myself to wander this place alone."

He tilted his head to the side. "Then why don't you believe it?"

How could I explain it in a way that didn't make me sound completely crazy?

"Because I heard her giggle. Nyrah—it sounded just like her." I held up a hand, stopping him before he told me something I already knew. "I know it isn't her. She wouldn't abandon me to wander. She would come find me just like I would come find her. But what if it's all just wishful thinking? What if in my desire to not be left behind, I conjured you instead?"

"You're far more advanced at dream walking than I ever thought you would be as a novice, but I doubt you can create something from nothing—even in this place. This church? It exists in my memory. I assume it still stands not too far from where we fell asleep. This place is real."

"So, you're saying the woman I could see giggling out of the corner of my eye is real, too? You're real?"

That wasn't good.

"Everything might not be what it seems in a place like this, but yes. Just like how you can get hurt in these dreams, and items can be brought into reality, what exists here, in some way shape or form, exists out there, too."

Dread yawned wide in my belly, stealing any relief I'd had.

"It's not her, is it?" I whispered, the echo of a giggle sending a chill down my spine.

Gently, he shook his head. "No. There might be someone out there, but it's likely not your sister."

That still didn't tell me if he was really him, though. "Tell me something only my Idris would know. Tell me something that only we share."

A hint of a grin lifted the edges of his lips, and with that faint smile, his entire face changed. In that single instant, he wasn't drowning in grief like I was or worried for my safety. He was simply a man with a salacious secret.

"Sometimes when you don't guard your thoughts from me, you think about what our bonding night will look like," he admitted, curling his arms around me and pulling me in. "Sometimes we are alone, and you contemplate what I'll do to make sure you come screaming. Others, all four of us are together, worshipping your body, making you come over and over and over again."

Shock curled in my belly. There were only a few times I'd let myself consider what our wedding night might look like. When we spoke about the ceremony, everything seemed so formal, so bound by rules and regulations and royal protocol. There had been so few times where Idris and I had been alone together without anger or fear separating us.

"You've been snooping again."

"And like I have told you time and again, it's not snooping if you're yelling at me. But I'll tell you a little secret. It's only going to be you and me on our bonding night. Every night after, I'm open to making all your fantasies come true, but that one night? You're mine, Vale. All of you."

His voice was like sugar on my tongue and honey down my spine. It reminded me of my first dream walk with him. We'd been in his bedroom, and somehow, I'd ended up wrapped around him with his fangs at my throat. I'd woken from that dream wrapped around Kian and Xavier, my need so acute, I'd started kissing them in my sleep.

That one dream set everything into motion, and it seemed like it was starting all over again. It was as if he were seducing me, stealing my thoughts, my worries, my...

I didn't realize until it was almost too late but his grip on me was iron, and he was pulling me away from that church, moving me through the space, stealing me away. Roughly, I pulled my arm from his grip.

"What do you think you're doing?" I hissed, trying to get my bearings.

"I'm trying to get you out of here while I still can.

You haven't strayed far from your body yet, but we still need to get back."

And then it was as if light dawned in my brain. "We're closer to Direveil than we were in the castle, right? We're closer than we've ever been. Meaning, we don't have to go back—not yet."

Idris dug in his heels, his strength making it so much more effective than when I did it. "What are you talking about?"

How could he not remember?

"The book. My family's book. It has all the information on the Luxa."

Guilt threatened to drown me as I considered all the knowledge I could have had already if I hadn't been too scared of the truth. Had I just finished reading it, maybe Xavier wouldn't be dying, maybe I wouldn't have lost Nyrah, maybe...

"If Selene was telling the truth, then my parents stole the scrolls of the Luxa and hid them. What if it's in that book? What if all of this could be solved—your curse broken—if we found it? I can pull objects from the Dreaming, right? I did it without even trying before. What's to stop me from walking right into Direveil and taking it?"

"That's a big if, Vale." Idris rubbed at the growing stubble on his jaw. "We have no idea whether Selene

was just trying to save her ass or not. We have no idea if the information she had was on the level or twisted to out traitors. If they're looking for that book, it won't be where you left it."

Something in my gut told me otherwise. "But you said that the church we were just at exists somewhere, correct? Even if it's just in your memory. I know that book. I know exactly where I put it—exactly where I hid it. If the answers we need are there, shouldn't we try? If we can break the curse, if we can save Xavier, if we can bring magic back to everyone, don't we have to try?"

I would beg if I had to. I would do anything if it meant he would survive.

"What about the bonding? Many have said that it—"

"If you believed that the bonding would break your curse, we would have been bonded days ago. You don't think it'll break your curse any more than I do. The only reason you're still going through with it, is because you believe it will bring me a modicum of protection. Fenwick burned the scrolls, so we have no idea if what he knew was even in the realm of truth. This is something to go on. This is something we can try."

Idris' jaw turned to stone, his eyes flashing from gold to red and back again. "It's too risky."

But I couldn't accept that—I wouldn't.

"What is risk if it means Xavier will die without it? Who gives a shit about risk if we lose him?"

Idris fisted his hands in his hair, the stress threatening to break him.

"And what good is any of it if we end up losing you? I know you care for us, but we love you—all three of us. Even Rune loves you. If you sacrifice yourself for us, how will any of it be worth it? How will any ounce of magic, any grip we have on power, how will it mean anything if you're gone?"

As much as his words touched me, I couldn't back down—not about this. "You can't stop me. I'm going to the mountain. I will find that book. You can come with me, or you can let me go, but you can't fucking stop me."

For the first time, tears welled in his eyes as despair etched itself into the lines of his face. "Don't do this."

"I have to. What if it has more than just how to break your curse? What if it has information on how to heal grave magic? How to stop it? How to do anything but just sit there at his bedside and watch him die? I have to do something. Please."

Gritting his teeth, a lone tear fell down his cheek. "I won't lose you both. Do you understand me? I won't."

"Then help me. Because I'm getting that fucking book if it's the last thing I do."

With a solemn nod, Idris relaxed his hold and folded me into his arms. "As you wish, my brave one," he croaked, before taking a shuddering breath. "It seems I can never say no to you."

CHAPTER 18

IDRIS

Quite possibly, this was the worst idea in the history of bad ideas. But I'd seen that look on Vale's face right before she jumped off a dragon and went headlong into battle. There was no changing her mind and a part of me fucking loved that about her.

I wondered when the exact moment was I'd fallen for Vale. Was it her steadfast defiance as she protected my closest friends in the caverns? Was it her unwavering dedication to her sister? Was it her sacrifice? Or was it just the kind heart that she tried so hard to hide?

Was it her vulnerability—that soft underbelly she kept protected at all costs? Compounded with her laugh, with her smile, with her determination, I'd been a goner from that very first day.

But seeing her now in the face of potentially losing Xavier, I knew she would sacrifice anything to keep him breathing. I just had to make sure she didn't sacrifice everything.

"If we're doing this, really doing this, you're getting a crash course in dream walking."

"I already know the first two rules," she said, narrowing her eyes. "What more is there?"

I fought off the urge to strangle her. "I don't have time to go into all the details, but just to reiterate rule one: If you get hurt in here, you get hurt out there." I pulled her hand up to show her the shallow cuts on her palm. "Like this."

The muscle in her jaw ticked. "I know. I got it."

"Rule two: Nothing, and I do mean nothing, is as it seems here. You and I are stable walking together, what comes when we get into an entire mountain filled with Lumentium? Who knows? Everything could go sideways on us."

"Except, I have lived my entire life with Lumentium around me. I should be fine."

While she had a very good point, and while she would likely be fine, I knew I wouldn't be. But there was no way I was leaving her alone for this.

"Rule three: Time works differently here. What can

seem like hours is mere seconds in some ways, in others, seconds can be hours in the waking world. It all depends on you and where you are. There is no consistent time structure here, so the best course of action is to get in and get out while you still remember you're dreaming."

That brought her up short. Twisting her fingers together, she firmed her jaw and gave me a hesitant nod. "Okay, I think I've got it. Anything else I need to know?"

There were a hundred other rules, but we didn't have the time. Already I felt the drain and we hadn't even gotten anywhere yet.

"Rule four: You are in control. This is your domain. This is your dream. You have the power here. But use it wisely. The farther you are from your body in the Dreaming, the more power it takes from you. The last time you were too far from your body, you stopped breathing. This means we don't have very much time. You used a lot of power to keep Xavier alive, you don't have much to spare."

Worry etched itself into the lines of her face before she locked it down. "Neither do you."

"Exactly, which is why we are going to get in and get out and pray to every god and goddess we know of that we don't get caught."

"Caught? Who the fuck is going to catch us in a dream?"

My laugh was mirthless as I realized just how little she knew of this world, even though she was made from it.

"The guild claims they don't use magic—that magic-users are a blight on this world, and yet, that entire mountain is powered by the dead. And grave magic isn't always as predictable. I have no idea what protections they have in place. Why do you think they don't care when you die? You're just another power source for them."

Vale shoved at my chest, the fire in her eyes one millimeter away from violence. "Are you kidding me? You wait until now to tell me that?"

We didn't have time for her rage—not with our lives on the line. "What good would telling you do? You were already upset that your parents had been taken from you. Me telling you that they likely power every bit of magic in that mountain probably wouldn't go over very well."

Gritting her teeth, Vale shot me a glare. "So how do we do this? How do I get us from here to there?"

"How did you get from the darkness to the church?" I asked, knowing she already had the answer.

"How did you know I was in the darkness?" she asked, crossing her arms over her chest.

"It's where you last saw your sister." I chose not to tell her that the likelihood of that small blonde being her baby sister was slim to none, but the point had been made. "You naturally would go back to the one place that brought you some small measure of comfort. Finding Nyrah has always been your goal—what has driven you this whole time. If you were going to be anywhere, you were going to be there."

"I don't like that you know that much about me, if I'm being honest. I wish I knew more about you—how you grew up, the life you've had, the things you've seen. It has to be better than how I grew up."

I wouldn't disagree with her on that point, but with the good, always came the bad. "I have seen many things on this continent. The one place I've never been, is where we're going, so we are relying on your memories of it. So, you think you can do that?"

She swallowed nervously before giving me a shaky nod. "I think so."

"That's my brave one," I murmured, pulling her into my arms as I pressed a kiss to her temple. "To get from here to there is the same way you left the darkness. Close your eyes and envision exactly where you want to be. What does the inside of the mountain look like? Are there tunnels? Torches?"

Her face paled slightly as she closed her eyes, hanging on to me as if her life depended on it. "It's dark under the mountain, always dark except during midday when the sun shines directly overhead of the crevasse. Only then do we really get any light. There are stone staircases everywhere, but hardly any of them have any railing, and most of them are open to the chasm below."

As she spoke, the church and the dark forest melted away, and we slid through space and time, her magic pressing in on my skin as she took us to the one place I'd never been. Direveil hadn't existed two hundred years ago. The mountain range, yes, but the guild's dark mountain appeared overnight, rising from the earth, akin to the finger of a god reaching for the sky.

Moments later, we were plunged into darkness, the faint flickering of torches barely lighting the narrow passageway beneath our feet. I couldn't help but stare at the skeletal innards of the guild's home.

Of my brother's home.

I didn't know what I thought I would see when I got here, but this wasn't it.

Crumbling pathways led to treacherous stairs, the cracked stone one errant move away from disinte-

grating altogether. In the vast darkness that I suspected Vale couldn't see through, was a wide chasm that seemed to never end, drilling all the way to the center of the earth.

She trembled in my arms as her hand blindly reached for the rough wall.

This explained why she was afraid of heights. Why she clung so tightly to railings and hated every single staircase she saw. This place was terrifying on its own, even without the threat of execution just for being a Luxa.

Death seemed to be on every path, around every corner, breathing down her neck.

And mine. I'd told her how Lumentium affected me, but I'd downplayed it. Even in the Dreaming, the poisonous mineral seemed to cut into me on all sides. My breaths felt like I'd swallowed razors.

Choking down the pain, I clutched her to me, holding her tight.

"I won't let you fall, Vale. I promise. You are in control."

She peeled her gaze from the edge of the chasm, her wide fearful eyes glowing with her power. Even here, surrounded by poison, she was the definition of strength. Only someone boldly facing their fears could walk into the lion's den like this.

"I'm in control. This is my domain. This is my dream. I have the power here," she whispered to herself as she straightened her spine. "This way."

Taking my hand, she led me up a wider staircase carved into the side of a disintegrating stalactite, two hundred years of water eroding the limestone into almost nothing. Luckily, the trip was short, and it guided us to a wide stone corridor lit by fading torches. Off the sides of the passage were darkened caves, the echoes of snores emerged from their depths as if the occupants had long since stumbled into slumber.

At the very end of the corridor, we turned left, following the maze of paths to a tucked-away hole in the wall. It was deserted, luckily, but the detritus of what remained littered the floor. In the corner lay a pile of rags disguised as a sleeping palette, and I realized just how little she'd had before coming to the castle.

Before she became mine.

Before she agreed to be my Queen.

"It's not much, but this was home."

There were no chairs, no tables, barely a cushion underneath disintegrating blankets, and even those were thin as paper.

"All four of you lived here?" I asked, astounded anyone could live like this, let alone a family. I ducked

to fit under the ceiling, the space little more than a hovel.

She shook her head as she moved to the farthest corner, her fingers trailing the rock as if she were searching for something. "No. When my parents were alive, we had a bigger sleeping chamber, but when they passed, we were moved."

If I knew my brother—and I knew his depravity well enough—he put them in this hole as punishment for their parents' perceived crimes.

"I used to sleep in a hammock up off the ground, and it was almost nice. It wasn't anything like the castle, but we made do with what we had. We used to have a kitchen back when the guild would grow crops. My mother did what she could, and it wasn't so bad before they died."

She dipped her hand into a nearly invisible hole in the wall and drew from it a thick parcel wrapped in fabric. With shaking hands, she unwrapped it and breathed a sigh of relief. The leather binding looked ancient—at least five hundred years old—and when she gently opened it, she lovingly ran her finger down a list of names.

"This is it," she whispered, closing the book before re-wrapping it in the fabric.

Blinking away tears, she wiped her nose, the back of her hand coming away red.

We were officially out of time.

"Well, look what we have here. My long, lost Luxa and the brother I didn't get a chance to kill all wrapped up in a little bow. I didn't know it was my birthday."

A chill raced down my spine. I hadn't seen Arden in two centuries, and yet, I would know his voice anywhere. Spinning on my heel, I faced my brother down, trying to put myself in front of Vale.

"I'm going to enjoy burning you alive, little Luxa. And this time you can't wriggle free."

Arden was a vastly different man from the one he'd been centuries ago. Dark sigils marked his cheeks, his flesh tattooed with binding magic. His eyes glowed with the gold of his dragon, the animal slithering beneath his skin, caged with all the Lumentium so close. But worse, the youth and light he'd had as a boy was long gone.

All that was left was madness.

I had no idea how he knew we were here, but this exact scenario was what I'd been afraid of. Direveil was powered by the dead, and we were treading a thin line in the Dreaming.

Somehow, he'd known we'd come here. Maybe that

had been his plan all along. Why he'd taunted her with her sovereign name at the ball, all the attacks.

He'd wanted her here.

"That's a lot of words for 'I suck at my job,'" Vale taunted, her body unfortunately out of my reach. "How many times have you tried and failed to kill me? Aren't we at four now? Or is it five?"

Arden's jaw clenched as his pupils elongated to the slits of his dragon. "You're like a cockroach, you filthy little witch. And I'll crush you like one. Him, I need alive. You, not so much."

Her laugh echoed around us, as light bloomed under her skin. "You couldn't kill me when you had the knife in your hand, you weak, spineless sack of shit. And as smart as you think you are, you're forgetting a very important fact."

Arden didn't wait for her to continue, he lunged into the room, only to get thrown backward by a wall of magic.

Golden light poured from every inch of her skin. "I'm the Luxa. This is my domain. I have the power here, not you."

Rage washed over Arden as orange scales radiated from his skin. His body grew, crumbling the stone around him. As his claws erupted from his fingertips, his bones snapped and cracked. Mid-shift and growing by the second, he blocked our only exit.

We had no way out of here.

Eyes wide, Vale lunged for me. Her body collided with mine, knocking us off our feet.

The world slammed back into focus as our consciousness knocked us both into our bodies at the same time. Sucking in a huge breath, I held her tight to me as I tried to get my bearings. We were still in that chair at Xavier's bedside, only night had fallen, and a quiet darkness surrounded us as low mage lights lit the still space.

Heart thundering in my chest, I cupped her cheeks, pressing a kiss to her trembling lips.

"You saved me, my brave one. You saved us both."

Someone yanked Vale from my arms, stealing her away, and I nearly lost my mind before I realized it was Kian.

"Gods, woman, what did you do?" he growled, his anger failing to disguise his fear. I couldn't blame him. Losing her would end us all—curse or no. "Don't we have enough to worry about without you trying to hurt yourself?" He clutched her to his chest, squeezing her tight. "Please. I can't—"

"I'm fine," she said, her voice muffled by Kian's

jacket. She wriggled from his hold, her eyes shining bright with a familiar bundle still in her arms, the tattered cloth protecting precious cargo.

A smile bloomed over her face, the first time I'd seen it since Xavier had gotten hurt.

"I got it."

CHAPTER 19
VALE

Kian's amber gaze fell to the bundle in my hands, his irises igniting as if he'd like to set the book on fire. "Please don't tell me you spent twelve hours dream walking for that."

My gut bottomed out as the world tilted. "Twelve hours? We were in there for an hour at most. What do you mean twelve hours?"

I couldn't believe it. Then again, I knew I'd overused my power. Tossing Arden away, keeping him from killing us, it had taken nearly everything I had.

Blackened scales rippled across Kian's flesh, his animal too close to the surface for him to contain it. "I have been sitting here on my own, praying none of you died on me for half a fucking day, counting the minutes until you came back to me. Watching your nose bleed, watching your breathing slow, listening to your heartbeat, and praying it didn't fucking stop."

My heart wrenched in my chest. I had no idea that we had left him alone in this. Dropping the book on the side table, I reached for him, doing my best to reassure him that I was still alive.

"I'm so sorry. I thought it was minutes at most. I would never do that to you on purpose—never leave you to pick up the pieces." I swallowed down my tears, trying to get myself together. "I got my family's histories. Maybe they have something about the curse. Maybe it has information so we can still save him."

Kian let me go, and instantly my heart felt like it was turning to ice. Shuffling backward, his jaw hardened to granite as he got himself under control. "It's fine. I understand what you did and why you did it, just— Could you stop hurting yourself, please? I can't take losing you, too."

I wanted to reach for him again, but it didn't seem like he wanted my touch at all.

"It's not her fault," Idris rumbled, coming to my side. "The Dreaming is dangerous, but we took a calculated risk. You should have seen her. There hasn't been a Luxa in hundreds of years who can do what she did."

While the praise made my heart soar, I also felt like the biggest asshole in the world for leaving Kian alone. I just hoped it was worth it.

Shakily, I stood next to Xavier's bedside, hanging on to the frame for dear life. I didn't want to tell Idris or Kian this, but traveling to Direveil had taken more out of me than I thought I could spare. Hands trembling, I gently placed the book at the foot of Xavier's bed, untying the bonds of the tattered fabric that had protected it for so long.

The binding was nearly broken, the thick leather tome held together by a hope and a prayer, but it had withstood the trip back from the Dreaming. Finally— through all of this—I'd managed to do something right. So many times I'd failed, but this once, I'd made a plan and fucking stuck with it.

With tears in my eyes, I tried to focus on the cover, but my sight wavered, blackness encroaching on the edges of my vision.

"Vale?" Idris called, his warm touch at my shoulder.

"I'm fine. I just need a minute."

I'd just faced down my torturer, and I was about to open a book I had shut away for years. There was no way I could fall apart now. This curse had to be broken. I had to save Xavier. I had to get my shit together and fucking focus.

"I'm fine," I repeated, though, I doubted anyone believed it, least of all me.

Gently, I lifted the cover, running my fingertip over the list of names of all the Luxa in my family. Now that I knew we were a bloodline and it wasn't some magical curse bestowed upon me because I hadn't been a good enough daughter, I realized each sovereign name was a form of protection. Each one was a way to keep us hidden, to keep us safe.

There were many before me, and it hurt my heart that so many were dead because of this curse.

But I was about to break it.

Turning the page, I skimmed the histories of Luxa —the bastardized version of the fabled story Idris had told me what seemed like eons ago. In this account, there was only a king cursed to live alone, unhappy with his fate as the keeper of all magic. I knew if there were ever a story like the one Idris shared with me, I would have paid a hell of a lot more attention to this book.

Few remember the true origins of the Luxa, and perhaps it is for the best. The blood of the light witches was woven with powers meant only for those who would understand the peril they inherit. But in time, all things hidden must surface.

As much as I had told him I hated the history of his ancestor, a part of me loved it, too. I loved how someone could care for another so much that they were willing to sacrifice their entire world for them. The longer I spent with my mates, the more and more it made sense.

THE LUXA WERE BORN OF THE LIGHT AND THE DARKNESS, BLESSED AND CURSED TO WALK THE BOUNDARIES BETWEEN REALMS. NOT BOUND TO ANY REALITY, NOR MAY CALL ANY HOME, FOR THE PULL OF BOTH WILL SEEK TO RECLAIM THEM.

Then the history morphed into what I'd always hated—the twisted recounting of Idris and his curse —the story of two brothers letting the world burn over their desire to possess a single woman. How the

Luxa refused to let herself come between them and banished one brother while cursing the other.

It said so little about who they were as people, and even less about the banished brother. All it did was give dire warnings about why breaking the cursed king free of his bonds would bring the end to us all— that only a Luxa could free him.

> *There is a shadow over the Luxa, one which grows darker with each generation. Beware the one born of dreams, for she will be the harbinger of great change and ruin. When she rises to her power, the boundaries between realms will weaken, the Beast will be freed, and the Cursed One shall be unshackled.*

I wished I would have known about my abilities far sooner. Wished my parents had thought to tell me what was coming—what I was. Of all the things they prepared me for, this had never been one of them. They had to have known what I would become.

Betrayal was a difficult emotion to swallow, especially when those that betrayed you were dead. But I didn't have time for regrets or recriminations. We had a curse to break, and I had a mate to save. I needed to read this damn book no matter if it tore me up inside.

Hastily, I kept flipping pages past the parts I knew and on to what I didn't. But there was so much to wade through that getting to the meat of everything seemed almost impossible. Some of the entries were in diary format, some of it was simple chicken scratch. The difference between my parents' writing was obvious, even though I'd read so little of it.

My mother's handwriting clogged my throat, the tears of loss choking me as I allowed myself to run my finger over the indent of each word.

"My mother wrote this," I whispered, trying not to sob at the unhealed wounds their deaths had left.

I wanted to tell them all about her, and what she meant to me. How she made the awful life with the guild bearable. There was so much I'd never said, so much they didn't know. There were so many bad times under the mountain, but there had been good times, too.

When we were all together.

When we were safe.

But that safety had always been an illusion—the truth was a bitter pill to swallow. Selene hadn't been lying for once. My parents had stolen the scroll of the

Luxa histories and potentially transcribed it into this book, hiding it away for years under the guild's nose.

What might my life have been like had they told me what I was—what I'd always been destined for? Would I have been prepared for the trials? Would I have been more amenable and less hostile to the dragons I'd fallen in love with?

Would I have wasted so much time?

Or would I have died like all the Luxa before me?

I guessed I'd never know.

But as my mother's handwriting fell away and my father's took her place, the text became more frantic, more illegible, and the deeper into the book I got, the less his words made sense.

WHAT WE HAVE BROUGHT FORTH CAN NEVER CONTINUE TO BE. THIS MAGIC WILL BE OUR END—OUR RIGHTFUL EXTERMINATION. WE MUST LET THE HALLS OF DREAMS DIE TO ENSURE THE SURVIVAL OF US ALL.

Did they want to kill the Dreaming? Why would they want to destroy it? It made no sense. And yet... something about the way it was worded reminded me of the mage's warning.

I shook my head. Malvor was crazy and doing the

bidding of a maniac. What difference did his ravings make?

But when I turned the page again, my entire world fell away.

Gasping, I shakily ran my fingers over the jagged edges. Roughly cleaved from the spine as if someone had ripped them out in a hurry, an entire chunk of the book was missing. My stomach heaved as I hung onto the bed frame, praying it would hold me up as my knees threatened to give out. But there wasn't anything about how to break the curse—about how to fix anything. It was all warnings and bullshit—nothing substantial.

There had to be more than this. I didn't nearly get us all killed for... for... *this*.

"What is it?" Idris rumbled, his hand on my shoulder like he didn't know if he should keep me up or let me fall.

Funnily enough, I didn't, either.

"It's gone. The rest of the book is gone," I whispered, my gaze landing on Xavier's still form. He hadn't so much as twitched since I'd been awake, and now there was no way I knew of to help him—to help anyone.

What was it all for? The torture, the pain. What was it all for if I wasn't supposed to do good things—

if I wasn't supposed to right the wrongs? If I wasn't supposed to fix what was broken?

Fury pooled in my chest, igniting the blazing rage that I'd kept leashed for so long. A scream ripped up my throat as I threw the book against the wall, hating every single page that fell from the broken binding. Tears flooded my eyes, blurring my already-fading vision.

"I can't break your curse. I can't heal Xavier. I can't find my sister. I can't fucking fix it. I can't fix *anything*."

"Hey," Kian growled, his rough hands cupping my cheeks, making me look at him. "Focus, little witch. We're no worse off than we were before, but we will be if you don't calm down."

Ripping myself out of his hold, I fought off the urge to explode. I wanted to destroy something— anything. I wanted to take something precious and break it. I wanted... My gaze fell on Xavier. His big body was barely contained in the bed, the ends of his hair still bloody from the trip to this useless monastery.

He was here because of me, and I wasn't strong enough to heal him, and now he might not ever wake up.

"Being a little dramatic, aren't we?" a smooth

voice called from the doorway, but through my blurry vision, all I could see was the red hair. "It's one thing to throw a fit, but darling girl, you're about to take out the building. Dial it down a notch, yeah?"

Squeezing my eyes shut, I tried to clear my head. There was no way Freya could be here, and yet, when I opened my eyes, she was. How had she even known we were here?

"Dramatic?" I growled, just noticing the blazing light pouring from my fingers, the stone floor scorching as light flooded from my body. "My mate is dying in a hospital bed, and you think I'm being dramatic? Not all of us can be hard-hearted thousand-year-old vampires, Freya. Some of us actually feel things."

She had the gall to roll her eyes at me. I swore to everything holy, if she did it one more time, I would figure out a way to kill a vampire.

"These young doctors don't know the first thing about fateborn mate bonds," she said, calm as you please, waltzing into the room as if I wasn't one second away from losing it. "I know how you can heal him if you would just settle down and allow me to touch you."

"If you know a way to save him, I don't care what I have to do." I didn't. If there was a way to help

Xavier wake up, I'd do it. So what if I couldn't break the curse? At least I would be able to do one thing right—even if my family's book was a complete bust.

Squeezing my eyes shut, I tried to pull the power into myself, taking deep breaths to calm the rage boiling in my chest. But it lived in me—curled up nice and tight right where my heart should be.

Freya kept talking, an odd story I didn't particularly want to listen to, spilling from her mouth while I tried to concentrate. "Do you have any idea what it's like to have a giant dragon roar the castle down disturbing your beauty sleep? Or trying to understand his bullshit dragon sign language while wondering why he's covered in Xavier's blood? I have to say, this day has not been my favorite, little Luxa. Not at all."

Calming myself down couldn't knock me out of my own head, but finding out Rune went and picked Freya up to help us sure as hell did.

"He did what?" I squeaked while Kian and Idris stood there with their mouths open, staring at her like she had a brand-new hole in her head.

"Oh, yeah," she growled, her hands menacingly on her hips. "Did I forget to mention the part where he broke my balcony doors and yanked me out of my bed naked into the freezing courtyard? I was entertaining a *guest*. Not only was she terrified, but I got frostbite in places one should never get frostbite."

I couldn't help it, I snorted. Imagining Freya yelling at Rune for giving her frostbite the whole way here had to be the only funny thing to happen all damn day. Well, that and watching Arden's head bounce off the wall, but who was counting?

"Now that you've officially calmed down in the face of my misery, it's time to fix your mate," Freya grumbled, shooing Kian out of the way as she drew a dagger from her leathers. "While there hasn't been a fateborn mate in two centuries, there were plenty before Zamarra fucked us all over. And it wasn't too uncommon for mates to occur across species. I might be an Ashbourne, but I'm not a dragon. Ever wonder why?"

Actually, I hadn't wondered why at all, I'd just assumed there were many different species in the Ashbourne line. "Not really. I assume you're going to give us all a history lesson?"

Freya squinted her eyes at me before giving me a little smile. "Fair enough. My father was a dragon, but my mother was not. She was a vampire, and when I was born, I inherited the magic from the dragon line and a fraction of the vampirism, which made me ill and my power unstable. Eventually, once

I realized I would never shift into a dragon of my own, I embraced my mother's vampirism."

"How long ago was that?" I asked, curious about Freya's origins. I hadn't realized how long she'd been alive or what she might have seen through the centuries.

"Over a thousand years ago, but the important part is once upon a time, my father was very sick, and no matter what my mother did, no matter how much power she infused in him, she could not heal him. Until one day, she let her vampire side take over and she fed him her blood. Granted, I fully believe she planned on turning him, but she didn't have to.

"It didn't take very long until my father was healed, his wounds fading away as my mother's blood filled him. While no, you aren't a vampire, and this very well might not work, but if it'll save one of my closest friends, we're sure as hell going to try it."

She held out her hand for mine, and I gladly gave it to her. Without so much as a warning, she sliced through my wrist, the wound pouring blood in an instant. She yanked me forward, pressing my flesh against Xavier's lips as my lifeblood flowed down his throat.

Kian and Idris cried out, but I knew this was our only shot. If I had to lose my life for Xavier, I would do it, and Freya knew it, too. Dizzy, I wilted into Xavier's side, resting my head on his chest. His heartbeat thrummed through my ear as the world whirled around me.

Kian lunged for her, his talons extended as Idris lifted my legs so I didn't fall off the bed, but all I could hear was Xavier's heartbeat getting stronger. And when the world faded away, I knew she'd been right.

I could heal Xavier.

I just might have to die to do it.

CHAPTER 20
XAVIER

"For the last fucking time, it was necessary," Freya growled, shrugging off Idris' golden bonds and straightening her flight leathers. "You think I wanted to hurt her? There was a choice to be made, and I made it. If you'd actually listen to me instead of losing your shit, you'd probably agree."

I considered how much trouble I'd be in if I shifted into my dragon and just ripped Freya's head right off. Instead, I buried my nose in Vale's hair and took in her scent. Granted, it didn't lessen my anger one bit, but at least I could reassure myself that my mate was still alive. Vale had yet to stir in my arms since I'd woken, the coppery tang of her blood still lingering in my mouth.

It reminded me of when she'd been in my arms on the way to Tarrasca—her small body clinging to me as I wondered if I would ever see her beautiful green eyes again. And just like then, I had to fight off the urge to find the person who'd hurt her and rip them limb from limb.

"You slit her fucking wrist without warning anyone—least of all her—and let her bleed enough that not only did she pass out, but I can scent death on her," I hissed, hanging onto sanity by a thread. "Please tell me in what world would her mates *not* be absolutely livid?"

"It's not my fault that you took forever and a day to wake up. I was saving your life. You're welcome. If you're so pissed that she hasn't woken up yet, maybe you should heal her yourself. You and I both know her blood is powerful enough that you're at tip-top shape. Why don't you stop whining at my methods and realize that I'm right."

It didn't matter that she was right. Energy thrummed through my body, racing up and down my limbs like a brushfire. The ache of the wound at my side was long gone, the only irritant the stitches I no longer needed. But through it all—through the scents of incense and herbs from the maesters' tonics and potions, through the perfume of blood and death, was just the sweet scent of Vale in my arms.

"She trusts you," I growled, clutching Vale close to my chest, willing her to rouse. "Did you ever stop to think that she has never had another female figure in her life other than her own mother to rely on? Never had anyone teach her? You're a thousand years old. You should be smarter than this."

Freya dabbed at the rapidly healing scratches at her neck, while Idris held Kian in a half-broken chair, the golden ropes of his power preventing another violent outburst.

"She could have fallen back into the Dreaming. She could have been stuck there, unable to get back," Idris murmured, fear etched into every line of his face. "She could have gone where I couldn't reach her. Arden could have taken her—you don't understand how fragile her power is—how special. She's connected to the Dreaming in a way I've never seen. Not since—"

Zamarra.

Not since Zamarra.

All roads led back to that woman, and I hated that Vale was caught in the middle of all this shit.

"Do you think I don't know that?" Freya fumed. "I

took a calculated risk based off the information I had."

"I suggest you," Kian rumbled, still fighting against Idris' bonds, "think for once bef—"

Freya's cool gaze flicked to Kian. "I *suggest* you listen, you big idiots, before we take too long and end up on the wrong side of fucked. While I'm still pissed at Rune, I'm glad he came to get me. Flying back here, I caught sight of a battalion of Girovian mages moving for Tarrasca."

That had me sitting up in earnest and Kian fighting his bonds tooth and nail.

"How close are they?" Idris growled, his attention never once leaving Vale's still form in my arms.

"Two days at least—maybe three if the wards hold," Freya said, tossing the bloody gauze she'd used on her wound into the bin. "So I need you out of this hospital, on the back of a dragon, and married in the next twenty-four hours. If the curse doesn't break, at the very least, it will show the people you're trying. Worse comes to worst, Vale will have the protection of the Crown."

Not that it would do her any good right now.

She was still as the grave, the only movement her chest as she slumbered. If what Freya said was true, we didn't have time to waste. Closing my eyes, I willed a fraction of the power she'd given me back to her, praying that she opened her eyes. And just like she had on the back of a horse what seemed like eons ago, Vale curled into my chest, rubbing her cheek against me like a contented cat.

"Did it work?" Vale mumbled sleepily, slipping her frail arms around my neck and burying her face in my shoulder. "I hope it worked."

Tightening my hold, I couldn't help but chuckle. "It worked, my love. Though, I would have preferred you hadn't been hurt because of me."

Pushing back from my shoulder, Vale's piercing green gaze fell on me. Relief I could sense through the bond filled my chest, as her eyes welled up with tears. A moment later, she fell into my chest, squeezing me tight like she thought if she didn't, I'd fade away from her somehow.

"I... We... almost lost you. I thought I'd lost you. Never do that to me again. You understand me? You can't leave me. I promised I wouldn't leave you, didn't I?" Her breaths came in short, panicked pants, her sobs wrecking my soul.

"I'm not going anywhere. I promise. You won't lose me."

She pushed back again, this time her nose was

bright red, and her eyes were puffy and tight. Still, she was the most beautiful thing I'd ever seen.

"This is touching and all, but..." Freya's words trailed off as Idris' bonds fell away from Kian's shoulders.

He stood from his chair, his scales rippling over his arms as his pupils narrowed to slits. But he didn't lunge at Freya or rip Vale out of my hold. No, Kian simply sat at the edge of my bed and brushed a strand of hair from Vale's face.

"You're just about the only woman who could cry her eyes out and pull it off."

Vale blushed and reached for his hand, pressing it to the side of her face. "But you're about to tell me bad news, aren't you? I can practically hear it buzzing in your mind."

Kian's smile was a little sad, but I chose not to see it for what it was. It was the same feeling in my chest when I thought of her marrying Idris and not us. When I thought of watching her promise herself in front of the whole kingdom, even though we'd never get recognized as her mates. It was a burn I wondered would ever heal.

"We need to move the timetable up on the wedding," Kian said, the ache in his chest echoing my own. "A threat is headed for Tarrasca, and we need you protected. And if that mage insisted that you should never bond with Idris, then I think you should do the opposite. It's a shit plan, but it's the best we have."

Vale's gaze went from Kian to Idris before falling to her lap. Her mind was eerily silent for once, like she'd shut us all out, carving out a small space for herself.

"How soon?"

Freya skirted the bed, heading for the door. "Tomorrow evening at the latest. I don't think the ward will hold much past that."

Vale nodded to herself as if she was coming to terms with everything. "Do you think you can get everything ready by then? I never did my dress fitting or study all the protocol you said I should learn."

I curled Vale into my chest, dropping a kiss to her temple. "We'll make it work. I promise."

Vale pulled back before slipping from the bed altogether. Standing on her own two feet, I watched as she donned the mantle of Queen in her mind. Her spine straightened, her shoulders set, she lifted her chin and regarded Idris.

"I'm ready if you are," Vale murmured, and it made my heart twist in my chest.

Idris took her hand in his and pressed a kiss to the

inside of her now-healed wrist, the faint line of the scar fading even now. "I've been waiting two hundred years to marry you. You could say I've been ready for some time now."

I'd like to say that it didn't rip my heart out of my chest to watch Idris usher her from the room, but I'd be lying.

The love of my life had just agreed to marry one of my best friends.

And I'd have to watch.

HOURS LATER WE ARRIVED AT THE CASTLE, THE trip exposing just how much energy it had stolen from Vale to heal me. Shifting back into my human form was smooth, and yet, I could feel every ache in her bones, every strain of her muscles as she dismounted from Rune.

Vale was exhausted, barely able to hold herself up as Idris carried her inside. Freya immediately went to work, peeling off to manage wedding plans with murmurings about expanding the guest list and making sure the council knew about the change in date. Kian also left, his focus on his soldiers and making sure the castle and Festia was as secure as he could make it.

I doubted either would sleep tonight.

I wouldn't, either.

I caught myself following behind my King and my mate, knowing that this would be the life we would always lead. I would forever be one step behind them, never recognized for who she was to me. I feared it was a sting that would grow over time, a cancer that would rot me from the inside out.

I'd always said that it was Idris' jealousy that had been his downfall. That had he not been blinded by his brother going after the woman he loved, he would have seen what Arden and Zamarra were planning. That had he opened his eyes, the continent wouldn't have been bound with this curse.

But watching them walk up the stairs to the castle entrance, I realized that maybe jealousy would be my downfall, too. I didn't mind the fact that Vale had three mates. I didn't mind sharing her. I minded the ring on her finger and the realization that I'd never wear a matching one.

I minded that her mark would never be on me.

I minded that if ever she bore my young, I would never get to claim them.

And yet I could never stand in the way of this wedding—not if it kept her alive.

Not if it kept the kingdom safe.

Not if it managed to break the curse.

The love of my life was getting married tomorrow, and it wasn't to me.

"Xavier?" Vale called, her voice barely above a whisper, but singing to my heart all the same. It snapped me out of my pity party.

"Yes, Love?"

Those gorgeous green eyes peered over Idris' shoulder. "Are you coming? I need to ask you for a favor—and Kian, too, when he gets a chance."

Her expression was so apprehensive, so nervous, it nearly brought me to my knees. How had such a little thing bent me to her will so easily? And why didn't I mind?

"You know I'd do anything for you," I murmured, catching up to them as we swept down the hallway. "Ask and it's yours."

Vale's gaze went from me to Idris, their faces close as if their minds had melded into one. She nodded, and a faint smile lifted the tips of her lips.

"Do you think you and Kian would want to walk me down the aisle tomorrow?" Her eyes flooded as she looked away, but no tears fell. "Freya said it was

custom for someone from your family to do it, but I
—" She shook her head. "I don't have anyone except
Nyrah. And you and Kian are my family now in a
way, and I thought—"

"I'll do it," I said, cutting her off.

Giving her away would gut me, and yet I couldn't
say no.

Not to her.

Never to her.

And even if I had to call in every favor and twist
every arm, Kian would tell her the same damn thing.

I'd make sure of it.

CHAPTER 21
VALE

My hand shook as I reached for the hairbrush, my nerves getting the better of me despite the crushed lavender sachet Briar had stuffed into my hands when she'd brought me breakfast. The brownie had taken one look at me and gasped in horror—something no one wanted to hear on their wedding day.

I couldn't blame her.

Despite Xavier and Kian curling around me while Idris made sure I didn't dream walk, I hadn't managed to sleep more than a handful of minutes the whole night. I was too worried about the mage advance, too focused on the convoluted bullshit in my family's book, too scared that I couldn't live up to what a Luxa really was to fix anything. It didn't matter if I was warm and safe in this castle—the coming war would change the face of Credour, and I had no idea who would come out on top.

Briar said the lavender would calm my nerves, but so far, it had only made the room smell nice and gave me something to pummel.

As it was, I avoided the dressing table mirror altogether, handing the brush off to Freya. If I was walking into my wedding looking like a zombie, I'd prefer not to know. She was working on a complicated hairstyle, and I was trying to calm myself down.

Only one of us was successful.

My gaze fell onto the dress hanging from an intricate hook in the dressing room. In mere minutes, Freya would cinch me into the beautifully delicate thing, and I would become a whole new person.

Not a poor miner from Direveil.

Not the starving-child-turned-mother too soon.

Not the broken sister.

I would be a queen. Idris' Queen. Credour's Queen.

Of all the things I did not want to fail at, this was at the top of the list.

The golden and silver threads of the dress converged into a shimmering fabric, the intricate beading catching the light and cascading into a work of art that only the finest dressmaker could create. It was made of magic, and I didn't feel worthy of wearing it.

Freya fit the last pin in my hair, arranging a lock of it just so. "You sure are quiet, little Luxa. Penny for your thoughts?"

Kian and Xavier were still pissed at her for last night, but I wasn't. She might not have gone about it in the right way, but I couldn't argue with the results. Since I'd met her, Freya had been the big sister I'd never had. Still, she was Idris' family and telling her I was nervous to be marrying into the Ashbourne line would *likely* still be considered rude. There was so much I still didn't know about my mates—so much I needed to know—and yet I'd run out of time.

"There isn't much to say, is there?" I murmured, my gaze not leaving the dress. It hurt my heart how perfect it was. "None of this feels real. It's like I'm dream walking again, only this time there's no one to wake me up."

Freya's chuckle did what the lavender could not, easing my nerves by a fraction. "I hate to break it to you, but all weddings feel like that. I remember my first marriage. It was a whirlwind of duty and protocol, only it was simply a business relationship for us. I wasn't in love with the man I married. You are."

I opened my mouth to deny her, but that single red eyebrow kept me from lying outright. "I feel like I don't know him, and yet... I don't want to disappoint him. All my life I've been warned against breaking his curse, and now I know that all of it has been a lie —one lie on top of another in an avalanche of misinformation and half-truths. Nothing I knew—not about me, not about my parents—none of it is real. How do I know if what I'm feeling is?"

Her smile sent a blanket of comfort to my jangling nerves. "Because even when you were convinced you hated him, you still stayed. You can say it's for Nyrah, but you and I both know you hate the injustice of what was done to him."

"Not that I know the bulk of it."

"True. But there isn't much to tell. He fell in love with a Luxa, and he thought she loved him back. Instead, she was in league with his brother to steal his crown and drain him of every ounce of power he had. The lore spouts a story of warring brothers, but the truth is much worse. Arden and Idris did fight over Zamarra, but her curse was never meant to stop it."

The faint glow from my hands filled the room before I could pull it back.

"See? One mention of someone hurting him, and

you go all glowy. You *looooove* him. You're going to marry him, break his curse, and have little dragon babies with him and the rest of your mates, and everything will be fine."

I choked on air. "Excuse me," I wheezed, trying to process her teasing. "Dragon babies?"

Freya's cheeks colored as she pressed her lips together to keep from laughing at me, but this was serious. "Never fear, little Luxa, that will happen many years down the road. Dragons take ages to reproduce if they do at all. It's a wonder the species isn't extinct."

My heartbeat thrummed against my ribcage, aching to take flight. "Don't scare me like that. It's bad enough I have to go out there in front of all those strangers, let's not keel me over before I even get my dress on. This day is going to be hard enough as it is."

Freya put a quelling hand on my shoulder. "Strangers or not, in this dress or in a potato sack, you will be their Queen. You are more than just a Luxa, more than just a witch or a woman or a sister. You're a beacon, Vale. Just like your light, you will guide us home. I have faith in you—even if you don't have it for yourself."

Blinking away tears, I fought off the urge to

smack her. "If this makeup runs because you made me cry, I don't want to hear shit from you."

"Yeah, yeah."

Minutes later, I was cinched into the dress, the delicate fabric so beautiful I almost made good on those tears but managed to hold myself together. With no other option, I let my gaze fall to the trio of full-length mirrors. In it was someone I didn't recognize but knew all the same. Crystal pins held my mass of hair in an intricate arrangement, gleaming in the flickering light.

But it wasn't the shimmering beauty of the dress that held my attention. No, it was the way the high, transparent back of the cape exposed my scars.

The heretic brand stood out against the translucent fabric, a dark and jagged mark between my shoulder blades. Around it, smaller scars twisted across my flesh like fractured lightning, each one a reminder of where I'd come from.

"You look perfect," Freya said softly, stepping back to admire her work.

My throat tightened as I stared at the brand. The symbol burned into me had once been a mark of shame, meant to strip me of my dignity, meant to break me down, meant to keep me a slave forever.

Now, it was on full display for all to see—a stark, unflinching declaration of what I'd survived.

Unlike the ball, I didn't have a quick entrance to save me. I would be up on a stage for all to see, all to witness. I struggled to swallow as I fisted my gloved hands.

"Do you think they'll accept me?" I asked quietly, the question slipping out before I could stop it.

Freya's hands stilled again, and she placed them gently on my shoulders, turning me to face her. Her gaze was steady, filled with the kind of certainty I wished I could bottle to save for a rainy day.

"It doesn't matter if they accept you or not, Vale," she said firmly. "What matters is that you stand there as you are—unapologetically. Not a brand or scar in the world can take that away from you."

"That's a lot easier said than done," I admitted, my voice barely above a whisper.

Freya smiled faintly and picked up the veil resting on the edge of the table. The delicate fabric was woven with silver and gold threads, catching the light like the stars had been sewn into its folds. She placed it gently over my head, her touch reassuring. "You've done harder things," she said simply. "And you'll do this, too."

The door creaked open, and we both turned to see Kian and Xavier standing there, their black dress uniforms hugging their shoulders like I wished I could. Kian leaned casually against the frame, his sharp grin made of mischief as his amber irises glowed with his power. To anyone else, he would seem cool as could be, but I knew better. He was putting on a brave face for me, but I knew he was worried about the mages headed our way, about potential attacks at the wedding, about a whole host of things he would never tell me because he didn't want me to worry.

Xavier stood beside him, his icy gaze locked onto mine with an intensity that sent warmth curling through my chest. The last few hours, he'd locked himself away from me, and as much as I hated it, I knew he was protecting me in his own way. He was just as worried as Kian was—as we all were.

"Well," Kian drawled, his eyes caressing every inch of me, "if the goal was to make Idris lose his fucking mind, I'd say mission accomplished."

Xavier moved closer, his expression softening as he reached out to brush his knuckles along my cheek. "You're breathtaking, Vale," he murmured. "More than he deserves."

"Exactly," Kian quipped. "You sure you want to do this? I know a dragon or three who could fly you out of here, no questions asked." He waggled his eyebrows, and I managed a shaky laugh. I knew only part of him was teasing.

"You two are supposed to calm me down, not make me more nervous." It was bad enough there were mages on their way to Tarrasca. I couldn't even joke about leaving the kingdom and Idris to deal with this alone.

Kian smirked and held out his arm. "That's what we're here for, little witch. Let's get you to that courtyard before Idris comes storming in to fetch you himself."

Freya stepped back, smoothing the folds of my dress before resting her hands on her own gown. "You'll do fine," she said, her voice soft but sure. "Now go show them all why you're the queen."

I took a deep breath, slipping my arms around Kian's and Xavier's as they led me toward the door. My heart was pounding, but as I glanced at them, I felt a flicker of courage take root.

I wasn't walking into this alone.

The faint rustle of my gown against the stone floor was drowned out by the ringing in my ears, the trek through the castle not quelling my nerves one bit. It felt as though there were hundreds of people in this hallway with us, all with their eyes on me, and yet I saw no one.

"I don't know if I can do this, Rune," I whispered through the bond to the one person who could likely snap me out of this.

I caught the mental snort, and I could practically feel him rolling his eyes. *"I could have sworn you were the woman who broke a siren queen's jaw a few days ago. Maybe that was another Luxa. If so, you should probably fess up now so that one can get married instead."*

Irritated, I wished I could flick the overgrown pigeon in the nose. *"You know damn well it's one thing to fight for my life and another to get married. Everyone will be staring at me."*

"Yes, and I'll be staring at them. No one will so much as say 'boo' to you. You'll see."

"You're doing fine," Xavier murmured, his voice a low rumble of reassurance, like he could hear my heart fluttering in my chest. "Focus on us."

I tried grounding myself in the steady cadence of their steps, but I could still feel the eyes on me. Kian's grip on my arm was firm, and when he caught me glancing at him, he winked. "Almost there, little witch."

His abilities made illusions almost real, and I

narrowed my eyes at him. "There are people in this hallway, aren't there? You made them disappear for me."

He gave me an impish grin as he held a finger to his lips. "A little present to calm your nerves. I won't tell if you won't."

The heavy double doors leading to the courtyard came into view, and my heart went from fluttering to a full-on gallop. The soft murmur of the gathered crowd filtered through them, their anticipation palpable even through the thick wood. A pair of guards moved to open the doors as we approached, their ceremonial armor gleaming in the torchlight.

The moment they parted, the world seemed to shift.

The courtyard was almost unrecognizable, transformed into a breathtaking winter landscape under a protective dome of magic. Snowflakes drifted gently against the translucent bubble, melting as they touched its shimmering surface. Within, the air was warm, filled with the scent of citrus and pine and something wonderfully floral.

I could barely see the stone walls through towering trees blossoming with delicate white flowers, while enchanted lights floated through their branches like tiny stars. The aisle was lined with tall wrought-iron candelabras, their flames flickering softly in the still air.

At the end of the aisle, Rune sat perched on a raised platform near the altar, his massive red form gleaming like molten metal under the magical lights.

"I told you you'd see. You're safe, my Queen. I promise."

Idris stood beside him, his broad shoulders squared, his golden eyes fixed on me. Even from a distance, I could see the faint curve of a smile tugging at his lips, the private expression meant only for me.

"Ready?" Kian asked, his voice softer now, but I shook my head. "I can make them disappear, too, you know. If you want."

Looking up into his liquid amber gaze, I nodded shakily. With a kind smile and a wave of his fingers, the guests, the council, everyone except us melted away. Instantly, my heart went from hammering so loudly I was sure they could hear it, to slowing to a crawl, the relief nearly making my knees weak.

"Let's do this," I whispered, taking my first step, Kian and Xavier's support making the trek bearable.

When we reached the altar, Idris stepped forward, his hand outstretched. Kian and Xavier paused, each leaning in to kiss the golden swirls of our mating mark on my shoulder. The warmth of their lips lingered as they pulled back, giving me one last look before they stepped away to take their seats.

I placed my hand in Idris', and the world seemed to quiet around us.

"You're stunning," he murmured, his voice low enough so only I could hear.

The courtyard was silent except for the faint crackle of Rune's scales shifting behind us, the only reminder that this wasn't a dream. The magical bubble overhead sparkled faintly as the archbishop stepped forward, his crimson and black robes brushing against the altar as he raised his hands. Aged but kind, the withered man gave me a benevolent smile before he began the ceremony.

"We gather here," his voice resonated, deep and commanding, "to witness the union of Idris Ashbourne, King of Credour, and Duchess Isolde Vale Tenebris, Grand Luxa of Tarrasca. This is not merely a union of hearts and fate, but a binding of magic, of power, and of purpose. It is a union that will shape the future of this realm."

I forced my breaths to steady, though my fingers trembled in Idris's hand. His golden eyes searched mine, warm but unreadable, as if he could sense the storm raging inside me. I had agreed to this—chosen it, even—but that didn't mean I didn't question everything. My life, my freedom, my very future—everything would change with this moment.

Idris turned to face me fully, and the intensity in his gaze stole the breath from my lungs. He reached for my other hand, his warmth seeping through the delicate fabric of my gloves as his thumbs traced small, soothing circles against my skin.

"Vale," he began, his voice low and steady, yet brimming with emotion. "You are more than I ever expected. More than I ever deserved. You are strength, power, and light. Today, I vow to stand beside you—not just as your King, but as your ally and protector, and to never falter in my faith in you. I vow to fight for you, to honor the magic that flows between us, and to build a future where we both stand strong."

My vision blurred with unshed tears, his words sinking deep into the cracks I thought I'd hidden so well. I swallowed hard, the lump in my throat making it almost impossible to speak.

"Idris," I said, barely above a whisper, though I knew he heard me. "Your voice found me when I was lost and scared and alone. It kept me alive when I'd thought that feat was impossible. I was afraid of this, of you, but you've shown me that strength isn't about fighting alone. It's about trusting someone to stand beside you. Today, I vow to be at your side—not as your Queen, but as your fateborn mate, your partner. I will honor the trust you've placed in me, to wield the strength I've found within myself, and to fight for this kingdom—for all of us."

A soft rumble from Rune behind us rippled through the courtyard, almost like an acknowledgment. For a moment, Idris's eyes softened, but he didn't speak. He simply lifted the small onyx band from the archbishop's outstretched hand. The jewels in the band gleamed faintly, their red swirls pulsing as though in time with my heartbeat.

"Rings are the symbol of eternity," the archbishop intoned. "A promise with no end. As you place them on one another's hands, so too do you bind your lives, your hearts, and your magic."

"With this ring," Idris said, sliding it onto my finger, "I bind myself to you, in fire and in life, for as long as my soul burns."

My hands trembled as I took his ring, a solid band of blackened metal engraved with intricate runes. I slid it onto his finger, the metal cool but quickly warming under his touch. "With this ring," I whispered, "I bind myself to you, in light and in shadow, for as long as my soul shines."

The archbishop raised his arms again, his staff

glowing brighter. "By the power of magic and the will of the realm, I pronounce you bonded, mates, and sovereigns united. You may seal your vows."

Idris didn't hesitate. I barely had time to draw a breath before he closed the distance between us. His hands cupped my face, his touch impossibly gentle as he leaned in. When his lips met mine, the world seemed to tilt, the emotions he'd held back from our bond flooding through me as his joy lifted every bit of trepidation from my heart. His tongue swept into my mouth, curling my toes as he laid his claim. The best I could do was hang on as I fell into the kiss.

Funny, I'd always been afraid of falling before, but as Idris wrapped his arms around me and lifted me off my feet, I knew he'd be there to catch me.

When we pulled apart, the crowd erupted into cheers, the veil of Kian's magic lifted as the sound echoed through the courtyard. Rune let out a low, rumbling roar, and the magical barrier above us shimmered as if in celebration.

Idris leaned close, his lips brushing against my ear as he whispered, "You're mine, Vale. And I'm yours."

The air in the throne room was different. Heavier. The blooming trees and floating lights were replaced with harsh stone columns and flickering mage lights. The wide chamber was filled with people—council members, noble families, and emissaries from every province. Somehow with no notice, they'd all managed to be here, each of them standing silently, their gazes fixed on me as I stepped through the massive double doors.

A few days ago, I'd blown those doors to pieces, and now I was walking through them as a queen. Beside me, Idris's presence was steady, grounding. He held my hand gently in his as we walked together, but when we reached the raised dais, he let go and took his place beside the throne.

The throne.

I hadn't even dared to look at it directly—not once. Made of obsidian and gold, it loomed like a black sun at the end of the room, its edges carved with an intricate dragon that looked a lot like Rune, the golden inlays shimmering in the torchlight. It wasn't just a chair—it was a declaration of power, of rule, of responsibility.

Next to it rested another throne—one that hadn't ever been there before. Absent was the dragon scales and sharp teeth. No, my throne was made of shining obsidian, threaded through with silver and gold, the back drawn into a sunburst of gold flowing into swirling carvings of shadow. Idris' handiwork, I realized, his magic imprinted in every detail.

The archbishop's voice rang out, breaking the silence. "Queen Isolde Vale Tenebris, you stand before the throne of Credour, not as a Luxa, not as a witch, but as a sovereign. Do you accept the responsibility of this crown? Do you vow to serve this realm, its people, and its magic with all that you are?"

"I do," I said, my voice loud and clear despite the knot in my stomach.

Step by step, I ascended, each one heavier than the last. When I reached the top, Idris strode forward with the crown—silver and gold accented with onyx and ruby.

"Bow," he instructed, and I bent into a curtsy. His golden eyes held mine as he placed it gently on my head, the weight both grounding and daunting.

"Rise," he murmured through the bond. *"Rise as their Queen."*

I stood, adjusting to the weight as he turned to address the crowd. "Behold your Queen," he proclaimed, his voice resonating with authority. "Queen Isolde Vale Tenebris, Light Bringer, Curse Breaker, Grand Luxa of Tarrasca, and ruler of Credour."

The room erupted into cheers, the sound echoing off the stone walls.

"You did it, my Queen."

I nodded, swallowing the lump in my throat as I turned to take my seat. The obsidian was cold beneath me, the high back curving slightly to support the weight of the crown. Idris sat beside me, his golden eyes scanning the crowd before he spoke again.

"This is a new chapter for Credour," he said, his voice steady and resolute. "A chapter of unity, of strength, of hope. Together, we will face the trials ahead, and together, we will prevail. With our Queen beside us, the realm will endure."

Cheers rose again, but this time, I let myself take a deep breath and sit a little taller. I wasn't sure if I was ready for this, but I was here.

And that had to be enough.

Soon the crowd parted to make way for the royal procession. Idris offered his hand once more, helping me rise from the throne. My legs felt like jelly, the enormity of the movement making me unsteady on my feet.

Idris leaned in, his golden eyes warm and steady. *"One step at a time,"* he murmured through the bond. *"You've already won most of them over. The rest will come to adore you soon enough."*

I wasn't sure about that, but I nodded, letting him guide me down the dais. The procession was orderly, the council members bowing their heads as we passed, while the nobles curtsied with precision. I caught glimpses of admiration, skepticism, and outright distrust in their eyes, but I refused to let it rattle me.

Freya fell into step beside me, her sharp grin cutting through the tension like the decorative blades crisscrossing her back. "Well, little Luxa," she said under her breath, "you survived a wedding and a coronation. Now, let's see if you can stomach the feast."

THE SOUND OF LAUGHTER AND CLINKING goblets filled the grand ballroom, the air warm with the mingling scents of roasted meats, spiced wine, and honeyed desserts. The celebration was in full swing, yet all I could feel was the weight of every gaze that landed on me.

I sat beside Idris at the head of the table, the sheer opulence of the banquet enough to make my stomach churn. Golden platters were piled high with food I couldn't name, enchanted lights dancing above us, and musicians playing a lilting tune that seemed almost too cheerful for the tension lingering in the air.

War was on the horizon and a party of this magnitude seemed out of place. I understood why—there were deals to be made, alliances to strengthen, but it all seemed trivial in the face of what was coming.

"Eat," Idris murmured, his voice low enough that

only I could hear. He leaned in, his lips brushing the mating mark on my shoulder. "You haven't touched a thing."

I forced a small smile, my fingers brushing the edge of my goblet. "I'm not sure I can."

"Where's my brave wife?" he asked, his hand squeezing mine under the table. The gesture was subtle, but the steadiness of his touch sent a flicker of calm through me. "They're watching you, yes, but they're also trying to figure out how you managed to survive everything thrown at you."

His words brought a faint smirk to my lips. "When they find out, do you think they'll clue me in?"

Across the table, Kian and Xavier were deep in conversation with Talek, who seemed far too at ease for someone who'd just joined the council. I still hadn't forgiven him for letting us walk right into a trap with Selene. His sharp features and easy smile belied the calculating look in his eyes, and I made a mental note to keep an eye on him.

As the banquet continued, I found myself lost in the ebb and flow of conversation around me. Plates were passed, goblets refilled, and laughter rang through the hall, but I barely tasted the food. My gaze kept drifting to Idris, who was listening intently to one of the council members. His hand rested on the table, fingers threaded with mine in a silent reassurance.

Idris leaned closer, his voice a soft murmur against my ear. He could speak inside my head anytime he wanted, but I had a feeling he enjoyed the way my body reacted to him. "We've done enough, my Queen. We can leave whenever you're ready."

I glanced at him, startled. "We can just leave?"

His lips curved into a faint smile. "Queen's prerogative."

Relief washed over me, tempered only by the weight of what leaving meant. Every time I had been with someone before, it had been natural, unspoken, organic. This was different. This was deliberate—a ritual of sorts—and I didn't know what was expected of me.

Idris rose, his movement drawing the room's attention. "My lords and ladies," he began, his voice carrying effortlessly. "Tonight, we celebrate a new era for Credour. But my Queen and I must take our leave."

He extended his hand, his golden eyes warm and insistent. "Shall we?"

Taking his hand, I let him guide me from the

room. The applause followed us, a thunderous wave that faded as we stepped into the quiet corridor.

The cool air was a relief against my flushed skin, and Idris' thumb brushed softly over my knuckles, grounding me. "Are you ready?" he asked, his voice a blend of anticipation and promise.

I nodded, my breath catching under the weight of his gaze.

His rare, unguarded smile sent a flutter through me. "Good. Because tonight, you're all mine."

The words sent a delicious shiver down my spine, but with it, came a wave of nervous energy. My body reacted to his presence, my mating mark pulsing faintly where his lips had brushed earlier, but my mind wrestled with the weight of expectation.

By the time we reached his chambers, my nerves were wound so tightly I thought I might snap. The familiar dark-red walls of his bedroom glowed warmly under the flickering mage lights and the low crackle of the fire in the grate. It was exactly as I remembered it from the first time I'd seen it—when he'd rescued me from my first dream walk as I stumbled through the Dreaming, disoriented and afraid. Idris had been there, steady and unyielding, anchoring me, keeping me safe.

I'd wanted him then, though I hadn't understood

it at the time. And now? Now, I wanted him even more.

Idris closed the door behind us with a quiet finality, the sound sending a jolt of awareness through me. He moved with the easy confidence of someone completely in control, his golden eyes never leaving mine as he crossed the room. The tension in my chest tightened further as he stopped just short of touching me, his presence a magnetic pull that I craved.

"You don't have to be nervous, my brave one," he rumbled, his voice like silk over gravel.

I opened my mouth to deny it, to brush off the twisting in my stomach as something insignificant, but the way his gaze softened stopped me. He saw through me—he always did.

I hesitated, searching for the right words. I knew we needed to complete the bond—that it might help in some way—but the reasonings were so muddled that I didn't know which way was up anymore. I just kept remembering needing his kiss in Everhold as Kian and Xavier shared me. How right it had felt— how special. I'd wanted him with everything in me then—still did.

"I just..."

His lips curved into a faint smile, his hand coming up to brush a stray strand of hair from my face. "This isn't about expectation," he said gently. "This is about us. Nothing else matters."

His words settled something inside me, the sincerity in his tone wrapping around my frayed edges like a balm. Idris's hand slid from my cheek to the curve of my neck, his thumb tracing the edge of my mating mark as he circled me. The faint pulse of his magic brushed against mine, a subtle invitation. My heart skipped a beat, the tension in my chest shifting from anxiety to anticipation.

"I'll wait as long as you need," he murmured against my ear, his voice a low rumble that sent a delicious heat pooling in my sex. "But if you'll let me, I'll show you there's nothing to fear."

I swallowed hard, the warmth of his skin against my back grounding me.

"I trust you," I whispered, the words spilling from my mouth, ringing with truth.

"Good," he growled in my ear, his hand moving to my throat. His grip was light but firm and he tilted my head to the side. He ran his nose down the column of my neck. "I fucking love the way you smell when you're turned on."

Biting my lip, I covered his hand at my throat with my own, my fingers lightly tracing the scars that crisscrossed his flesh. His fingers flexed, tightening as he tasted my skin, and I fought off a moan. I'd always been attracted to Idris—even the first time I'd met him in a dream that was not a dream.

His presence—his desire—had always struck me, consumed me. From that very first time with his fangs at my throat, I'd been a goner. I'd fought, I'd argued, but somehow, I'd always known I would end up right here in his bedroom exactly where I started.

"It's almost as good as your scent when you come. I swear, it drives me insane how much I need you. Will you let me show you, my Queen?"

I couldn't help but nod—not knowing what he meant but needing to find out all the same. In the next moment, it was as if he'd pulled back the veil of his emotions, allowing everything to flow through the bond we already shared—the one that seemed so much stronger since he'd bitten me.

His desire was so strong, my knees buckled, the flames of need nearly burning me from the inside out. A moan escaped my throat, his yearning like a drug that threatened to drown me.

How had he been holding all of this back? How had I never noticed before? And why did being craved this way make me ache to let him do anything he wanted to me? Why did it make me lose all reason, all sense?

And why didn't I care?

"Do you see? Every second of every day, I need you like this. I'm nearly blind with it. Never in all my years have I wanted someone the way I want you, Vale. Will you let me have you?" His grip on my throat tightened, eliciting a needy whimper from my lips, even as he closed the connection in the bond. But just like a fire, once started, it wouldn't burn out easily.

My skin was on fire, my sex ached with need. My dress felt too tight, too hot. I needed it off, needed him to help me. I—

"I need the words, Vale," he growled in my ear, the vibration cascading down my body like a caress. "Tell me I can have you, and I'll help you out of that dress. I'll take care of you. I'll do anything you want me to."

It was a deal with the devil, but he was my devil— my husband, my Beast. Turning my head, I stared into those golden irises that had sealed my fate the first time I'd laid eyes on them. "Yes. But... don't shut me out. Give it back. I want to feel you—all of you. Let me see all of it."

His gaze darkened as he pulled back the curtain, and in that second, I knew I was absolutely done for. Idris could have whatever he wanted from me—

anything, everything. For the first time today, or maybe ever, I reached up on my toes and pressed my lips to his.

Idris wasn't taking, I was giving.

I just hoped it wasn't more than I'd be willing to lose.

CHAPTER 23
IDRIS

My wife wanted me on my knees.

She hadn't asked for it or even let the thought cross her pretty little brain, but the way she'd just cut me open, I would gladly kneel at her feet and give her anything she asked for.

Fuck.

I'd never let anyone in like I did her, and I couldn't say I regretted it. My fingers flexed on the delicate column of her throat, and the whimper that came from her nearly unmanned me. I'd been strung tight since she'd let me watch her come, sandwiched between my two closest friends.

Gods, I wanted to see that again. Her skin flushed with desire, her eyes half-lidded and glowing, her perfect lips swollen from kisses as her skin glistened with sweat. Only, I wanted to be the cause of her mindless need. I wanted to be the one she clung to, the reason she screamed.

But as much as I needed her naked and under me, Vale needed my care more. Still, that didn't mean I had to play fair. It was high time I used my magic for my own gain just this once.

Without so much as a snap of my fingers, the golden tendrils of my power curled around her, unfastening every button on Vale's dress, uncinching every tie. In seconds, she was free of the gorgeous if cumbersome confection. As I pulled her from the fabric, I ended the kiss, pulling back to admire my handiwork.

"*Fuck*, you are perfection," I groaned, admiring her white dragon scale corset, her lace underwear, her sheer stockings. Gods, she was wrapped up like a present, and all I wanted to do was stare at her. From the top of her head to the tips of her toes and everything in between, I was a gods-be-damned goner for this woman.

I'd seen it, I'd known it, and yet, I couldn't imagine my luck. Fate had decided to choose this amazing woman for me, and despite my flaws, despite my limitations, she still managed to care about me.

Dropping to my knees, I unfastened the clasp on her heels, pulling them from her feet before going to work on her stockings. With everything I removed, with every inch of skin exposed, I worshipped it with my mouth. And for tonight at least, I wouldn't have to share.

She was mine.

All mine.

Curling my fingers into the tops of her stockings, I relished the shiver vibrating her body as I ran my lips over the tops of her thighs while pulling them down and off. Her scent had my cock aching, the delicious perfume of her desire making me ravenous.

I had to taste her, needed her cream on my tongue. I'd been gentle with her dress, but this scrap of silk was shredded in an instant, my control slipping. I just had to get one taste—one taste and I could concentrate. One taste and I could go back to being gentle.

"Who said I wanted gentle?" Vale murmured, the throaty cadence to her voice nearly making my eyes roll back into my head.

"I didn't say anything," I replied, meeting her

glowing gaze. Had I said that out loud? I didn't think I did.

Her skin was lit from within, her magic rising with her desire. She tapped her temple. "What do you always say? It's not snooping if you're yelling at me. Not once did I say I wanted gentle. In fact, I'd prefer it if you weren't. I said I wanted all of you. Now give it to me."

Tilting my head to the side, I let my lips curve into an impish smile. "Tell me, my Queen, do you enjoy being restrained?"

Vale rubbed her thighs together, an answer in and of itself, but I'd let her tell me.

"Sometimes. Sometimes I want to touch."

Without giving her time to think about it, I latched onto her hips, bringing her sex to my lips. I didn't lick even though I needed to. No, I just let my breath skate over her curls, over the soaking wet cunt that needed my mouth on it. "So if I told you that the only way you'd get my mouth on you was if you kept your hands to yourself…"

"I'd need you to help me. I—I want to touch you. So much. I want to taste you, I—"

Gripping her harder, I growled at how vocal she was being. It was so fucking hot, I gave her a long lick as a reward. Her taste exploded onto my tongue, the pure honey from her cunt so godsdamned good, my cock pulsed.

I couldn't get enough—there would never be enough.

Before her knees could buckle, my magic wrapped around her wrists and brought her hands above her head. In an instant, she was trussed up to the post of my bed, and I had her legs over my shoulders.

"What about now? Do you like being restrained now?"

Breaths heaving, her perfect tits trying to escape her corset, the flush of desire blooming across her chest, I again knew the answer already, but I wanted to hear it, anyway.

"I... I... I like it. Can you..." She circled her hips, needing what only I could give her.

"Can I what, my Queen? Fuck you with my tongue? Make you come on my face?"

Gratefully, she nodded. "Yes. All of that. *Please.*"

I gave her another long, slow lick, this time circling her clit before sucking it into my mouth. "'Please,' you say? So polite. Say it again, and maybe I'll let you come soon."

Mulish resolve took over her expression. Her hips

bucked as her eyes flashed, but she didn't say please. My brave one had claws, but I'd always known that.

Smiling, I landed a solid smack to her exposed ass cheek, her surprise only interrupted by her moan. So my brave one liked to be spanked? I'd remember that.

"Good girls get what they ask for when they say please." I spread her wide, licking her from clit to cunt and back again. Then I landed another smack to her ass before filling her with my fingers.

She tried to buck her hips to take my fingers deeper, but I wrapped another thread of my power around her hips, locking her in place. "Say please and I'll give you everything you want. My mouth, my fingers, my cock. I'll fuck you until you can't breathe."

I licked her again, thrusting my fingers just once before stopping. Then I gave her the rest of my desire, ramping her up so high, I could feel her cunt pulse around my fingers. Sweat broke out over her skin and her eyes went glassy.

Trembling, she bit her lip, trying and failing to move. Then Vale released a moan that had me freeing my cock from my leathers just to get a little relief.

"Yo-you feel this? All of it?"

"Around you? Always."

Shakily, she nodded as she met my gaze. "Please. I'll beg if I have to. Please, Idris."

I'd told her good girls got what they asked for, and I'd meant it. She barely got my name past her lips before my mouth was on her, licking, sucking, tasting every part of her. I wanted her to drown me in her honey.

No, I fucking needed it.

Her greedy cunt sucked at my fingers, soaking them as she kept trying and failing to roll her hips. A smile curled my mouth, and I set more of my magic free. Soon that corset was gone, and I let my power roll over her skin like it was my hands, my lips all over her.

Thrashing her head, she couldn't stop shaking, the moans spilling from her throat music to my fucking ears. Then I released her hips and hung on, fucking her with my tongue as she fucked herself on my fingers.

Her release hit her in a flash, and then it was as if she were touching me everywhere. Her magic raced over my flesh, curling my need higher, my desire adding to her orgasm, prolonging it. I couldn't hold off any longer. I needed her under me.

Releasing her from the threads of my magic, she wilted into my arms. Instantly, her lips found mine, and she tasted herself on my tongue as she wrapped herself around me. Her magic wasn't as careful as mine was. She ripped at my clothes, the fabric shredding as she tore it away.

"I need you, Idris. I need you now."

As soon as her fiery skin met mine, I was lost. I'd give her whatever she wanted, whatever she needed. She pushed us, and I landed on my back on the floor, all thought of finesse long gone. Vale was ravenous.

It made sense. She had all her desire and mine.

Now I wanted hers.

"Pull the veil back," I whispered as I latched onto her hips, stopping her from moving us faster than I wanted to go. "Let me see your mind, your need. I can hear it, but I want to feel it."

Trembling, she opened herself up to me, crumbling every wall between us. Her desire slammed into me, compounding my own, driving me insane. Gods, how were we ever supposed to satisfy this?

"We aren't," she whispered into my mind, her sweet voice so much softer, so much clearer than it had ever been. "I'll always want you. You'll always want me. We'll never get enough."

Never get enough? I could live with that.

What I couldn't live with was fucking her on the floor. My Queen deserved a bed. I rose to my feet with a very naked Vale wrapped around me, her lips at my throat, her hands in my hair. Scraps of my tunic and leathers hung from my arms and legs, but it didn't matter.

What mattered was the look in her eyes when I fit the head of my cock at her opening. What mattered was her flushed skin and glassy eyes, the desire that raced down my spine as I thrust inside her for the first time.

This was right, this was exactly right. Nothing had ever felt this good, this perfect. Not in centuries had anything ever made me feel whole again, and yet, here she was.

Vale reached for my face, bringing my lips to hers. And as I kissed her, I began to thrust, aching to hear every hitch of her breath, every moan. The pair of us were insatiable, and I fucked her with abandon, powering inside as her walls closed around me like a vise.

"More. Please, Idris."

"So fucking greedy, my Queen. I fucking love how greedy you are."

Her fingernails raked against my skin, and I realized I hadn't even begun to see her greed.

"Gods, you fuck me so good. More."

She wanted more?

I'd fucking give her more. Letting my magic loose, I touched her everywhere.

"Yes, gods, yes. Give me everything."

She needed more?

The leash I had on my darker side snapped, and I gave in to my baser instincts, shedding my tenderness, my refinement, my carefully crafted control. As she requested, I wasn't gentle as I fucked my wife. My senses in tune with every hitch of her breath, every tremble, I let my power wash over her, kissing her everywhere, licking her everywhere, biting, tasting, she felt it all.

I drove her higher, further, her cries egging me on until all I could feel was her pleasure, all I knew was her scent, her moans, her body against mine.

Her back arched as her eyes rolled into the back of her head, her release barreling toward us so fast I became lost in it. I trailed my lips over her neck to her delicate collarbones to her dusky-pink nipple. Sucking it into my mouth, I raked my fangs over the stiff peak, laving the sting with my tongue. At the touch of my fangs, her hips bucked violently, her orgasm so close, I could almost taste it.

The urge to bite, to mark, to claim her raced down my spine.

"Please let me come. Please. Oh, gods, please."

Who could deny her when she asked so nicely? Curling my arms around her, I brought her mouth to mine, losing myself in her kiss. Her release slammed into us both, the sharp ache followed by bliss too acute, it could only take me with her. Groaning, I felt my fangs lengthen as my power rose. Without thought, I struck, my fangs sliding into her skin over her near-complete mating mark.

At the first taste of her blood in my mouth, my balls tightened, and I exploded, ecstasy washing over us in a blanket of pleasure. The lightning of the bond raced through me, changing every cell in my body as Vale took root in my soul.

Vale was my home, my life, my heart. She was everything I was or would ever be. She was forged into every pore of my skin, every bone. Even with Rune still connected to me, I'd never felt as whole as I did at that moment.

Pulling back, I watched as my magic infused into her skin, changing the mark from just a faint gold design over her shoulder to an intricate web of magic cascading down her arm and up her neck. It shimmered in the darkness, glowing like a beacon, calling me to her.

My lips fell to the already-healed bite, and Vale moaned, her sex pulsing around me as her need rose again. Or was it mine? I couldn't tell—didn't want to.

"I need you again, my Queen. Can you take me?"

Vale rolled her hips, her mouth too busy at my neck to reply.

Then again, her mind, her heart, her cunt was calling me.

I'd be stupid not to answer.

CHAPTER 24
VALE

"*Come to me.*"

Rune's voice tore through the peaceful bliss of slumber, startling me awake, but it was so faint, I struggled to discern if it had been a dream or reality.

Limbs heavy, the remnants of pleasure weighed me down as Idris' warmth flooded through every part of my body. His arm draped over my waist, his legs tangled with mine, his face serene in the faint light from the fireplace, there was no place I would rather be.

I'd never seen him so unguarded, so relaxed. It was as if the last two hundred years had been a terrible nightmare and now it was over. The golden shimmer of my mating mark pulsed in the darkness, the swirling design reaching from the back of my hand all the way up my arm and neck and into my hairline.

Idris showed me the full extent last night in the shower, his mouth and tongue tracing every line as he worshipped me again and again. The lines reminded me of Kian and Xavier and Idris' tattoos, taking pieces of them somehow and inking them into my skin, the golden marks showing the world who my heart belonged to.

The delicious ache between my legs had me considering waking him again. Maybe this time with my mouth. Watching him writhe right before he lost his mind was becoming my favorite pastime, especially since that link between our minds had yet to fade. Every swipe of my tongue, every circle of my hips had him coming undone, and I felt all of it.

"You can't ignore me, my Queen. There's no time."

The bond hummed with his urgency, pressing against my mind like a roiling thunderstorm ready to break. This was no dream. Any time Rune had woken me, it had been for a damn good reason. Slowly, I sat up, my gaze searching the room for danger. Other than the steady cadence of Idris' breathing, there was not even a hint of movement.

But still, a thread of danger filled every pore,

every cell of my being, making me reach for the jeweled dagger Kian gifted to me what seemed like ages ago.

"No time for what? What is going on?"

A frustrated growl filtered through the bond. *"I can't explain. Get dressed and get down here. Now. It has to be now."*

I slipped from the bed, careful not to disturb Idris, though every step away from his warmth made my chest ache. Moving to the dressing room, I quickly pulled on my leathers, managing not to forget my corset and boots as I grabbed my second dagger and belt.

"Rune, what is it?" I asked, hastily lacing the dragon scale tight to my chest. My boots thudded softly against the stone floor as I cut through the warding on the room, replacing it as soon as I passed through the door.

There was no answer, and soon I broke out into a run, racing through the nearly deserted hallways, the dregs of the party still winding down as the faint strains of laughter echoed through the castle.

My gaze lingered on the double doors I once destroyed, the throne room looming like a shadow in the corridor before I turned left, reaching for the entrance to the caverns. Days ago, I'd made this same trek, only I'd never reached my destination. Swallowing hard, I gripped the hilt of my dagger, Rune's fear threading through the bond like a death knell.

Gods, this had to be bad.

Shakily, I pulled open the cavern door and my stomach plummeted at the sight of the stairs. Darkness enveloped my path, and it was as if I were back under the mountain, headed to the overseer, praying not to fall to my death. Each step sent daggers through my heart, and the closer I got to Rune, the worse it got. The twisting, winding descent into the caverns seemed to take forever, the air growing colder with each step.

By the time I got to the bottom, I was sweating, shaking, nausea roiling in my gut. But only some of it was mine. White-hot agony lanced through my middle, making me cry out as I fell to my knees.

This wasn't me.

This was Rune.

Rune was in danger.

"What's happening? Why are you in so much pain? Why won't you answer me?"

Staggering to my feet, I shuffled forward, the pain only getting worse the closer I got to him. But I had to keep moving, had to get to him. Dread filled my belly with each step, spoiling every bit of happiness, every good thought, every sense of peace I'd ever had.

Rounding a giant stalagmite, the giant dragon came into view. He was on his belly trying to stand, but his legs wouldn't hold him. Instantly, tears filled my eyes because a part of me knew there was no fixing this.

"I've run out of time, my Queen. I thought I had more, but..."

Choking down a sob, I pressed my forehead to the side of his face. "What can I do? How can I help? Do you want me to call Idris? I—"

His response was immediate, his voice a low rumble echoing through my thoughts. *"There's no time for goodbyes or apologies. You've bonded with him now. The curse has loosened just enough for me to tell you how to break it. Will you help me? I can't do it on my own."*

My stomach churned, fear and sorrow warring within me as I tried and failed to swallow the lump in my throat. "A-anything," I croaked, tears falling down my face in earnest. "You know that. I can never repay your kindness, your protection. You've saved my life too many times to count. Anything you need."

His deep rumble reverberated in my head. *"I couldn't tell you before. Zamarra's curse wouldn't let me. But now that you've bonded with Idris, I can speak —though not for long."*

I stepped closer, the weight of his words settling heavily on my chest. *"Then tell me. Tell me how to break the curse."*

Rune's gaze bore into mine, and for the first time, I saw something in his eyes that I hadn't before— regret. *"The curse can only be broken through sacrifice."*

"W-what kind of sacrifice?" I stuttered, my heart hammering because I already knew. I knew it like I knew my own mind.

"Me," he said simply, the word a dagger plunging straight into my soul.

"No." I staggered back, shaking my head as tears cascaded down my face, dripping from my chin. "Not that. Never that. There has to be another way."

"There isn't," Rune growled, his voice resonating with unrelenting finality that shredded my heart. *"This curse was crafted to ensure Idris and I would remain fractured, powerless. Zamarra designed it to keep him weak, to steal all the power of the realm, to rule over the Waking and the Dreaming. To undo it, I must die."*

"I can't," I choked. "Rune, I can't do that."

"You have to," he said, his voice softening, though

the command in it remained. *"If you don't, Idris will never be whole again. He will never be strong enough to defeat Arden, and the realm and magic itself will fall."*

I clenched my fists, my vision blurring as the tears came faster. "Why does it have to be this way? Why does everything always have to cost so much?"

Rune's voice rumbled with quiet sorrow. *"Because that's the nature of power, my Queen. It forever demands a sacrifice. This time it's mine."*

I sank to my knees, the weight of his words crushing me. *"I don't want to lose you."*

"You're not losing me," he said gently, his massive head lowering until his glowing eyes were level with mine. *"I'll always be with you. Through Idris. Through the bond. Through the kingdom we've fought to protect."*

But I knew it was a lie.

If I did this, I would lose him forever. Rune had given me so much, but most of all, he'd given me his senses. I could scent the falseness before he ever said it. Before I could respond, the ground trembled beneath us, dust falling from the cavern's ceiling. Rune's head snapped up, his eyes narrowing. *"The castle is under attack. We have no more time. You must do it now."*

Panic surged through me, and I rose to my feet, clutching the daggers at my waist. *"By who?"*

But again, I knew that, too. Somehow the mages had moved much faster than we thought they could.

"I know Girovia wants to keep this curse unbroken, but we can't let them stop you. They might say they're here for Idris, but you and I both know they're here for you," Rune said, his voice grim. *"Vale, listen to me. You don't have time to think this through. If you don't act now, everything will be lost."*

I shook my head, stepping back as fresh tears streamed down my face. *"I can't, Rune. I won't."*

Before Rune could respond, the faint echo of footsteps reached my ears. I turned to see Idris, Xavier, and Kian entering the cavern, their expressions a mixture of fury and fear.

"Vale!" Idris's voice was sharp, his golden eyes narrowing as he took in the scene. "What are you doing down here?"

Choking down my sobs, I met their eyes—amber, ice, and gold—and my heart broke. "Rune knows how to break the curse. He needs my help."

All three of them froze, but Idris' power swirled around his body. "What?" His gaze flew to Rune and back to me. "All this time? How?"

I shook my head as I covered my mouth, doing

everything I could to keep him out of my head. He didn't need to share this with me. It wasn't fair.

Rune rumbled low, his eyes glowing brighter. *"You must kill me, Vale. Stab me right in the heart. And then you must stab Idris in his. Only through your power can we merge, and the curse be undone."*

My knees went weak, but I stayed standing by sheer force of will. That much power running through me wouldn't just be Rune's end. It would be mine, too. Agony lanced my heart as I looked at my mates, knowing I would be breaking every promise I ever made.

My promises to stay, to never leave them behind, to stay alive. All lies.

"Sacrifice," I murmured into his mind, realizing just how cruel Zamarra was.

Idris wouldn't share her, so she made it so the only one who could break his curse would be someone who had more than one mate. She wanted him alone, separated from his power, so the method of breaking had to kill the other half of his soul. And for just desserts, right when he fell for me, I would in turn sacrifice everything—my magic, my body, my life.

All for him.

Cruel was too kind a word for it.

Idris's expression twisted into rage, his steps eating the distance between us. "No. Absolutely not. You're not doing this."

I backed away, pulling my dagger from its sheath as my heart hammered in my chest. "I don't want to, Idris. But if I don't, the curse—"

"*No*," he roared, his golden eyes blazing with fury. "I don't give a fuck about the curse. Fuck this kingdom, fuck magic, fuck everything. I will not lose you. I forbid it."

Xavier moved closer, blue flames of his power swirling around his feet. His icy-blue eyes narrowed as he tried to penetrate my mind. I couldn't let him. None of them needed to feel this.

"Why are you shutting us out, Vale? There's too much at stake, my love. Please let us in."

Black scales rippled up Kian's flesh, his usual smirk long gone as he slowly approached, his hands raised. "Tell us what's going on, little witch. Please, just talk to—"

The castle shook once more, stalactites crumbling around us as the attack began in earnest.

Rune's voice was quieter now, his large body fading fast under the strain of the curse. *"Vale, there's no more time. You have to do it now."*

I looked at their faces one more time, knowing this might be my last.

"I love you—all of you. I want you to know that," I whispered, trying to swallow past the lump in my throat. I thought we'd have more time. My gaze turned to Kian and Xavier. "Find her for me when this is all over? Find her and keep her safe. Tell her I did this for her, okay?"

The look of betrayal on Xavier's face was enough to make me rethink my decision, and Kian's devastation was a knife to my heart. They'd never forgive me for this. As one, all three of them moved, trying to stop me, but they didn't make it very far. Raising my shield, I kept them all back, knocking them off their feet as they fought to breach my magic.

My heart shattered as I turned to face Rune, the weight of his trust and the enormity of what I was about to do crushing me.

"I'm sorry," I whispered, tears blurring my vision as I touched my forehead to Rune's cheek. "I'm so sorry."

"Your apologies are not necessary. It's been an honor watching over you, my Queen. I'm ready."

He lifted his head, giving me a straight shot to his chest. My small dagger wouldn't work for this. I'd have to do it myself. Sobs tore from my throat as I formed a sword of light in my hand.

"See you later, okay?"

Rune's body heaved, his breath rattling in his chest. We were out of time. Why was there never enough time? I screamed as I plunged the sword into Rune's heart, and his roar of pain mingled with my scream, shaking the very foundations of the castle. Blood poured from his wound, drenching my hands.

His massive form shimmered, seeming to dissolve into a cloud of smoke before my very eyes. The crimson cloud wrapped around me like a suffocating shroud, stealing my breath, my strength as it cut at every inch of my skin.

"No!" Idris' scream ripped through the air, his rage breaking through every barrier, every ward my mind had. He lunged toward me, he alone cutting through my shield, leaving Kian and Xavier behind as he sprinted for us. Kian and Xavier slammed against the golden barrier, their shouts muffled as I welcomed Idris.

"I'm sorry," I whispered again, my voice breaking as my knees buckled. "I-it's t-the only way to s-save you."

Idris' fury gave way to anguish as he got to me, his hands trembling as they reached for me. I leaned up, pressing my lips to his, pouring every ounce of love and regret into the bond we shared.

"Please, baby. Please don't do this. You can't leave us now. Please." He put a trembling hand to my face, brushing back my hair. "I love you, Vale. *Please.*"

Nodding, I pressed my forehead to his. "I love you, too. I w-want you to r-remember t-that."

Then, with a single motion, I drove a sword of light into his heart.

Betrayal and shock contorted his face, twisting my heart. The smoke that had once consumed me now surged into him, his body jerking as it enveloped him, filling his mouth, his nose. And when it left me, it felt like I was being torn in two, blood pouring from my nose, my mouth.

My heart slowed, stuttered. My breaths hitched. My sight dimmed.

"I'm sorry," I whispered through the bond, knowing there would be nothing left of me when this was all over.

Idris' form shimmered, shifting, and growing as the curse unraveled, revealing the true power that had been denied him for so long.

The last thing I saw before darkness claimed me was Idris, his body transforming into a massive red and gold dragon, his roar shaking the very walls of the cavern as the last of my magic died.

CHAPTER 25

XAVIER

The cavern was too still, the kind of silence that followed devastation, thick and suffocating. The world was falling apart around us, but it was right here in this little bubble, everything was dead, gone, ripped apart and broken.

Smoke and the sharp tang of blood lingered in the air, mingling with the acrid odor of spent magic. I knelt in the devastation, cradling Vale's lifeless body against my chest. Her head lolled, her black hair tangled and streaked with blood and ash, stark against the pale hue of her lifeless body.

She was cold. Too cold.

I'd felt death before—seen it too many times to count. But none of it had prepared me for this.

Not *her*.

"Vale," I whispered, my voice cracking as I pressed my forehead to hers. The warmth of my tears traced down her cheek, mingling with her dried blood.

She didn't stir.

She didn't move.

Behind me, Idris' massive dragon form shifted, his claws scraping against stone as he paced. The cavern trembled faintly beneath his weight, the heat of his presence palpable even from here. But he hadn't come closer.

Not once.

"She's gone," he growled, his voice low and guttural, vibrating in my mind through the bond we shared. *"I felt her die."*

My chest felt like it was caught in a vise, his words a blade twisting deep. "No," I rasped, shaking my head. "She's not gone. She can't be."

"You think I don't want to believe that?" Idris snapped, his voice sharper, angrier. His golden eyes burned as they locked onto mine, molten fury radiating off him. *"I felt it, Xavier. She's dead."*

"She's *not!*" My shout echoed through the cavern, loud enough to make Kian, who stood silent in the shadows, lift his gaze. My grip on Vale tightened, as though holding her closer would somehow pull her back from wherever she'd gone.

"Please, baby. Please. Come back to us."

Idris snarled, his wings flaring as he turned away. His massive form was tense, every muscle coiled tight as if the sheer force of his grief and rage would tear him apart. But he didn't come closer. He wouldn't. Not even as the castle rocked with another blast, as the ceiling above us crumbled.

"Idris," I whispered, my voice clogged with tears I didn't want to let free. "She broke herself for you. For us. And you won't even—"

Already I felt the surge of my power, the dam breaking as magic flooded back to us. I wanted so badly to heal her, to pull her back, but I knew it was above me now. And if he didn't believe in her—if he didn't trust that Fate would never be this cruel—we would never get her back.

"*Stop.*" His command was a growl, low and lethal. He turned his head slightly, one blazing golden eye fixing on me. "*If I touch her... if I let myself believe for even a second that she could come back... and she doesn't...*" His voice cracked, the words hanging heavy in the air. "*I won't survive it.*"

My throat burned with unshed tears, but I didn't look away. "You're her mate," I whispered, the words raw. "If you don't hold her now, you'll regret it for the rest of your life."

Idris didn't answer. He didn't move. He only stared at her limp form in my arms, her bloody fingers, her still chest.

Kian stepped forward, his boots scuffing against the stone. His amber eyes flicked to me, then to Vale, his expression unreadable. "She wouldn't give up on us," he said, his voice low and rough. "We won't give up on her."

"She's already gone," Idris muttered, the words almost too soft to hear. *"I can't—I love her too much. Please don't let me hope."*

"She's still *here*," I snapped, my frustration boiling over. "I can feel it."

Kian moved closer, kneeling beside me. His claws flexed, his gaze flicking over Vale's still form before meeting mine. Slowly, deliberately, he placed a hand over her chest, where her heart should have been beating. His eyes widened, and he nodded.

"Not a heartbeat, but magic," he murmured, his voice a mixture of wonder and desperation.

Idris froze, his massive frame going utterly still.

His wings folded tight against his back as he turned, his claws scraping against the stone. He loomed over us, his golden eyes narrowing as if daring us to lie.

"Check for yourself," I said, my voice raw as I stared up at him. "Feel it, Idris."

For a moment, he didn't move. Then, with a low rumble of hesitation, he lowered his massive head. His nostrils flared as he inhaled deeply, his gaze locked on Vale's lifeless form. Slowly, carefully, his snout pressed to her chest.

His golden eyes widened, and for a fleeting moment, I thought I saw hope flicker in their depths.

"It's there," he rumbled, his voice softer now, almost reverent. *"It's faint, but it's there."*

Relief surged through me, stealing my breath. My hands tightened on Vale's shoulders as I leaned down, my lips brushing her temple. "Vale, come back to us," I whispered. "Please."

But she didn't stir.

Idris stepped back, his wings twitching, doubt clouding his thoughts. *"She's gone too far,"* he said, his voice hollow. *"Whatever's left... it won't be enough."*

"You don't know that," I snapped, glaring up at him. "We've all come back from the brink before. Why is she any different?"

"Because she's dead, Xavier," Idris growled, his tail lashing against the cavern floor. *"Not dying. Not hurt. Dead. No bond, no heartbeat, no soul left to hold onto."* His golden eyes burned as they locked onto mine. *"I begged her not to. I begged, and still, she sacrificed everything. You think I don't want to save her? That I wouldn't trade places with her in an instant? But this—this is beyond any of us."*

I looked down at Vale, my tears falling freely now. Her chest didn't rise, her heart didn't beat, but there was *something*. A flicker of warmth, a faint hum of magic lingering beneath her skin. It wasn't much, but it was enough.

"She's not gone," I said softly, the words more for myself than anyone else. "Not yet."

The cavern fell silent once more, the oppressive weight of grief settling over us. Idris turned away again, his tail snapping as his gaze turned to the fight above us. *"I've lost her—my love, my Queen, my heart. I won't lose my kingdom with it."*

Kian rested a hand on my shoulder, his touch gentle despite the rawness of his emotions.

"We'll fight for her," he said, his voice steady. "Whatever it takes."

I nodded, though my chest ached with the weight of it all.

"Stay with her," I whispered, my heart aching, but

knowing only Kian could keep her safe right then. "I'll watch over him."

Whatever it took, I'd bring her back. Because losing Vale...

That wasn't something any of us could survive.

CHAPTER 26
VALE

Death was a lot more painful than I thought it would be.

I'd always assumed that once I left this world it wouldn't hurt anymore, but I couldn't be more wrong. The air around me felt like a dark blanket filled with stone, as though the magic that had just been unleashed still lingered, thick and oppressive. My body throbbed with echoes of my agony, my limbs leaden as the frigid ground of the cavern seeped into my bones. Each breath sawed through my lungs, every inhale scraping against my ribs like sandpaper.

But I shouldn't be breathing. I shouldn't be in pain. I—

And the pain wasn't just mine. Rune's presence still lingered, even though I knew he was gone. His essence

—his very soul—had surged through me, fracturing every part of who I was before it merged with Idris. I could still taste the metallic tang of his blood, feel the weight of his soul leaving mine, hear the agony of his roar as I... as I...

And now... now I was empty.

"Rune?" I whimpered into the void of my mind—into this dark, fractured place that should be death but wasn't. "Are you there?"

But there was no answer.

There wouldn't be.

Not anymore.

Because he was gone. He was gone, and I would never get him back.

I tried to think of what he would say to me if he were here now, but all I could do was curl into a ball as gut-wrenching sorrow tore me in half. I'd done it. I'd broken Idris' curse, and now I was paying the price. Because there was always a price to pay, wasn't there?

When my sobs subsided, I pressed my trembling hands to the stone and weakly tried to push myself upright. My body screamed in protest, my vision swimming as dark spots clawed at the edges of my sight.

A pulse of the bond with my mates thrummed faintly in my mind. It was distant, fractured.

And that was my fault.

I'd broken all of my promises, turned every vow I made them into a lie. And now with Rune gone, I—

The echo of a dragon's roar had me shoving from the ground in earnest as a lance of white-hot agony ricocheted through my whole body. The world tilted as I managed to get vertical, my back pressed against a jagged wall.

My fingers brushed over the blood that still stained my skin, Rune's sacrifice a visceral reminder of what I had done. My chest tightened, a sob clawing its way up my throat. I had killed him. I had killed Rune. And Idris... Idris had watched me do it.

I squeezed my eyes shut, tears slipping free despite my best efforts. How could I face him after this? How could I face any of them? I shattered everything—my bond with Idris, my trust with Kian and Xavier—all in the name of a choice I never wanted to make.

But I'd made it—I'd broken the curse.

Idris.

My heart fluttered in my chest, a spark of hope igniting. I'd watched him change, watched him accept Rune into himself. Maybe... maybe Rune was still alive inside him, and it was just me that...

Before the weight of my guilt could suffocate me entirely, a strange warmth began to spread through my chest. It wasn't the bond, nor was it my own magic.

This was something... else. Something brighter, purer. I gasped as the cavern around me blurred, the jagged walls and scattered debris melting into a haze of light so bright I had to shield my eyes from it.

When I could see again, I wasn't in the caverns anymore, and then I knew.

This wasn't death, and I wasn't on my way to meet Orrus. This was the Dreaming, and it was different from anything I had ever seen. Unlike when I'd been in the Dreaming before, this wasn't somewhere in Credour. It was twisted and bent, the whims of magic warping reality into this pocket of a place that didn't make any sense.

Starlit pathways floated in midair, their edges dissolving into streams of glittering light. Trees with crystalline branches stretched toward a sky that didn't exist, their roots anchored in nothingness. The air shimmered with an otherworldly hum, as if the realm itself were alive.

But something was wrong with this place. The edges of the Dreaming frayed, dark tendrils creeping in like ink spilled over water. That darkness coated everything, poisoning it. The crystal branches snapped and cracked, engulfed by the inky blackness, consumed by it. One by one, the stars died, the magic faded, until there was nothing but darkness.

The ground beneath my feet pulsed faintly, the cracks spidering outward as the oppressive energy I had felt earlier grew stronger. I... I'd been here before. I knew this place. It had been where I'd seen Nyrah, but—

"You shouldn't have come here."

The voice was cold and sharp, slicing through the dim like a blade. A cold light bloomed in the darkness, harsh and cutting. I had to shield my eyes from it until it dimmed ever so slightly. And just like when I'd been here with Idris, rocks cut into my palms as the tunnel finally came into view.

The blonde who had once been cowering at the end of the tunnel stood. I'd thought she was my sister, cold and alone, trapped in the darkness, but I couldn't have been more wrong. As soon as her cold gaze met mine, I knew.

Zamarra.

She stepped from the shadows, her smile just as cruel as the woman herself. Gone were the rags hanging from her skin, replaced with a gown of crystalline black, swirling around her legs like a living thing. Her eyes burned with an intensity that made my knees weak, her presence as commanding as it was terrifying. She wasn't just formidable—she was raw power, an ancient force that had been bound for far too long.

"Do you like my prison, cousin?" Zamarra hissed, her voice dripping with contempt. "Funny how life works out, right? All your toils, all your struggles, and look where it got you."

I stumbled back, my hands trembling as I reached for my daggers—daggers I no longer had. I called for my magic, but that, too, was long gone. I had nothing to fight her with. Nothing at all.

"I... I don't understand."

"Of course you don't," she spat, her lips curling into a cruel smile. "You're nothing more than a pawn in a game that's been going on long before you were born. But you've played your part well. And now, the Dreaming will pay the price for your interference."

My gaze fell to the jagged rocks at my feet, their iridescent sheen telling me exactly where I was.

Direveil. We were in Direveil and Zamarra had been bound in Lumentium. My heart stuttered as the truth slammed into me. Arden hadn't cared one bit about the mine. The rising quotas, the deaths, the tight fist of control.

We'd never been mining for Lumentium.

We'd been digging her out.

The ground beneath me trembled, cracks snapping through the ground, widening as the dark tendrils *spread farther. She stepped closer, her blue gaze melting into pure flame as it locked onto mine.*

"Do you feel it? The fracture you've helped me create? You've freed me, little queen. And now, there's no going back." She tilted her head to the side, her blonde hair flowing about her head as if she were underwater. "I really should be thanking you. And I will. Once you give me what I need."

Soon those tendrils of darkness latched onto my wrists and ankles, tethering me in place as she drifted toward me, her smile widening into a maw of sharp jagged teeth the closer she got.

"I don't have anything," I growled, fighting against the bonds. "And even if I did, I wouldn't give it to you."

"Oh, but you do. You always have. And make no mistake, you will give me what I want. Did you think I set this all up so he would get his freedom?" She clucked her tongue, shaking her head. "That there would be no consequences for denying me? Oh, no. If he thought that curse was bad, he really should have been paying more attention."

Zamarra lunged for me, her blackened fingers curled like claws aiming for my face. But before she could make contact, a blinding light erupted from behind me, forcing her to shield her eyes. My heart leapt, thinking it was Idris, but this felt so much different.

Hissing, Zamarra retreated, and I was hooked around my middle, the world swirling around me as I was pulled away from the poison of her magic. The light continued to bloom around me, swallowing the darkness, until my feet touched a soft tuft of grass so green it couldn't be real—none of it could.

I turned, shielding my eyes as the light grew even brighter, warmer, until it consumed everything. When the light dimmed, I found myself standing before a figure unlike any I had ever seen. She was made of pure light, her form shifting and shimmering like sunlight on water. Her presence was overwhelming, but not in the way Zamarra's had been.

This was... soothing.

Reassuring.

It was as if I'd been called home. Oh... Oh, no.

This was exactly what Idris had warned me about when he'd told me the story of how the Luxa was created. I'd drifted too far into the Dreaming, and it was calling me home.

"You're Lirael, aren't you?" I breathed, in awe of just how beautiful she was and just how terrible. "From the story."

I wouldn't be going home. I... I'd never see any of

them again. I... I'd drifted too far, done too much, and now I was lost.

Her smile was gentle, kind. "Indeed, my child. But why do you cry?"

She lifted a lone finger to my cheek, a drop of a tear balanced on the tip as she drew it away. She blew on it, and it burst apart into a cluster of shimmering stars that floated away on the wind.

"Because I don't know how to get back to them—my mates. I-I think I broke something in this realm, did something, and I don't know how to fix it. I don't know if I can fix it. I... I'm not enough. I can't—"

"You are more than you realize," Lirael said, her voice echoing like a melody in my mind. "But your light has awakened what should have remained asleep."

"Zamarra," I managed to whisper, my voice trembling as I rubbed at the raw skin of my wrists.

Lirael didn't answer. Instead, she stepped closer, her radiant hand reaching out to touch my chest. A warmth spread through me, soothing the aches and pains that had lingered since Rune's sacrifice. My breaths came easier, the weight on my chest lifting as her light seeped into me.

"You are so much stronger than you realize," she said, her voice soft but resolute. "But strength alone will not be enough for what lies ahead. The balance

has been disrupted, and you must find a way to restore it."

"Restore it? How?" I asked, my voice cracking. "I don't even know what I've done."

Her gaze was both kind and sorrowful. "You've awakened more than just Zamarra, Vale. You've set events into motion that cannot be undone. But you are never alone. Remember that. And when you need me, call on me. I have never answered my daughters, but I will answer you."

"But why?"

"The book, my daughter. You must go back to the book."

Her smile stretched wide. Before I could ask her anything else, the light began to fade, the Dreaming dissolving around me.

A faint, rhythmic pounding echoed in my ears, dragging me from the weightlessness of the Dreaming. My chest no longer ached, my limbs no longer weak, and for a moment, I thought I was still cradled in the warm light of Lirael's embrace. But no—the cold stone beneath me, the copper tang of blood in the air, and the sounds of chaos shattered that illusion.

I gasped, the world roaring to life around me.

The cavern walls shook violently, dust and debris

cascading from the ceiling. Magic crackled in the air, the searing clash of fire and ice filling my ears. My vision swam as I opened my eyes, the dim light of the cavern punctuated by bursts of violent spells. It was chaos—pure, unrelenting chaos.

And then I felt him.

Kian's body was draped over mine, his broad shoulders blocking my view of the battle. His black dragon scales rippled along his exposed arms and back, deflecting a barrage of magic that should have torn us both apart. His claws dug into the stone at either side of me, his snarl a low, menacing rumble as another blast struck him squarely in the side.

"Kian," I whispered, my voice steadier than I'd expected. He didn't respond, too focused on shielding me from the Girovian mages pressing closer. His molten amber eyes flicked down to me briefly, relief flashing through them, but he didn't dare take his attention away for long.

"Vale?" His voice cracked on my name, a mixture of disbelief and desperation. "Gods, you're awake."

Another explosion rocked the cavern, and Kian's body tensed, his wings—now partially formed, his body mid-shift—flaring out to shield me further. Freya's fierce battle cry rang out, and I turned my head to see her slicing through the tendrils of magic aimed at us. Her twin blades moved with deadly precision, their silver edges catching the flickering light as she spun to take down another mage.

"Stay down, little Luxa," Freya barked over her shoulder, her voice sharp but tinged with relief. "We've got this. Just don't move."

But I wasn't weak anymore.

The warm hum of Lirael's magic still lingered beneath my skin, her light thrumming faintly in my chest. My muscles, which should have ached after everything I'd endured, felt whole, steady. I flexed my fingers, expecting pain, but there was none. Even the bond with my mates pulsed stronger, clearer than before.

"Kian," I murmured again, trying to sit up. He pressed a hand to my shoulder, keeping me down as his eyes raked over me.

"I felt you go," Kian rasped, his voice breaking as his claws flexed against the stone. For a moment, he looked lost, his molten eyes flickering with disbelief before the roar of an approaching mage pulled him back to himself.

"I'm not," I said, my voice firmer this time. "I'm here, Kian. I'm fine."

His amber eyes narrowed, his gaze roving over my face, searching for some hint of weakness. "I held you," he said, his voice raw. "You weren't breathing. You were cold. I—" He broke off, his jaw tightening as his amber eyes flicked away. "You were gone."

"I was healed," I said softly, though my voice trembled. "In the Dreaming. I—I can't explain. It was Lirael. She sent me back."

Kian's eyes widened, his claws flexing involuntarily, crumbling the stone in his large hands. "The goddess? She—"

"Can we save the reunion for later?" Freya snapped, her blade deflecting a surge of green magic. "I love a good miracle and all, but we're still in the middle of a godsdamned battle."

Kian snarled, his wings flexing as he rose to his full height. "I'm not leaving her."

"You don't have to," Freya shot back, slicing through another wave of attackers. "But we need to get out of here. Now."

I pushed myself up on trembling arms, brushing past Kian's attempts to hold me down. "I told you, I'm fine." To prove my point, I rose to my feet, the lingering hum of Lirael's magic steadying me as the cavern spun. "And I'm not leaving. Not while we're under attack. A Queen does not run."

Kian growled, his hand darting out to steady me as another explosion rocked the cavern. "I don't give a fuck what goddess patched you up—you're not fine. You fucking died. I watched you." He slammed his fist against his chest. "I felt you go. You were gone."

"For the love of fuck, let her prove it," Freya snapped, slicing through a mage's spell with an almost reckless ferocity. "If she's up for it, great. If not, I'll drag her out myself. Either way, we're not losing her again. Not today."

Kian shot her a glare, but I didn't give him a chance to argue further. Reaching deep inside myself, I called on my magic—and it readily answered. I raised my hands instinctively, and golden light flared bright and sharp, erupting from my hands brighter than ever before, forming a barrier so solid it felt almost alive. The mages' spells shattered against it, fragments of magic dissolving into sparks. My power surged, foreign and familiar all at once, as if Lirael's light had fused with my own.

The warmth Lirael had left in my chest pulsed faintly, like a second heartbeat, steadying me even as the cavern trembled around us. My body should have been weak, aching from the toll of Rune's sacrifice and the Dreaming's pull, but instead, I felt... whole.

Golden light surged through me, sharper, clearer than ever before. It wasn't just my power—it felt layered, ancient. Like Lirael had left a piece of herself behind, a steady flame to guide me through the dark.

"I told you," I snarled, the molten fury of battle thrumming through my veins as my magic surged through my limbs. It was bigger now, somehow more than it had ever been. "I'm not broken."

Kian let out a low growl, his heated gaze locking onto mine. "You're infuriating, you know that?"

"So I've been told," I shot back, stepping closer to him as Freya carved a path through the mages. "Now, are we getting out of here, or are you going to keep arguing with me?"

His lips twitched, the ghost of a smile breaking through his frustration. "Fine. But if I see even a hint of blood, I'm throwing you over my shoulder."

"Deal," I said, the hum of Lirael's magic surging in agreement.

Kian rushed forward, his claws tearing through the tendrils of magic that reached for us as Freya covered our flank. The bond with my mates pulsed in the back of my mind, and I could feel Idris' fury blazing like wildfire above us. Xavier's icy determination was closer, his magic carving through the enemy as he cleared the upper tunnels.

But even as they pushed the Girovian forces back, I couldn't shake the feeling that something was wrong. Lirael's words echoed in my mind, her warning a constant hum in the back of my thoughts. This wasn't just an attack—it was a distraction. A prelude to something far worse.

Zamarra's venomous gaze lingered in my memory, her voice like a shadowed whisper, taunting me. I couldn't shake the feeling that she was watching, waiting—her tendrils already sinking into the cracks we'd left behind.

As the battle raged on, I knew the real danger had yet to reveal itself.

And when it did, I would need to be ready.

CHAPTER 27
VALE

Echoes of the battle ricocheted through the cavern, an ear-splitting clashing of spells and roars of fury. Kian's fiery gaze darted toward me, his wings half-unfurled, shielding me from an incoming blast. Freya fought like a dervish, her twin blades carving through the onslaught, but their numbers were relentless. I was shielding them as best as I could but there were so many.

Then the air shifted.

It wasn't just the chill of magic. It was the oppressive weight of something darker. The mages faltered, their violet eyes wide with fear as shadows coalesced at the far end of the cavern. Even they feared what was coming, which could not be a good thing.

And from the darkness, a familiar mage emerged

—one I hadn't had a chance to kill. One who'd escaped before I could end him.

Malvor's presence was suffocating, his black robes flowing like living shadows. Inky magic slithered along his fingers like snakes as his pale lips curled into a cruel smirk. Even Freya paused, her grip tightening on her blades.

"Well, well, well," Malvor drawled, his voice sharp enough to cut stone. "The little queen survives. How... *disappointing*."

Freya stepped in front of me, her silver blades gleaming with magic. Kian snarled, his dragon scales shimmering as his claws flexed. But Malvor's eyes were locked on me, cold and unrelenting.

"You should have listened to me," Malvor hissed, his voice calm and condescending. "I told you not to break the curse. I warned you what would happen if you meddled. But you just couldn't resist playing the hero, could you?"

"I did what needed to be done," I said, forcing strength into my voice. "The curse is broken. Idris is whole. Rune is—"

"Dead," Malvor interrupted, his smirk twisting cruelly. "Your little pet is dead, and you've unleashed something far worse in the process. The chains are breaking, little queen. Every realm trembles because of what you've done. But don't worry—you won't live long enough to see the full extent of the consequences. I'll make sure of that."

Before I could respond, Malvor's hand shot out, grave magic surging toward us like a tidal wave. My power ripped through me, flooding from my skin as I tossed up a shield, but the spell struck with enough force to send me stumbling.

"We need to move," Freya barked, her eyes darting toward the cavern's exit. "If we stay boxed in, we're dead."

Kian didn't hesitate. His claws wrapped around my arm, and with a powerful beat of his wings, he propelled us toward the cavern's entrance. Freya followed, her blades flashing as she deflected spells from the mages still pursuing us.

The moment we burst into the open air, Idris and Xavier were already there, their magic wreaking havoc on the Girovian forces. Idris—still in dragon form—let out a roar that shook the ground, his crimson scales shimmering under the pale light of the moon.

Xavier's ice-blue eyes burned with fury, and frost crackled at his fingertips as he unleashed a barrage of ice spikes at the approaching mages. Several impaled the oncoming barrage, running them through like swords.

But something was different—something I couldn't ignore. Xavier had never wielded frost magic before. His flames had always been blue, searing and precise, but now, ice seemed to flow from him as naturally as breathing, carving through the air with devastating precision.

My breath hitched. The lifting of Idris' curse—it had done more than restore the king. It had freed all of us in ways we hadn't even begun to understand. Whatever chains had bound Xavier before were gone now, leaving his magic raw and unrestrained. He was stronger than ever—and the Girovian mages didn't stand a chance.

"*Vale.*" His voice cut through the chaos, relief and urgency mingling as his gaze found mine. He moved toward us, his magic forming a protective barrier as more mages descended from the tree line.

There were too many. How had they gotten so many to fight?

Idris, however, didn't speak. His golden eyes burned with fury as he turned his massive frame toward Malvor, his claws digging into the earth as he unleashed a blistering flame.

"*This ends now,*" he growled inside my mind, his

voice a deep, resonant snarl that sounded so much like Rune it made my heart soar.

Malvor emerged from the cavern, his expression almost bored as he surveyed the chaos. "Ah, the king." He sneered, his gaze flicking to Idris. "Or should I call you half a king? You may have your dragon back, but you're still nothing compared to what's coming. You should have stayed broken. Now we're all dead."

Idris lunged, his claws slashing through the air, but Malvor vanished in a swirl of shadows, reappearing several feet away. His laughter echoed as he raised his hands, summoning tendrils of black magic that lashed out like whips. But those whips weren't aimed at us.

No, they landed on the fallen mages, each one rising from the snow, their bloody limbs and broken bodies brand-new fodder for Malvor to use.

"Do you like my warriors? I know I do. You should have never meddled in this, little Luxa. Because she's not coming for me and mine—not yet. She'll be coming for you and yours. Every shadow, every darkened corner, every time you fall asleep, she'll be there. The best I can do is stop her before it's too late."

As one, the fallen mages attacked, their forms

mingling with the live ones as they moved to box us in. With the steep slope at our backs and the caverns in front of us, there were little options left.

Kian growled, his claws raking the ground as he moved to flank Malvor. Xavier's frost magic collided with the shadow tendrils, severing them from the fallen mages, but the live ones still pressed closer, their own spells raining down like a storm.

"Enough of this," Malvor roared as he raised his arms. The shadows around him expanded, forming a dome of writhing darkness that swallowed the narrow battlefield. For a moment, the world went silent.

And then the screaming started.

But it wasn't us—no, it was the souls of the fallen powering Malvor's magic, the darkness swelling from his body, filling the narrow space with inky blackness that reminded me of Zamarra's magic.

"Kian," I shouted, clutching at his arm as the shadows closed in around us. "We can't fight him like this."

Kian's molten eyes met mine, a flicker of determination cutting through the chaos. "Then we won't."

He raised his hands, and the air around us shimmered, twisted. The oppressive darkness wavered, and suddenly, it was as if it were no longer there. The shadows moved past us, searching, but they couldn't find their targets.

Kian's illusion magic had cloaked us, hiding us from Malvor's magic. His amber gaze met mine, determination flickering behind the strain etched into his face. A bead of sweat slid down his temple, his claws flexing. "It won't last long," he said through gritted teeth. "He's too powerful. You need to end this, Vale."

"Protect him," I snapped at Xavier and Freya as I stepped forward, the warmth of Lirael's magic surging through me. Golden light flared in my hands, cutting through the illusion just enough for me to confront Malvor.

"You think you can stop me?" Malvor sneered, his gaze locking onto me as the illusion faded. "You're nothing but a child playing with powers you don't understand."

"Maybe," I said, my voice steady, despite the storm raging around us. "But even a child can end you."

I unleashed a flood of golden light, brighter and stronger than anything I'd ever conjured before. It collided with Malvor's shadows, burning through them with an intensity that made him stagger. He snarled, his dark magic flaring as he countered, but

Lirael's power swelled within me, knocking him to his knees.

"You've grown stronger," Malvor admitted, his tone laced with pain. "The goddess' touch suits you. But even her light won't be enough to stop what's coming. You think breaking the curse was the end of your troubles? Zamarra is clawing from her prison as we speak, little queen. And she's already set her sights on your precious baby sister."

My heart froze. "Nyrah?" I whispered, my voice barely audible. "What does Zamarra want with her?"

Malvor's smirk widened. "Oh, you'll find out soon enough. But by then, it'll be too late. Zamarra doesn't just want you, Vale. She wants everything."

His words sent a rush of fear and fury through me, and I lifted my hands, golden light pooling from my palms. "She won't touch her. And neither will you."

Malvor laughed, a cold, mocking sound. "You can't protect her. You can't even protect yourself."

With a roar, I unleashed the full force of my magic, golden light exploding from me in a blinding wave. Malvor tried to counter, his inky magic surging to meet mine, but it wasn't enough. Lirael's light burned through his defenses, driving him to his back.

He gasped, his eyes wide with shock as the light

began to burn him. "Y-you think this changes anything?" he rasped, his voice weak but filled with venom. "Zamarra's game is far from over. And you... you're already too late."

Rage burned through me, and I poured every ounce of my magic into my next strike. The golden light speared forward, piercing Malvor's chest. His eyes widened in shock as the light consumed him, his body trembling before it collapsed in on itself, burning to ash and dust. The gust of his magic shattered his withered form, his ashes floating away on the bitter wind.

The moment Malvor fell, his connection to the Girovian mages shattered. Many screamed, clutching their heads as their spells backfired, their noses and eyes bleeding as they collapsed into the snow. The ones who survived fled into the night, their retreat chaotic and desperate. Idris let out a final roar, his crimson wings flaring as he slashed through the last of the stragglers.

The silence after the battle was deafening. It pressed against my ears, louder than any roar of magic or clash of weapons. The Girovian forces were gone—those who hadn't been destroyed fled into the shadows, leaving behind a trail of shattered lives and broken ground.

Freya sheathed her blades, her sharp gaze scanning the battlefield. "Well, that's one way to start the night," she muttered, though her usual bite was absent. Her steps were sluggish, her stance tense as though she expected more attackers to come crawling from the darkness.

Xavier moved to my side, his frost-blue eyes surveying the scene with grim determination. Idris stood a short distance away, his massive dragon form glowing faintly in the moonlight, steam rising from his nostrils as he surveyed the chaos. Kian leaned against a tree, his wings tucked tightly against his back, his amber eyes locked on me.

"Back to the castle," Idris growled through the bond, his voice resonating through my mind like a command. *"Now."*

I nodded silently, my body moving before my mind caught up. I couldn't tear my gaze away from the devastation around us. The clearing that had been our battlefield was littered with bodies, the snow stained red. The air smelled of charred flesh and magic, the acrid tang clawing at my throat.

We moved as a group, the weight of our silence heavy. Idris shifted back into his human form, his magic weaving armor from thin air, his posture unyielding. He walked ahead, his strides purposeful, but I could feel the simmering rage rolling off him in waves. I felt all of it, his emotions too big to hold in, and yet, he hadn't so much as looked at me once.

I'd betrayed him—I'd betrayed all of them—and I had no idea if he could forgive me.

Xavier followed close behind, his hands glowing faintly with residual frost magic. Kian brought up the rear, his gaze flicking toward the shadows as though expecting an ambush.

When we reached the castle gates, my heart sank. The walls bore the scars of the attack, great gouges torn through stone and steel. Guards were strewn across the grounds, some injured, some completely torn apart. Faint cries of the wounded drifted through the air, mixing with the crackle of dying flames.

I stopped in my tracks, my chest tightening as I took it all in. This wasn't just a battle—it was a warning. A declaration of war.

"Vale," Xavier said, his voice softer now. He placed a hand on my shoulder, grounding me. "We need to keep moving."

I nodded, though my legs felt like lead. As we stepped into the castle courtyard, the full scope of the damage became perfectly clear. Soldiers rushed in all directions, carrying the wounded, shouting orders, and extinguishing magical fires that seemed to burn without end. The once-pristine cobblestones were smeared with blood and ash. The air buzzed with the hum of strained magic as the wards were being hastily repaired.

Freya let out a low whistle, her expression grim. "Looks like they hit harder than we thought."

Idris spun toward me, his golden eyes blazing. "This is what happens when we're distracted. When we're not prepared."

But I hadn't been the one to demand a wedding. I hadn't been the one to throw a party in the hopes that war wasn't coming.

"This wasn't distraction," I said, my voice steadier than I felt. "This was a message. Malvor knew exactly what he was doing."

"And he used us to do it," Kian muttered, his claws flexing. "He wanted us divided, focused on him while his forces tore through the castle."

Xavier's gaze darkened. "It worked."

I swallowed hard, guilt clawing at my chest. This wasn't just about us—it wasn't even just about the castle. It was about the realm. The chaos Zamarra wanted to unleash had already begun, and I'd played right into her hands.

"I need to see the wounded," I said, my voice firmer now. "I need to see who we lost."

Idris hesitated, his jaw clenching. "Vale, you—"

"You already blame me. I can fucking feel it. Why not let me see it for myself?" I cut in, my eyes locking onto his. "They fought for us, Idris. They fought for this castle. They need to see that I at least know what it cost."

He stared at me for a moment, his expression hardening with each passing second, but then he nodded. "Freya, go with her. Kian, Xavier, see to the defenses. I want every ward restored, every weak point fortified. We won't let this happen again."

Then he turned, dismissing me as if I hadn't married him hours ago, as if I hadn't sacrificed everything for him, as if I were nothing. Except for the brief hesitation, the flicker of something I couldn't name in his golden eyes before he walked away.

If it had to be that way, fine.

The courtyard was a sea of chaos, but as Freya and I moved amongst the injured, the reality of what we'd faced hit me like a blow. Soldiers with burns and broken limbs lay on makeshift cots, their groans of pain echoing through the air. Healers worked tirelessly, their magic glowing as they mended wounds and whispered reassurances.

"Vale," Freya said softly, her gaze scanning the courtyard. "We won, but we're bleeding."

I nodded, my throat tight. This wasn't victory. It was survival, and barely that.

As we reached the great hall, my steps faltered. The long tables that usually held feasts were now filled with the wounded. The room smelled of blood and desperation, and the low hum of healing magic thrummed in the air.

Freya placed a hand on my arm, her sharp eyes softening. "You don't have to—"

"I do," I said, cutting her off. My voice steadied as I straightened, scanning the rows of wounded. "This is my fault, Freya. Malvor warned me, and I still—"

"Enough." Freya's voice was sharp, slicing through my spiraling thoughts. She moved closer, her face a mask of determination. "You think you're the only one who made mistakes? The only one who underestimated them? You think Idris, Xavier, Kian, or I had nothing to do with this?"

I blinked, caught off guard. "But—"

"No buts." Her voice lowered, but the intensity didn't fade. "We all knew they were coming. We all thought we had more time. You think this is your fault because Malvor pointed a finger at you? Fuck that. You don't get to take all the blame just because it makes you feel like you're in control of the chaos."

Her words hit me like a slap, and I opened my

mouth to respond, but she held up a hand, silencing me.

"You feel guilty? Good. That means you give a fuck about this kingdom. But don't stand here and act like the rest of us didn't make the same damn miscalculation. We're bleeding because this is war, Vale. It was never going to wait until we were ready."

Freya's hand fell away, and she exhaled a sharp breath, glancing over the hall. "You can't save everyone in war, and thinking you can, will get you killed. You want to help? Then stop blaming yourself for things you couldn't control and start doing something about the things you can."

Her words should have been the slap in the face I needed, but they weren't. Not when I knew the truth. Not when I could feel Zamarra's presence creeping closer, not just the threat in Malvor's words but in the way the air seemed colder, heavier. Like she was already reaching for me, her claws sinking into every single thing I cared about.

Freya was right about one thing: I couldn't save everyone.

But I could save one.

The castle had settled into an uneasy silence as the night bled to day and back into night. The air still carried the weight of what had happened. The stone walls bore scorch marks and cracks from the battle, and the lingering scent of ash clung to everything. The wards had been repaired, the gates fortified, but none of it seemed like enough.

I hadn't seen Idris once since he'd sent me with Freya. He'd managed to avoid me all day, his presence in the bond distant and cold. Not severed—never severed—but strained enough to make my chest ache. All of our bonds were damaged, hurting, and I didn't know if they could ever be repaired.

I could feel them now, though, a constant pulse of

anger and fear simmering beneath the surface of my skin. They were in the war room, waiting, though for what, I wasn't sure. A faint flicker of hope bloomed in my chest that maybe they were waiting for me, but as I pushed through the heavy doors, I knew that wasn't the case.

Idris, Kian, and Xavier were gathered around a wide table, their voices low but tense. The air crackled with unspoken frustration. Idris was standing at the head of the table, his arms braced against it, golden eyes fixed on the map spread before him. His conjured armor had been discarded in favor of simple black leathers, but there was nothing casual about his posture. He was a king ready for war—focused, unyielding, and furious.

"You're late," he barked, his voice cutting through the tension like a blade. He didn't look up, his gaze fixed on the map as though it might hold the answers we'd all been searching for.

"I wasn't aware this was a meeting."

The bond pulsed faintly between us, his irritation spiking like a lance in my heart. And he wasn't the only one on edge. Kian and Xavier's fear and pain and rage bombarded me, muddling my thoughts, making everything ten times harder than it needed to be.

"It isn't," Xavier murmured, his gaze softening as it met mine. He was seated near the fireplace, his posture more relaxed but no less watchful. "We're trying to figure out our next steps. Malvor's attack wasn't just a raid—it was a message. And we need to be ready for what's coming and that's difficult to do when over half the council is scattered to the wind. Most of them fled when we were attacked. The ones that stayed are banged up but breathing. We're running on a skeleton crew, and we need to regroup. We never expected Girovia to align with Direveil."

"They didn't. Malvor was working on his own. And what's coming is Zamarra," I said, moving closer to the table. "Malvor made that clear enough."

The dark mage's words echoed in my mind, a poison I couldn't shake. *Zamarra's chains are breaking, little queen. Every realm trembles because of what you've done.*

He'd been right. The moment I broken Idris' curse, I'd felt it—a shift in the magic of the realms. It wasn't just the return of Idris' dragon or magic flooding back into the continent. It was something older, darker. A fracture deep within the Dreaming. I'd seen it myself when I'd confronted Zamarra in the jagged black edges of her prison.

And then there was the shadow I'd felt since. The

oppressive weight of her presence pressing against the edge of my mind. I hadn't told the others, but I'd felt her watching me, her claws scraping at the corners of my thoughts. She was free. Not fully, not yet, but it would only be a matter of time.

And Nyrah—gods, Nyrah was in her sights.

"Wait." Xavier froze, his icy gaze pinning me to the spot. "Zamarra? What do you mean, Zamarra?"

"She's coming back," I said, the weight of the truth settling on my shoulders. "She's breaking free. Malvor wasn't here for us. He came because of her—to stop her by killing me. This battle—all this death, was to kill me, to prevent her from digging her claws into the Waking world. And she doesn't plan on stopping with me. Nyrah—she's next. He told me so."

There was a beat of silence, the tension thick enough to choke. Kian's expression darkened, his sharp gaze darting to Idris. "Please tell me this is some kind of cruel joke."

Idris' jaw tightened, his golden eyes narrowing. "How do you know this?"

"Because I've seen her," I said, my voice steady despite the storm raging in my chest. Freya had been so wrong. All of this was on me. "In the Dreaming. After Rune, I— She was there. And she's not just after me—she's after everything. The Waking, the

Dreaming, all of it. Breaking the curse didn't just set you free. It didn't just free your magic. It loosened her chains, too."

Kian swore under his breath. "So Malvor was her pawn?"

I shook my head. "He was trying to stop her. But now he's dead, and she's coming."

Idris let out a bitter laugh. "And what exactly do you propose we do?" he snapped, finally looking up, his gaze no less cutting than it had been since I'd stabbed him in the heart. Those golden eyes burned with fury, but there was something else there, too. Guilt? Fear? I couldn't tell, and he didn't give me any time to figure it out. "You unleashed her, Vale. You broke the curse, and now the realm is at risk. So, tell me—how do we fix this?"

I flinched, his words cutting deeper than I expected. "You think I don't know that? You think I don't feel the weight of it every second? I didn't have a choice, Idris. I did it to save you. To save us."

His laugh was cold, humorless. "Save us? Take a look around, Vale. The castle is in ruins, the wards are barely holding, and the kingdom is on the brink of collapse. Tell me again how this saved us. And now we're supposed to believe she's targeting your sister?"

"Enough," Kian growled, moving between us. His

amber eyes flashed as he placed a hand on Idris' shoulder, forcing him to take a step back. "This isn't helping."

Idris shrugged him off, but he didn't press further. Instead, he directed his gaze back to the map, his jaw tight as silence fell over the room.

I exhaled shakily, my hands curling into fists at my sides. "Zamarra isn't just a threat to the realm. She's a threat to my family. Malvor said she's after Nyrah, and if she gets her hands on her—"

"You have no clue what she wants with Nyrah or if this bastard of a mage was telling the truth," Idris interrupted, his tone icy. "And running off to find her will only make you an easier target. I've already mourned you once. Do me a favor and don't make me do it twice."

His harsh words cut like a blade, but I stood my ground, meeting his golden glare with every ounce of strength I could muster. "What do you suggest I do? Sit here and wait? Watch as Zamarra tears apart everything I love?"

"I suggest you trust us," Xavier cut in, his voice calm but firm. "You think you're the only one who wants to protect Nyrah? You think we don't care about what happens to her—or to you?"

"That's not what I—" I broke off, my hands

landing on the daggers at my hips. I couldn't do this. Not with them. Not now. "You don't understand."

"Then make us understand," Kian said, his amber gaze steady and unwavering. "Let us help, Vale. Whatever it is you think you have to do alone, you don't."

But I couldn't. Because this wasn't just about Nyrah or Zamarra or even the kingdom. This was about me. The choices I'd made, the lives I'd cost, the bonds I'd fractured. Idris couldn't even look at me without his anger bubbling to the surface, and Xavier and Kian... they were trying, but I felt the strain.

They didn't trust me—not fully. And why should they? I didn't even trust myself.

Pained silence stretched between us, thick with tension and unspoken words. Idris finally broke it, turning back to the map with a frustrated sigh. "This is a waste of time. If Zamarra's really coming, then we need to fortify the castle, regroup the council, and prepare for war. Chasing ghosts won't save anyone."

His dismissal cut deeper than I cared to admit. I swallowed hard, forcing the words that burned on my tongue back down. What was the point? He'd already made up his mind, and I wasn't about to fight a battle I couldn't win.

Without another word, I turned and left the room,

the heavy doors slamming shut behind me. The cold, empty corridors stretched ahead, each step echoing in the silence. My chest ached, the weight of everything pressing down on me until I thought I might shatter under it.

They didn't understand.

They couldn't.

But that wasn't their fault this time. It was mine. I'd shattered their trust when I broke the curse, and now I was breaking them again. The bonds that had once been so bright and steady, now flickered weakly, strained by anger and fear and everything I couldn't say.

I reached Idris' chambers and shut the door behind me, leaning against it as I tried to catch my breath. The room was dark, the only light coming from the faint glow of the moon through the window. My gaze landed on the small, worn satchel I'd packed earlier, hidden beneath the edge of the bed. I reached under the mattress, pulling the worn, half-broken book from its depths. Lirael's words echoed in my head as I stuffed it into the satchel.

The book, my daughter. You must go back to the book.

I'd known this was coming. From the moment

Malvor had spoken Nyrah's name, I'd known what I had to do. But knowing didn't make it any easier.

I moved to the window, my fingers brushing against the cold glass as I stared out at the night. What I would give to hear Rune's voice right now.

Gods, you bastard. Why did you make me do this? He'll never forgive me now.

But Rune didn't answer. Of course he didn't. I was alone. And until I found Nyrah, I would always be alone.

The castle below was quiet, but the scars of the battle were still visible—the broken walls, the blood-stained snow, the flickering wards. This was my doing. My choice.

But Nyrah didn't have to pay for it. I could still save her. I could still do something right.

The bonds with Idris, Kian, and Xavier pulsed faintly in the back of my mind, a reminder of everything I was leaving behind. A part of me wanted to reach out, to tell them the truth, to ask for their help. But I couldn't. Not when I was the one who had broken us in the first place.

I turned away from the window, grabbing the satchel and slinging it over my shoulder. My heart ached as I took one last look around the room. Just hours ago, I'd shared that bed with Idris, cementing the bond that I feared would never be repaired.

But there was no room for hesitation.

Not anymore.

Swallowing down my tears, I moved into the corridor, the silent castle suffocating me as I picked my way through the wreckage, my heart breaking just a little more with every step.

When I reached the ward, I carefully sliced through it, repairing the cut once I slipped past, adding a little more power to the magic so the protection would hold as long as it had to.

This side of the ward, I almost couldn't feel my mates at all, and the first tear raced down my cheek as the loss hit me.

I'd done what he'd always needed me to do. I'd broken the curse—I'd freed him. He didn't need me anymore. And Kian, Xavier? They'd find someone else—someone better. Someone they could trust.

I wiped away my tears. There was no time for those—not if I wanted to save my sister. Readjusting my pack, I slipped into the shadows and disappeared into the night.

I had a sister to find.

Thank you so much for reading Stolen Embers. I can't

express just how much I love Vale, Kian, Xavier, and Idris along with their ragtag bunch of friends. And we aren't quite done yet!

Next up is **Broken Fates** *and all the crazy, dragon shifter shenanigans that is to come. I hope you're buckled in to see Vale & company contend with their crazy mate bond, the raging war, and the aftermath of breaking the curse!*

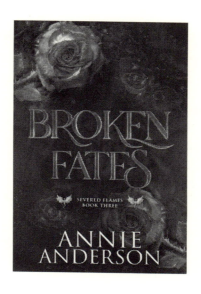

BROKEN FATES

Severed Flames Book Three

Queen. Savior. Sacrifice.

The realms are fracturing—and Vale Tenebris stands
at the center of the storm. With chaos spreading
across the continent, Vale must harness the magic
she barely understands to protect her kingdom and
the ones she loves. The bonds she shares with Idris,
Kian, and Xavier have been tested, and the forces
threatening to tear their world apart grow stronger by
the day.

As ancient powers stir and secrets come to light, Vale is thrust into a race against time to stop a war that could consume the realms. But with enemies in every shadow and betrayal waiting at every turn, survival will demand more than magic—it will demand everything she has.

The fate of the realms lies in her hands, but at what cost?

Preorder your copy today!

BOOKS BY ANNIE ANDERSON

SEVERED FLAMES

Ruined Wings

Stolen Embers

Broken Fates

IMMORTAL VICES & VIRTUES

HER MONSTROUS MATES

Bury Me

SHADOW SHIFTER BONDS

Shadow Me

THE ARCANE SOULS WORLD

GRAVE TALKER SERIES

Dead to Me

Dead & Gone

Dead Calm

Dead Shift

Dead Ahead

Dead Wrong

Dead & Buried

Soul Reader Series

Night Watch

Death Watch

Grave Watch

The Wrong Witch Series

Spells & Slip-ups

Magic & Mayhem

Errors & Exorcisms

The Lost Witch Series

Curses & Chaos

Hexes & Hijinx

THE ETHEREAL WORLD

Rogue Ethereal Series

Woman of Blood & Bone

Daughter of Souls & Silence

Lady of Madness & Moonlight

Sister of Embers & Echoes

Priestess of Storms & Stone

Queen of Fate & Fire

PHOENIX RISING SERIES

(Formerly the Ashes to Ashes Series)

Flame Kissed

Death Kissed

Fate Kissed

Shade Kissed

Sight Kissed

ACKNOWLEDGMENTS

A huge, honking thank you to Shawn, Barb, Jade, Angela, Heather, Kelly, and Erin. Thanks for the late-night calls, the endurance of my whining, the incessant plotting sessions, the wine runs... (*looking at you, Shawn.*)

Every single one of you rock and I couldn't have done it without you.

ABOUT THE AUTHOR

 Annie Anderson is the author of the international bestselling Rogue Ethereal series. A United States Air Force veteran, Annie pens fast-paced Paranormal Romance & Urban Fantasy novels filled with strong, snarky heroines and a boatload of magic. When she takes a break from writing, she can be found binge-watching The Magicians, flirting with her husband, wrangling children, or bribing her cantankerous dog to go on a walk.

To find out more about Annie and her books, visit
www.annieande.com

facebook.com/AuthorAnnieAnderson

instagram.com/AnnieAnde

amazon.com/author/annieande

bookbub.com/authors/annie-anderson

goodreads.com/AnnieAnde

pinterest.com/annieande

tiktok.com/@authorannieanderson

Made in the USA
Middletown, DE
27 February 2025

71928559R00245